And God created great whales, and every living creature that moveth, which the waters brought forth abundantly, after their kind, and every winged fowl after his kind: and God saw that it was good.

Genesis 1:21, King James Bible

All Weather Is Passing

Rachel Wade

Fisher King Publishing

Fisher King Publishing
fisherkingpublishing.co.uk

Cover image courtesy of furuno from Pixabay

For my parents, my anchors.

One

Whitby, 1973. Day had faded to dusk, the sky transfiguring into a vast canvas of sooty smudges, hazy greys and inky blues seeping into the leaden sea, void of winged companions and dappled instead with flocks of frantic debris. On the clifftop the land itched and bristled, once familiar shapes wavering and wilting, mutating into mysterious shadows amid the dying glow. The trees bowed to the brutal force of the wind while the grass shimmered as if electrified. Within minutes, the earth had become an unknown landscape, swelling then sinking, bleeding colour and light. This would be no ordinary storm.

Emil peered across the vista framed within the chipped white wood of his window, his wide eyes like two amber beads. He imagined a similar scene from the garden at the back, the stretch of turf dipping down into the belly of the bay where his boat was moored, a weathered trawler tethered among its kin. In his mind, he could see its emerald form being pitched and plunged, the salty swell licking greedily along the length of her hull. He held his breath, visualising each heave and sway as the pewter-grey surge seeped in from the estuary and flooded towards the expanse of sea, its pace and ferocity galvanised by the mounting tempest.

The thin glass of the kitchen window rattled in its surround, a meagre barrier against the will of the wild.

Night was falling. He could only hope his boat would be safe – out of sight, out of mind. He cast his gaze closer, noticing particles swarming before pelting the surface inches from his face. He saw a seed become suspended in a web before both were snatched away, lost in the endlessness. He wondered if he too could disappear so fleetingly, taken by a wisp of wind then carried into the great unknown. He yearned and feared the fantasy, acutely aware of his own mortality.

Clenching his left hand into a fist, Emil tried to concentrate on the weather, but his mind wandered unwillingly. He was thankful not to be able to see the harbour, to have to spot his own ship among the other struggling silhouettes beside the shore. His pride, his only joy. He pictured himself standing on the slippery deck, feet wide apart, anchored by his thick leather work boots. He could feel his thighs tensing with learned effort as he imagined his boat aching against the enduring commotion, her curves creaking with resistance, his own bones groaning in sympathy. Even in the shelter of his home, his ears could sense the whip, snap and strain as she battled, the binds barely holding.

"Hush, *mitt barn*," the fisherman whispered. "Hush."

Emil had never intended his life to be this way, isolated on a cliffside with only an aged fishing boat to concern him. Since withdrawing from society, he had come to care for her alone, above his own interests or those of another. He had settled in the North Yorkshire seaside town as a young man, grateful to find the comfort he had always craved. The remote cottage and the ever-changing landscape. The quaint quay and the amiable inhabitants. His steady work as a fisherman, a childhood ambition realised. Over the past decade, each day had echoed the last and foretold the next, providing a passive consistency that suited his nature and eased his visions. But his seclusion had come at a cost.

The storm was now seething, its visual violence matched by an unearthly rumble, then a single flash of bright white light. Emil felt a stab of regret having left his beloved to her fate. He should go down with his ship like a true sailor, he thought, not hide away in his house before burying himself and his nightmares underground. But there was no time for self-admonishment. For his own survival, he had to move – at once and with speed.

Rushing to the front door, Emil grabbed his waterproof from the hook and slipped it on, stumbling as he stooped to change his footwear. He donned a woollen cap and scarf knowing the bunker would be as cool as a freshly caught herring. There were provisions down there already, but they had not been checked in months. Hastily, he filled his pockets – bread and cheese wrapped in a handkerchief in one, a box of matches and a chocolate bar in the other. There was nothing else needed save for the strength of mind to batten the holds, hide and wait.

The previous tempest had been seven months ago and almost twice as long had passed since the one before, though neither had been quite like this. Tonight, Emil could feel an air of foreboding, a discomfort that made his skin prickle and his throat burn, symptoms which reawakened memories of his life before. Another place. Another time.

The fisherman paused, listening to his body – yes, it felt the same. The sharp plucking of his heart, the weighty ache of warning in his abdomen, the voracious panic that left him perspiring and trembling, on heightened alert. He felt under threat, though he feared neither the adverse conditions nor his potential demise – instead, it was the power of his own mind that he dreaded. The twisted thoughts, the cruel imagery, the apparitions that would turn his flesh to ice. The idea that he was being hunted – that he would one day pay for his sins.

In the small Norwegian village where Emil grew up, the intense storms had been rare but keenly remembered, like visits from distant relatives or ancestral phantoms, their legacies touching the tip of every local storyteller's tongue. Despite their radios and toasters, pick-up trucks and washing machines, most of the residents still believed in the old ways, the traditions and tales that would reignite at the turn of the tide. Not merely wind and rain, thunder and lightning, but the devil himself. A thing of such malevolence and power that it could whisk women from their feet and snatch children from their beds, dragging them, plunging them deep down into the eternal bitter waters.

Whenever a storm had approached, young Emil and his five brothers would follow their mother down to the cellar while their father hovered by the front door, wordless and morose, tugging on his hide jacket and battered stompers. As the families hid, the men would take to the boats. Brave men, noble men: fathers, sons, uncles, grandfathers, brothers, friends, neighbours, all risking their lives for their community. Yet despite the danger, there would always be something in Pappa's eyes that only Emil could see, or perhaps dared to notice. An expression of longing and anticipation, of adventure to come. A look he only wore when there were whales to be snared.

Banishing the recollections, the fisherman refocused on his plight, turning back towards the room for one final glance through the window. The landscape now resembled another planet, dangerous and hostile. He looked away, the gears of his brain slowly starting to spin as he hastened to the bookcase beside the fire. Emil slipped his hand above the unloved volumes to retrieve the rusted tobacco tin, its lid dented by the tip of a knife puncturing the once colourful slogan. He unbuttoned his coat to slip the box into his shirt pocket, momentarily soothed by its dull rattle. Once the sound had settled, he noticed another – the heady thud of his own pounding heart. Emil marched towards the door to the beat of his panic.

As soon as he removed the key and turned the handle, the door swung inward, slamming him in the chest and stomach, one hand still grabbing on to keep himself upright, his mind and body fighting against the formidable gale. With a heaving effort, he left the cottage and wrestled the door back shut, the wind tearing at his limbs as he tried to turn the key in the lock. Grimacing against the elements, he moved along the side of the building towards the stack of wood, his temples throbbing as a deafening drone thrummed against his ears.

Nostrils flaring and eyes watering, Emil tried to ignore the feeling of his body being beaten. For a moment, he wondered if this was what it felt like to drown. He lurched towards the first window, taking up a plank of wood, cradling its weight in his elbows as his mind drifted back to his childhood. He could recall one particular evening when the storm had seemed alive, like a physical being, a looming menace he could see and hear, touch and smell. It had been a night when time itself had felt frozen, the sky plagued with a peculiar nocturnal prickling, the ether hung with uncertainty as the land pulsated from its core.

Despite being the youngest and weakest of the brothers, Emil's father had pulled him outside by the shoulder of his shirt and taught him how to secure their homestead. He had been nine years old. Even now, he could still remember how sore and splintered his hands had been, always so small compared to Pappa's, the wounds having long since faded amid the traces of countless other cuts. Twenty years on, Emil could prepare his own dwelling alone, but there would always be the voices.

Prying his eyes open, the fisherman dragged up the next plank, focusing on his father's echoing commands fixed firmly inside his memory. One by one, he heaved each of the wooden supports into place, swift and deft, his slight frame packed with tight muscle from years of hard graft. Wisps of white salt stuck to his skin as the gale threw his tawny hair into a thorny crown. He wavered, reed-like, trying to assess his work through the darkness. Beamed, boarded, bolted; his home was finally safe. The outbuilding would survive, the boat would take care of herself. He could do nothing more.

Clawing his way towards the front of the cottage, Emil knelt to take the heavy metal handle that raised the hatch door leading into the bunker. He let it thud against the stone wall before beginning the climb down. Though the voice in his head still rang with urgency, he could not help but pause in his descent for one last look. The wind had quickened, now tyrannical, tinged with a metallic edge. He could barely stand as he squatted and squinted into the distance. The scene had become fully obscured by the night, but he could still feel something out there, across the water, veiled below the waves. Were they here? Did they know? Could they too feel the change?

Emil nudged his wrist against the wiry bristles of his three-day-old beard, head heavy with thought, breath paused with expectation. He told himself to see sense, righting his spine in defiance, pulling his gaze from the view. It was time to go down, he knew, yet his ears still strained for one telling sign, for just one low bellow from the depths beyond. Proof. Confirmation that he was not alone.

Despite his memories, he would often look for them. For a ripple, an echo, the faint outline of a shady shape halfway between the harbour and the horizon. Occasionally while fishing, he would feel a presence, undefinable yet unmistakable, down below the water, under the very spot where he stood on the deck. It was as if they knew he was there – the stranger, the hunter, the enemy. No different from the numerous other men their ancestors had encountered for hundreds of years. The same blood that ran through Emil.

For as long as he could remember, they had swum into his dreams, emerging within fantasies of both warning and wanting. Images of majestic creatures gliding smoothly through the currents, traversing thousands of miles across stretches of water no human could ever hope to cross without aid. Out there in the deep blue, their bodies bounded through the ocean with such ease and agility that there could be no doubt of whom the sea belonged to.

Eyes streaming from the whipping wind, one hand shuddering with the ebbing strength of holding the hatch door aloft, Emil conceded – his time had come. As the tempest threatened to reach its crescendo, the scene now smothered by a thick black veil, he shuffled down the rickety steps and closed the entrance, disappearing into the dank innards below ground.

At the base, he found the wooden stool and the aluminium cool box beside it. Inside was a bottle of water, a pack of crackers, a thin blanket, which he placed on the seat, and a candle. He retrieved the matches, holding his breath as he blindly lit the wick, watching the muddy walls as they became illuminated. He placed the candle in its holder on the box lid, seating himself as his eyes traced the studded surface in front. Pebbles, shells, the snaking remnants of roots. Centuries of forgotten life, a hidden world.

The fisherman tucked his wrists under the warming widths of his upper arms still pulsing from his toil, eyes slipping closed as more memories resurfaced. He had never known why the bunker had been built, during which time or by whom, but he was grateful for its existence. Despite the rarity of natural disasters here, there would always be a need to hide.

Staying safe in a storm was one of the few lessons Emil had been glad to receive from his father. The rest he had needed to learn for himself. Even though he was not like his elders or brothers – damaged, deformed, cursed, they called him – he had his own talents. Strong-minded, keen and clever, he chose to observe rather than to speak, watching with honey-coloured eyes and sullen features set as if etched in wood. Capable beyond his years, his ambition had led to an apprenticeship at the age of thirteen before leaving eight years later to become a fisherman. Despite his impediment, his perseverance had earned him a steady income and a life of independence. But no amount of knowledge could guarantee success in a storm. He had learned that the hard way.

For now, there would be no need to work. Deep in the bunker, he would not have to worry about a blade shooting from his grasp or a rope slipping through the crook of his elbow. In the dim cavern, he was unable to labour over broken nets and corroded pulleys, prepare tinder for kippering or pore over maps and readings. Too cramped, too cold, too dark, even with a candle or the battery-operated bulb he had installed. But there was something else, another reason for his inactivity. When the storms came, it was more than a warning of the weather. He knew it to be a sign from beyond. A message he could not ignore.

Despite Emil's distance from his childhood home, the beliefs of his forebears still pressed as heavy as iron chains around his limbs, forcing him to recall the many myths and legends he had tried to forget. The ghouls would usually appear in his sleep, in those darkest, deepest moments when his mind would be allowed to wander, but when the weather turned and he was forced into the bunker, out they crawled to greet him. Whether he toiled or slept, prayed or wept, they would not cease, ever eager, ever present.

Ten minutes. An hour. Three, perhaps more. Time stood still. Emil huddled into himself, forehead resting in the dip between his knees, eyes clamped so tightly that they ran. He tried to focus on the noises, attempting to read the tempest's progress, but his hearing could only narrow on the creak of the door above. The whining of the wood, the scratching of the metal. What if he could not open it? What if the storm raged to such an extent that trees fell and boulders rolled, covering his hideout, sealing him in this crypt? He would be trapped. Unable to escape, unable to be heard. The locals would take days, perhaps even weeks, to notice. It would be too late. A missing person. Disappeared.

The fisherman hunched his body tighter. With quaking fingers, he reached into his pocket and pulled out the corroded tin. Knowing its contents intimately, it was unusual for him to open the lid and retrieve what slid back and forth inside. Only in desperate times would he do so, in those singular instants when his logic wavered and his faith reappeared, distant yet determined.

Emil emptied the shape into his palm, began rotating

the small pale form between his chilled fingertips, its miniscule indentations clearly defined with even the softest touch. He muttered in his native tongue, choice words now only heard in his dreams, sacred sentiments sent upwards for the sea and the sky, for his ship and his settlement, for the creatures of the deep. Hoping. Wishing. Pleading.

In his makeshift shelter, the fisherman held his charm and imagined a place of safety, of reassurance and calm – his old kirke. He pictured below him the granite flagstones worn smooth by generations of believers; above, the curved dark beams offering a comforting echo of their daily toil and livelihoods. The pews appeared identical, yet each held indentations both specific and spiritual. And there, before the congregation had amassed or after prayers, Emil would rest, pacified not by his belief in the Almighty but by the incomparable luxury of an all-embracing silence.

But this was not his kirke, nor even a vast vessel upturned. As the slim shape continued to turn between his fingers, his inhalations rich with the peaty stench surrounding him, Emil felt himself swallowed. Eaten alive. He was in the bowels of a monster, a colossal thing he could not escape. Without warning or will, his mind conjured flesh and bone, blood and brine, above and below, consuming him entirely. In his palm, he could feel the handle of a blade, a flensing knife, sturdy and secure in his grasp.

Now he could hear the men, their voices reverberating a dialect seldom spoken by his own lips yet still so clear in his mind. Stab and slice, they told him. Stab and slice the beast. The monsters of the seas. The ones that come with the storms, meandering below turbulent waves, filling his quaint and peaceful community with a determination so venomous that they would spill litre upon litre of blood in the name of tradition, then toast their success in the firelight.

Running away had not been enough, Emil knew; he would never atone for the sins of his former life. Consumed by Mother Earth, she would soon have her vengeance, take back what was rightfully hers – the animals he had watched since he was a boy, had spotted from the window of the cottage, were perhaps even out there right now, riding the storm. Gentle beings, decades old and immense in size yet seamless and serene as they navigated the waters. He had always admired them, respected them, but never once had he said 'no'. Never had he tried to stop their slaughter. As if in reply, the candle snuffed its final breath.

The stone slipped from his grip, tumbling down into the shadows. Emil tried to stare through the blackness, furiously fumbling his hand amid the cool soil before eventually retrieving his prize, clutching it tightly, protectively. He left the candle unlit, noticing the faint scent of smoke along with the strange absence of sound. Focusing on his senses, the fisherman sat with his breath held, listening for a sign, hoping that the storm had perhaps passed. That he had survived.

Gripping the talisman, he remained in the bunker repeating his idle prayers, the taste of seared whale flesh haunting his tongue like a branded bruise.

Two

The storm had not yet passed, the streets and buildings eerily empty. Inside the church, the other segmented wooden box pews were vacant. No sound encroached on his memorial. Yet despite the silence, Hamish had not found sanctuary. Not today. Not when he needed it the most. Every sound, smell, sight and sensation seemed to set him on edge. The tapping at the windows. The whistling through the roof. The glow of the candles in an otherwise hollow, hallowed void. No voices nor footsteps, only the incessant hum of his own thoughts and the steady hiss of his breath. This was his favoured post, his place of peace, but today he could not settle, could not trace the shape of the carved cross without considering how things were, how they might have been.

It had been over forty years since Hamish had first entered St Mary's Church on Whitby's East Cliff. He had never been religious; he came only to converse with himself, returning once a month or so to reflect on that initial visit, the day when the empty grave had been dug and the false headstone raised. Even after all these years, he could only stand before the weathered slab and glimpse at the crudely carved letters for a few moments before the ache became overwhelming. He would then retreat into the church itself, take a seat in one of the plainer pews and silently survey the scene.

Permit the memories to rise, the dead to return.

As with many of the seafarers' stones in the graveyard, they had never found the body of the missing fisherman. Row on row of memorials to the lost, men drowned at sea on their quests for riches and more lucrative hauls, but this man was not like the others. Despite the tomb, Hamish knew that somewhere, somehow, the fisherman might still be alive. Wrinkled and stooped, forever spurred by his longing for the son he had discovered, the child he had rescued on the day of the famous storm nearly fifty years ago.

Hamish had been so young – just six years old – yet the memories were still crisp in his mind, the happiness still warm in his blood. So long as he maintained hope, the fisherman would never be forgotten. So long as he continued with his search, the fisherman could still be found. It was all he had lived for these past few years. But now everything was about to change.

A crack and a thud, a slammed wooden door, an ancient pane rattling in its fragile lead setting. Hamish started, eyes darting to the furthest and largest stained glass window. Shadows frolicked across its surface – a weather warning, the tide turning. The storm outside was rising and swelling like an animal released from capture. The thought filled him with fear and delight, sporadic emotions recovered after years of detachment. He recalled the bunker by the cottage, the damp, dark hole he had heard of but not yet found. A frightful place where memories and monsters flourished, friends and foes indistinguishable, searing into the soul. The fisherman had told them as fairy stories, but Hamish had always known otherwise.

Sliding his body further down the seat, he rested his head back and peered through misty eyes at the roof above, said to have been fitted by ships' carpenters. Indeed, it closely resembled an upturned boat, creating a cocooning welcome for the congregation who had lived and died by the sea, the generations of townsfolk whose lives had depended on the fishing and whaling industries centuries ago. He could picture the families gathering under the bowing bands of wood, subdued in prayer or singing in praise, lulled within their safe space. A heritage, a community, a history Hamish felt akin to but somehow distanced from. He considered himself a local man, at one with the sea and the earth, the elements and the atmosphere, the ancestors who had built the town stone by stone and coin by coin, yet he had never been able to find comfort here, had never felt contented.

Every time he looked up into the gently curved hull, he felt trapped. Confined, cornered, swallowed whole. Not a ship but the ribcage of a beast, ensnaring him deep within its stomach. Surrounded by the cold, consumed by the darkness. Was this how it had felt inside that bunker, waiting out the storm? Hamish imagined the panic and the solitude as he tried to recall the fisherman's face, but today all he could see was her. Despite the fish supper sat on the pier, the steady trudge through the wind and rain, the uncomfortable pause at the empty grave and the twenty minutes in the bowels of the sacred building, Hamish had thought only of her. Noa. His daughter.

Estranged for eight years, irregular phone calls and visits for ten more, they were neither close nor committed. Yet she had decided to come and live with him. Now a grown woman, an aspiring writer, a perfect human being whom he had had no part in nurturing, soon to be his ward. Her careful words of explanation had rendered him speechless, hanging from the end of the phone like a fish on a hook. He had not known what to say, think or do, had ended up mumbling his agreement and putting down the phone in bemusement. And still, with her arrival imminent, the right response alluded him. She was due tomorrow shortly before lunch, making her own way alone by train before meeting him at the flat. Their flat. The bedroom was ready, the fridge-freezer filled. He had cleaned and tidied, placed a newly framed picture on the wall. Yet it all still seemed too much. Too much for him to bear.

A gasp, a figure, a woman paused beside the pew with a pale hand gripping the ruffled neck of her cream blouse. The Maid of the Church chuckled, commenting on Hamish's appearance, his almost perfect camouflage against the dulled wood, dark flagstones and muted walls. Hamish raised his head, running a clammy hand through his mop of mousy-brown hair, the same shade and style since childhood. His clothes had not changed much, either – plain and practical, made of cotton, wool and corduroy, relics of a bygone era. The only flash of colour came from his eyes – golden and glowing, like the ochre waters of a moorland gully. He gave a polite nod, an enforced smile, masking his irritation at the shattering of his reverie.

Hamish had met the Maid, a woman called Gail, many times over the years. She had been there the day of the burial and was the first person he had questioned over the disappearance of the fisherman. This was where it had all started. The investigation. The yearning to solve the mystery. How could a man he had only just met have disappeared a few days later? He had returned to see Gail on account of his work as a journalist, checking the facts of the next church fete or a fundraising campaign for a new weathervane, and every time, he would always slip in his own enquiry, just one more query about the man they called 'Lefty'. A cruel nickname but said with such affection by the locals that Hamish had never countered their words.

He wondered now whether he should speak to Gail again, encourage her into revealing a clue he had somehow overlooked, but he was distracted. As she talked, he began to notice the resemblance to his grandmother. The eyes, the expression, the subtle smells of talc and toast. Yes, he could just about remember. Her presence, her voice, her house and his seclusion. Just a short walk to the cliff edge, yet it had felt like a foreign land. An island prison of two inhabitants, with his grandmother his keeper.

He could not recall the house he had lived in before, the one he had shared with his mother. He had not kept any photographs, had long forgotten her face. She had gone just a few days after the fisherman, leaving only his grandmother to take care of him. The night his mother had left, sitting in the kitchen with cups of tepid pea soup, his grandmother had suggested that his mother and the fisherman had eloped. Hamish had looked up the word in a dictionary, his insides twisting at the thought, his mind quickly coming up with his own preferred truth. It seemed simple enough – his mother had abandoned him, but not the fisherman. He would never have left him willingly. And so Hamish had made a vow. He would wait for him, search for him. He would never stop believing that the fisherman might be alive.

Despite now being much older and a little wiser, Hamish still felt more like a boy than a grown man. He seemed broken, damaged, somehow lacking inside. It was an emptiness that as an adult he had filled with hope for the fisherman's reappearance, the fateful spotting of his green boat or his figure on the cliffside. Surly-faced, tight-lipped, his right wrist hidden inside a sleeve. The faint tang of salt and sourness, his clothes and hair dotted with white. The image was so clear, Hamish could almost believe it to be real. Not a ghoul but a person, fully formed, brought back to life by his faith.

Gail continued talking, commenting on the changing seasons, the balmy summer evenings now replaced by the wilder pre-winter winds and choppy seas, speaking as if such shifts had never occurred before. Nature replied from outside by bellowing its cautionary cries, rapping its knuckles against the delicate stained glass, the rainbow hues rendered black by the fallen light. There came a screech, like the desperate cry of a panicked bird – a curlew, Hamish realised. Its call was said to be a weather warning by day and a bad omen by night. He drew his arms tighter across his body, fingers gripping into the fabric of his coat.

Nodding absently, one ear on the woman beside him, the other on the ever quickening wind, Hamish ran his palms down his thighs, preparing to leave, but there was no need; the Maid said her goodbyes and began walking back along the aisle. The sudden movement caused a flutter in the lefthand corner of the space among a sequence of paper shapes on strings. They reminded Hamish of the ones he had hung at Christmas in his grandmother's house, carefully cut from old newspapers and tied with kitchen twine. Their presence had been a rare source of delight, one of the few childhood moments he could recall without regret.

The decorations in the church, an installation by the local primary school, were cut into the forms of fish and loaves of bread – the Feeding of the Five Thousand. Hamish knew the story well. A miracle. A fairy tale. As he watched the flickering forms settle back into stillness, he wondered if Noa had ever read the Bible. For ten years now, he had posted paperback books in the hope of swaying her interest towards modern fiction and meaningful truths, to reveal through their pages the world as it was, in all its beauty and cruelty. He pondered whether her mother had taken her to church, if her former faith had withstood the pain. Though he had slowly grown to know his daughter, Rosa remained only as a figment of his past. Fleeting, nearly forgotten, now brought back in the face and hands and mannerisms of their child, Noa. Her name still made him smile inside. One day, he would tell her why.

One of the cut-outs caught his attention. Not a fish but something else, a distinct shape with a Mona Lisa smile, all swirls of blue and grey poster paint from a thick brush. Hamish had once loved to draw, especially animals. As a boy, he would snaffle unwanted notepaper, used envelopes, takeaway leaflets – any surface he could imprint with sketches copied from books, postcards and his own imagination – and the whale had always been his favourite. How many hours had he wasted staring out to sea, hoping he would spot one? He had collected all the illustrations he could, searched for pebbles in their shape, visited the museum and quizzed the fishermen by the bay. Yes, there are beasts in these waters, they had told him, and he had nodded, mouth agape, his young mind swollen with enchanted possibilities.

It was at the age of thirty-three when he finally saw one. It had been during an assignment for the newspaper, a dull and drizzling Monday morning spent on a new pleasure boat excursion he had been asked to review. The vessel's owner had barked a few responses to his questions as the handful of passengers looked glumly across the stretch of ocean, their frowns echoing the same sentiment – not today. Hamish had quickly given up hope too, returning to his seat to watch the clouds thickening above and the water quickening below.

Twenty minutes later, there came a shout followed by another. Even the ship's owner paused to raise a hand to shield his eyes. Every head was turned in the same direction – then he saw it. Hamish had to blink away the disbelief, but it was no illusion. It was a single sperm whale, riding the waves. Magnificent, majestic, the creature had brushed the surface of the sea, given an elegant cry, then disappeared again. Hamish had leaned over the side to watch, felt his jaw dropping, his pulse racing, reduced to a little boy once more. Awe-struck by God's creation. For days, weeks, months afterwards, he could not help but wonder if he had finally found the answer. If he had witnessed the spirit of the lost fisherman in another form, if the man he had longed for had at last returned. Always, he seemed to be nowhere and everywhere, as if playing a game. A game Hamish wanted to win.

Even this morning, with his hands around the vacuum handle, his shopping bag weighted with overpriced vegan produce, making the bed with the best linen he could find in the local charity shop, washed and ironed with his own fair hands, Hamish had found his mind irrepressibly drifting back to the past, to his childhood self, to those few days of peace. They still seemed more authentic than his current reality, the thought that tomorrow his daughter would arrive. It felt intangible, transient, meaningless. Unlike his memories.

The whale sighting had been one of the stories Hamish had told his daughter when they first met. After years of silence, Rosa had called him unexpectedly, her voice floundering with nerves. He had felt the same, their conversation filled with more pauses than words, but eventually she had revealed the reason for finally making contact, having come to realise that Noa, their child, could not grow up without knowing her father.

'Child?' Hamish had mumbled back, his world

suddenly imploding, confusion giving way to shock. Rosa had said goodbye and cut the call; he had clung to the phone until the revelation caught up with him. Almost as soon as he replaced the receiver, it rang again. 'Monday, midday, under the archway,' she had said. It might have been poetry, but the thought did not soothe him. Hamish would soon meet his daughter, the family he had never known about. He did not sleep for days.

Monday, midday, under the archway she had stood – a girl of eight wearing a red coat with a matching jumper underneath, dark denim jeans and shiny red shoes, all impeccably clean and neat. She was short for her age, like her father, but there the similarities ended. She stood with perfect posture, one hand stroking the end of a thick braid that hung across her shoulder, shining like a rope of polished mahogany. Her wide eyes and unwavering smile suggested a natural confidence, and perhaps an attempt to conceal the eager anticipation she felt bubbling inside as her gaze drifted across the bay.

Hamish could not help but stare at the figure on top of the cliff; she was her mother in miniature, a being from a past life, an apparition from a different world. His daughter, their daughter, the unmistakable emblem of a time he had tried to forget. Now, there would be no hiding from his past.

Realising the girl was waiting, he had continued up the steps, slowing his pace as he carefully observed her from a safe distance. Approaching the archway with the caution of a hunter nearing a wild deer, their roles became reversed as the girl caught his eye and smiled.

Trapped by her stare and expression of recognition, Hamish froze. He could sense but not control the slackening of his body, his movements muddled, his right foot hovering above the walkway as if solidified. Before he could continue, she had said his name, loudly and clearly, carefully elongating the first vowel as if learning the word for the first time.

He took the final few steps towards her, nodding his head, then without quite realising his actions, he stretched out an arm, pointing towards the curved structure above. 'It's whalebone,' he had said, the only response he could think of. He quickly averted his eyes upwards, grateful for the excuse to look away from her face, from his future, and instead trace the shape of the bowhead's jaw.

He then explained how, in centuries past, there had been several whalebone archways across the town, all since corroded by the elements or removed and vanished. The cliff site had held an archway since 1853, the most recent example having been raised the year before Noa's birth. Here he had paused in the tale, watching his daughter as she turned to gaze up at the spectacle, while he privately recalled the day the new archway was unveiled, him never even knowing he was about to be a father. But that was a story to come, a mere grain of sand within a handful of memories he hoped to share with his child.

For what seemed like hours, they had sat on the bench together overlooking the bones and the bay, licking vanilla ice-creams as they watched the gentle tumble of activity below. Noa's mother had looked on from the window of the hotel opposite where they were staying overnight. Perhaps that was why Rosa had dressed her daughter in red, Hamish had thought – so she could be easily seen. Despite everything that had happened, all they had been through together, he was still not to be trusted.

Noa had seemed oblivious to her mother's concerns. She liked him, the man she had been told about only a few weeks before. The one with the unusual eyes. Over the years growing up, there had been careful hints and subtle suggestions, but the eventual admission had proven a release for both mother and daughter. For Rosa, it had been a secret finally surfaced; for Noa, an answer to the question she had long been told to stop asking.

As a relatively mature and unassuming eight year old, she had listened to her mother, nodding in understanding. She had no concerns over the past or the possible future that might come from suddenly having a father. Noa already knew her heart too well, was still enveloped in the wants only a child could prioritise. At that time and as that person, she cared only for the sea she so seldom saw and for the promised visits that would preface every birthday and bank holiday for the rest of her childhood. Hamish was less a parent and more an excuse to escape the city and her place within it. It was only through going away that she could learn how much she wanted to go back.

In the early years, Noa embraced the novelty of somewhere and someone new. Hamish was so different to her mother, not only in character but in how he treated his daughter. Unlike Rosa, he did not pass comment on the state of Noa's hair or the marks on her clothes. He let her choose which ice-cream flavour she wanted and always asked which seat she preferred. And he would tell her stories – not morals or lessons, but elongated narratives with proper plots and memorable characters. After hearing about the archway that first day, Noa knew her father was a born storyteller. Quiet and cautious, yes, but with an enthusiasm she could see in his eyes and hear in his voice.

Hamish had enjoyed retelling the tales too, old yarns he had picked up in his childhood and adolescence that had always stayed with him. Stories of the iconic whalebones and their origins, of Captain Cook's statue and his infamous sea voyages. The thirteenth-century abbey ruins and the former Saxon monastery that had stood there, Caedmon's Cross and the literary vampire legend. The lonely lighthouse with its one-armed ghoul, the spooky black dog that prowled the streets. At every planned meeting, Hamish always had a different history to tell, another local secret to reveal. And the more he shared his knowledge and enthusiasm, the more riveted Noa became, just like Hamish had during those precious few days up on the cliffside with the fisherman. One day, he would tell her that story too.

An hour and ten minutes later, Noa had thrown the nib of her ice-cream cone to a passing pigeon and looked at her wristwatch – silver, ornate, an heirloom she had promised to take care of – then rose and said goodbye to her father. Hamish had nodded helplessly, watching as the figure in red carefully crossed the road to the safety of the hotel and her anxiously awaiting mother. He had stayed on the bench, slowly finishing his cone, staring out to sea with his heart still hammering as his head swam with thoughts. His body coursed with both new and familiar emotions, not all of them unwelcomed. She had told him the precise date of her birthday, he remembered. Three numbers he would never forget.

As the vista grew subtly darker, the crowds dispersing, the mellow hubbub easing, Hamish had sat and thought about his favourite books, the ones he had devoured as a child through to the many others he had studied at university and discovered as an adult. Golding and Conan Doyle, Faulkner and Hemingway, with their tales of heroes and leaders, adventurers and travellers – explorers of lands, life and love. He had an idea. He would buy a paperback for her birthday – for Noa, for his daughter – every year. Perhaps at Christmas too. It would be something they could share, a thread of mutual interest tying their separate lives together. A bond he could build from a distance. Something to remember him by.

But as Noa grew up, she began to source stories for herself, always turning up on her visits with more novels than clothes in her backpack. She would take them into town, finding solitary benches or secluded spots on the sand to indulge in her private pursuit. When her arms and legs began to tingle with inactivity, she would amble around the picturesque cobbled streets, observe the boats trundling in and out of the bay, then watch the wide stretch of sky pass from day to night before heading back to her father's home.

As the years passed and the hoped for bond failed to flourish, Hamish learned to keep his distance. He had been much the same at that age, could relate to the pull of the imagined, the endless possibilities of a written fictional narrative. He would not do or say anything to appease his daughter, merely wait silently by should she ever need him. He continued to send novels by post, hand-selected with the greatest care, never knowing whether they were the ones his daughter packed for her visits or if she read them at her other home, snubbing her mother as she did him. Over time, it became less about the books and more the act of sending them that mattered to Hamish. They were tokens of a sentiment he knew no other way to express.

His meandering thoughts were broken by another sudden crash punching through the silent void, violent and insistent against the window, as if something had been hurled from outside. The storm had arrived; he needed to leave. Packing away the memories into the far corner of his mind, Hamish scanned the empty church then made his way quietly towards the exit. He could already hear the rain pounding away at the door, smacking against the boards with vigour. He once more wondered about the fisherman in his bunker, safe yet trapped. Had a tree fallen from above, he might not have made it, might never have rescued him as a child. The idea caused Hamish to feel physical pain before he could muster his resolve to pull at the heavy handle.

With his hood up and jacket zipped, he left the church and stepped into the downpour. Night had fallen, the glare of the lampposts illuminating the pathway towards the hundred and ninety-nine steps, followed by the two cobbled streets that would lead him towards home, but Hamish found the way blocked. On the wet stone slab before him was a large bird, its neck contorted at an ugly angle, a small pool of black blood beneath its head. He realised the sound he had heard inside must have been its sturdy body slamming into the glass. He leaned closer, his face furrowed with pity. A black-browed albatross. Very rare, a splendid example. He would have to report it, but not now. Not with his head already swimming, drowning, clinging on to a life he knew was about to change.

Another bit of folklore resurfaced as Hamish leaned down to survey the rigid form, its eyes still open, wings splayed wide, almost Christ-like. They used to say that the men who died at sea would find their souls reborn within a seabird, and that to kill one would bring about bad luck. It was one of the first tales he had told his daughter, all those years ago. She had seemed to enjoy the macabre traditions as much as he did, though whether she still felt the same, he did not know. There were many things he would have to learn about Noa, and she about him. He sighed heavily, cautiously toeing the soggy corpse as he mumbled the few related lines of Coleridge he could remember from school. First the curlew and now the albatross. It seemed that nature was trying to warn him.

The wind continued to howl, the evening air feeling ever more chilled as the rain pelted harder and faster and louder. Pulling his hood down further, Hamish peered out to take one last look at the bird, pushing aside his anxiety as he strode over the body then quickened his pace towards the steps. He did not believe in fairy tales.

Three

It had only been yesterday afternoon when Noa had said goodbye to her old home, but already she could feel herself changing, her world transforming. It had started on the platform of Leeds station, a grand construction of steel and concrete ablaze with artificial light. As she waited for the train, Noa had closed her eyes to the commotion both around and inside of her, becoming absorbed by her surroundings. She found relief in the invisibility she felt stood within the infinite torrent of bustling bodies, the whirr of their movement and murmurs lost amid echoing announcements, chugging contraptions and repeat alarm calls, man and machine moving and pulsing, teeming with activity. For eighteen years, she had valued her place within this vast organism, but now, she had to leave it behind.

Growing up, Noa had always felt like she belonged here, motivated by city living with its speed and vibrancy, its sense of progression and possibility. She loved its bulk of closely clustered buildings, the old rubbing shoulders with the new, while unexpected glimpses of greenery, history and identity revealed themselves round every corner like an eternal playground, an endless empire for her to discover. But as she entered her teenage years, Noa began to see cracks in the once gold-paved streets. She had always known there would be a shift when she turned sixteen, some form of personal evolution that would see her grow from girl to woman, infant to individual, and spending time away from the city had felt like a part of that process. But then the planet went into lockdown.

The global pandemic forced Noa to celebrate her milestone birthday in isolation, her future clouded by new unknowns. With strict instruction to stay at home, she found herself craving change of a different kind. The natural world seemed to offer the escapism she needed, places and experiences she had only ever seen on a screen. And while the sprawling forests and flawless sandy beaches she coveted were in short supply locally, she was able to find opportunities to engage with the great outdoors in other ways. Between home schooling, video calls with classmates and her mother's attempts to teach her how to cook, Noa had filled her ample free time with her new passion. Numerous notebooks were covered with numbers marking the many wildlife species she had seen from her bedroom window. She made bird feeders from orange skins to hang in the garden or donate to neighbours. And when restrictions and the weather allowed, she walked to Roundhay Park, noticing the colour of the leaves or the shape of the clouds in the sky.

As the months slipped by, Noa had found the activities becoming much needed lifelines, simple ways to calm her mind and soothe her spirit as she tried to come to terms with both a world in chaos and her own anxieties. In nature, she had found a way to evade the past and the future, somewhere she could focus on the moment, no matter what the 'new normal' might bring.

Invigorated by her interest in the planet, Noa soon replaced her social media addiction with obsessive scrolling of a different kind. She began rushing through homework to search ecology journals for the latest statistics, swapping her favourite films for protest videos and documentaries. She would cut short video calls with family and friends to hunt out facts and figures, using up her data allowance to download podcasts and campaign speeches. With each new discovery, there came a surge of something – excitement, intrigue, concern, hope – each burning in her abdomen, fuelling her to find out more, to extend her knowledge in the belief that she could somehow help. That one day, she would be able to make the world a better place.

At the beginning of her final year of school, Noa felt more determined than ever to be a part of the global change she had spent so many months absorbing from a distance. Yet every time she looked in the mirror, she saw only her mother's daughter – the same eyes, the same face, the same doubt she had always sensed behind Rosa's moments of silent brooding. Noa knew she could be anyone and anything, but the responsibility felt too much and too soon. She found herself wavering between potential prospects, oscillating like an ocean, always moving but going nowhere. It was as if she no longer knew herself, that the person she was before lockdown had somehow disappeared, leaving a shapeless, helpless form in its wake. Something had to change. Then one day, she remembered the scissors.

After their last mock exam, Noa had left her friends celebrating with chai lattes at the local coffee shop and returned home. Changing into her loungewear and slippers, she made a cup of blueberry tea, turned up the latest playlist on her phone and tiptoed to retrieve the weighty fabric shears from her mother's sewing box in the spare room, the very pair she had always been warned about as a child. She took a final sip of tea before heading to the bathroom, locking the door behind her.

The blades had sliced through her charcoal braid with a satisfying crunch, the silky threads slipping quickly to the floor. The eight-inch strands splayed themselves on the monochrome bathroom tiles like a vanquished enemy, like serpents slain. Noa had stared at them, amazed at the simplicity of the deed, then plucked them up and tossed them out of the window into the garden, hoping the birds would find the hair among the foliage and use it in their nests.

Turning back to the mirror, she had carefully studied her altered reflection. There was a delicate curve to her jaw, the uneven globes of her earlobes, a long length of slender neck – still her mother's daughter, but different too. She looked unique. Just as she began to breathe in the scent of victory, Noa stiffened. The back door thumped open then shut, a call echoing up the stairs. Her mother had returned home early.

For Rosa, beauty was everything. As the youngest daughter of an ardently patriarchal family and the single parent of an only female child, she had always believed that young ladies should appear and behave in a certain way, even (and perhaps especially) if they did not feel that way inside. In her case, growing up in a new country with unfamiliar rules and expectations, the ideal had led her to create the persona of an affable but independent woman. Confident and considered. Smart without arrogance. Loving but never love-struck. As an adult, Rosa came to expect nothing less from her own daughter – after all, beauty was a gift from God and deserved to be appreciated. She did not consider whether she might be right or wrong, and there was no one to tell her otherwise.

Being raised by such a woman in a very different world and generation, Noa had tried to navigate her mother's terms with difficulty in her early years, never quite managing to look and feel like her own person. She had come to think of herself as spiritual rather than religious, but while her mother recited Bible verses and moralistic fables, Noa cared more about being able to define her own values and beliefs, her own idea of beauty and merit. With each small action, she felt herself taking another tentative step on her path, a journey that would lead to liberty and self-discovery, even if that meant having to leave her mother behind.

Next to change were Noa's outfits and habits. She disposed of the tight and short clothes many of her peers (and even her mother) admired, instead favouring androgynous styles and vintage finds rummaged for in local markets and charity shops. She wore colours based on her emotions, replaced cheap make-up in favour of vegan beauty products and donated her jewellery to a charity shop, keeping only a pair of silver hooped earrings. Rosa's fashion magazines remained unread on the kitchen table, the recommended creams and lotions in the bathroom unused, the suggestions for shopping trips and spa visits ignored. And with each decision, Noa felt more empowered.

Sometimes she wondered if she was being a bad child, disappointing and perhaps even offending her beloved mum, her dear Mama Rosa. But no matter what she did next – taking more clothes to Oxfam, refusing to use the designer body wash, chopping off her long and luscious hair – her mother would sigh, shrug, then suggest a 'girly night in' together. Noa would order a takeaway on her app, mother and daughter greedily scrapping the insides of the cartons with chopsticks, before Rosa reached for her CD collection, all her old favourites, and then they would dance.

With the volume turned up and the sofa pushed back against the wall, they would strut across the open space, swivelling hips and rotating hands, their fingers working like shining stars. With hearts beating and faces beaming, they would then sit at the kitchen table and paint one another's nails in the brightest shades, just like when Noa had been a little girl and the dream of being a glamorous woman seemed not only possible but inevitable. All because her mother believed it would be so. Noa still needed that hope more than ever.

They had begun discussing plans for Noa's future in earnest shortly after the new year and her return to school. Mother and daughter already had their own ideas, inevitably finding themselves fighting from opposing corners – Noa on the side of further education and personal freedom, Rosa determined to have her only child married and settled by the time she reached twenty-five, if not before. They were cautious in their arguments, yet neither would concede. Every time, Noa would end up begrudgingly silencing herself, sloping off to her bedroom and slamming the door with instant regret.

She would often call her great aunt Isobel for advice, but the insistence that she would 'find her own way' only added to Noa's frustration. The rest of the family had proved equally unhelpful, either agreeing with Rosa or making other unappealing options – becoming a doctor or a lawyer, or even staying at home forever as her mother's carer. They would never understand what it was like for her, Noa thought, the difference she could make to the world.

She had not wanted to raise the issue with her father either, though there had been the opportunity to during her visit in the February half term. It had been the first time they had seen one another in nearly two years, and he had been more distracted and disinterested than ever. Even the most ordinary topics of conversation had felt impossible, let alone a heart-to-heart about her future. It was clear to Noa that she would have to make her decision alone.

By the time summer had arrived, she felt physically and emotionally spent. The months of studying by day and worrying by night had left her no closer to forming a plan, but she at least had her trip to Europe to look forward to. With Rosa replacing her dating advice with travel warnings, still reluctant to let her daughter leave, Noa knew the distance and time would provide the distraction she needed to finally find a solution.

It was the first time Noa had ever been abroad and away from home for so long. Six weeks of exploration beginning in France and ending in Norway, during which she and her four friends had avoided the most popular locations in favour of a handful of smaller communities and hidden localities neglected by the holiday brochures. There they had witnessed real life, meeting people and visiting places outside of and in contrast to their cocooned existence in England, a life Noa now knew was safe but secluded, shielding her from reality. Having experienced such freedom, she had returned home eager to learn more. She wanted to be a part of the world, to understand it, to feel rooted deep within the earth. Her eyes had been opened; her heart finally felt full. She was determined to make a change.

Next, she needed to decide how she could help, but all the ambitions of her equally eco-conscious friends seemed unattainable. Noa did not have the confidence to be a politician or to start her own business, nor could she imagine herself leading rallies or planning protests. She had neither the grades nor the drive to become a great biologist or ecologist. But she could write reasonably well, she realised. And she had a voice. She began to research the idea of becoming a journalist, and the more she read, the more she realised the power of the pen, the ability to use words as weapons, to recount what she had seen and could not keep silent.

With summer a distant memory and autumn rapidly approaching, Noa had edged closer towards a career plan but still lacked a final decision. Her mother had agreed to her taking a gap year before studying English Literature at university, but only on the condition that she would spend the twelve months productively, earning as well as learning, pursuing her dreams but also fulfilling a purpose. Noa had agreed, knowing it made sense, and happily began preparing her CV and searching online for opportunities. But as she had sat in the kitchen one evening, arms stretched across the table as her mother finished her manicure, she became suddenly overwhelmed by the idea. A year was a long time, and a big responsibility. Despite all she had been through, she was still trying to understand herself. Her personality, her perspective. She needed space and time, to step back from everything she had seen and been, to grow into her own skin. What Noa needed more than anything was to escape.

While Rosa's expert fingers kneaded moisturiser into her daughter's left hand, Noa had reached across the table with her right for the television remote. A news report appeared blaring light and noise, a scroll of statistics moving ceaselessly below as a male voice tried to describe the scene amidst the uproar. The jovial atmosphere in the kitchen had quickly faded as they both became engrossed, Rosa's movements growing slow as she tried to continue the soothing circles against her daughter's skin. They had watched wordlessly as the crowd chanted, raising banners with slogans scrawled in red and white, some displaying grotesque images of bloodied animal carcasses so deformed as to be almost unrecognisable – but Noa knew them well. 'Hamish,' her mother had said suddenly, cutting through the silence. She stopped her motions, slipping her hands into her lap. 'He was like that.'

Noa had continued to stare at the screen, wondering what her mother had meant, noticing the use of his first name. Always Hamish, never 'your father' or 'my ex'. She knew they had not married, imagined they had perhaps only dated for a few months. She had never seen a photo of them together, nor heard Rosa say anything other than a few trivial comments about his clothes or where he lived. Sometimes Noa wondered if they had even been an item, if his existence and her birth had been rolled into one illusion to satisfy Rosa's need for closure. An easy explanation to conceal a more painful truth. Maybe her mother just wanted to forget the past, to keep the sense of distance that the use of his name implied.

Noa had said nothing to the comment, resting her damp hands on the table, pushing her fingertips firmly into the surface as she continued to watch the screen. Another man emerged in front of the crowd; bright eyed, his head too big for his body, slender in a dark green waxed jacket and grey checked shirt, his pallid face and dusky hair both weathered beyond his years. His gaze looked everywhere but at the camera, his arms holding a large placard raised above, his small mouth moving open and shut in an unheard chant.

Mother and daughter held their breaths – for all they knew, it could have been him. But the man Noa had come to know as her father was not a protestor; he would never have let himself be seen on live television. He was a nobody living alone on the North Yorkshire coast, spending his days writing dull local news stories and his evenings reading the same tatty novels. She pressed her fingers deeper, harder, until they began to tingle. Her mother's sigh was an alien sound. 'That's how we met,' she said, in almost a whisper, 'Me and Rebel Man.'

Noa had turned to Rosa, working the phrase over in her mouth, mimicking her voice as she tried to pick up on the hidden secret behind the words. She could not believe it, but there it was – Rebel Man. The person they were watching, the one that had made her flinch in recognition. Was her mother saying they could be one and the same? That all this time, Noa had more in common with her father than she had realised? It was as if someone had passed a needle through her skin, running a ragged thread through her flesh, tying her to this failing father figure. It did not seem real. Rebel Man? A fighter, a warrior? Or just another fallacy of her family life. She had snatched up the remote, turning the screen to black.

As Noa packed away the nail varnishes while Rosa prepared her special hot chocolate, she silently considered the possibility. If her father had been a protestor and was now working as a journalist, maybe it could be her calling too? Something inherited, the same ambition running through her veins. Her mother had never understood her veganism or second-hand clothes, her two-minute showers or homemade birthday gifts. But her father seemed to – at least, he had never said anything otherwise.

Thinking back to her visits, Noa realised she had

never really asked Hamish about his work, nor his time at university when he had met her mother, or even his interests and ambitions. If Rosa could compare him to an activist, he could already have written about all the things Noa had researched: glaciers melting and depleted natural resources, greenhouse gas emissions and polluted ecosystems. Perhaps he knew about them all and more, could even teach her how to describe them, to turn her impassioned pleas into impactful articles. The more Noa thought, the more convinced she became. Within the space of twelve minutes, her decision had been made.

Sipping her spiced almond milk hot chocolate, she had cautiously shared her idea with Rosa. She would become a journalist, documenting the ecological concerns that were destroying the world, but first she would learn how to be a great writer. Noa would move in with her father in Whitby, maybe even gain work experience alongside him, allying herself with local campaign groups while continuing her own online research, perhaps penning a paper or two. Six months, then she would go back home. It would be the ideal beginning to her gap year.

Rosa had sniffed, hiding her gaze in the comforting liquid of her mug. Her little darling had grown, her fledgling wanted to flee the nest, but what was to be done? It was a bold decision, another independent choice from her determined child. Noa had already explored northern Europe alone, so why not live a few miles away with her father for a while? Grow to know him as a person rather than through his calendared cards and gifts. As a mother, Rosa felt compelled to refuse, to send her daughter to bed so that she might wake in the morning and be six years old again. But as a woman now living with another adult – so beautiful, so spirited – she could only say yes. A million times yes. It was her maternal duty; it was God's will.

With the faintest nod, Rosa had set down her cup and reached across for her daughter's hands, curling her warmed fingers over the tender flesh. 'Go. Live. Make the world a better place,' she told her. Noa had thrown her arms round her mother, then hurried to retrieve her phone and notify her father, who, after several minutes of stunned silence, had finally replied with quiet acceptance. She had then pulled out her tattered travel bag, prepared a to-do list and spent over an hour online sharing the gossip with her friends. She had made her choice. A new chapter awaited.

Now here she was, travelling between her old home and the new, her gap year plans finally underway. While Rosa usually drove her to the coast, Noa had been adamant that she would make her own way, seeing a symbolism in journeying alone. With no direct train route to her destination, she had been grateful when Aunt Isobel had offered her an overnight stay and the excuse to make a long overdue visit. So after an emotional goodbye to her mother at the station, Noa had sped through city and countryside then back into the city again, alighting in Middlesbrough to spot the welcoming face of her cherished relative.

Despite being in her early seventies, Noa's great aunt still looked radiant, her hair and clothes effortlessly chic, her warm and cheery smile a beckoning beacon in an unfamiliar place. Aunt Isobel strode like a gazelle to envelop her great niece in a hearty squeeze, filling Noa with the reassurance she had been craving for weeks. Once she had climbed into the back of her aunt's tiny white Fiat, watching yet more scenery pass by, Noa realised that she already felt so far from her previous life. She kept her gaze averted during the short drive, gripping the handles of her stuffed backpack on one side and her new black satchel on the other, a post-exam gift from Rosa, personalised with her favourite keyring.

Having spent the train journey from Leeds lost in thought, Noa planned to quiz her relation on the many unknowns that still plagued her, but after a short nap and rejuvenating shower, she was glad to leave her troubles temporarily behind. Instead, she enjoyed the distractions provided by Aunt Isobel, savouring the taste of her homemade butterbean tagine and sticky poached pears, then watching a comedy film together wrapped in blankets before shuffling off to bed like a dutiful houseguest in the hope of an early night and a soundless sleep. It seemed the perfect interlude before her final day of travel, the day when Noa would leave for the coast to be reunited with her father and begin her new life. Yet despite the confident smile and carefree demeanour she had worn all evening, her hands would not stop shaking.

At a little before eleven o'clock, while her aunt prepared for bed – a tiresomely long routine, much like her mother's – Noa finished the last line of her journal and switched off the bedside lamp. The thin strip of light beneath the blind at the far side of the room distracted her; within minutes, she had crawled to the foot of the bed and raised the cover to reveal the view outside. After her eyes had adjusted, she took in the silhouettes etched in darkest blue. Rooftops and chimneys, tower blocks and powerlines. The odd flurry of foliage, a single sprig of bare branch. And there, high above, was a crescent moon.

Noa rarely saw the moon at home; its unexpected appearance now made her feel both nostalgic and safe. It reminded her of the first night in Paris when, after the long trip from the UK, the friends had finally found their hostel, removed their packs and headed out into the night. They had paused by the Seine to watch the mirror image of the silver curve gently rippling in the waters below. They had taken photos, looked up the translation on their phones and were instantly bewitched by the phrase – *croissant de lune*. It became one of many wonderful travel memories for Noa, one which still made her beam every time she remembered it. And now, the crescent moon's reappearance felt like a sign, a positive portent for what was to come.

A new place, a new life, she thought, settling herself back into bed, the moonlight casting a gentle glow over her unfamiliar bedroom, one of the many she had claimed during the year. Like an unexpected view of a *croissant de lune*, she hoped the next few months with her father would reawaken the enthusiasm and optimism that had so quickly faded since returning from her excursion, six weeks that had seemed so long yet had vanished all too soon. Seeing the Hamish lookalike on screen had given Noa fresh hope; despite her nerves, she had never felt more certain about her future. She knew there had to be more to her father than his posted books and mumbled phone calls – after all, her mother had called him 'Rebel Man'. The phrase had already changed Noa's view of him, a secret history she was longing to uncover – and tomorrow would be just the beginning.

Four

Though the tempest had passed at sunrise, Emil continued to wait. Buried in the bunker below ground, his instinct remained sharp with caution. Once his breathing had slowed and the slick of salted sweat across his skin had dried, he rose from his crouch. Finally, the danger had eased – even in the depths of the land, he could tell that the air had altered again, an imperceptible shift he could never describe with words, only sense in every part of his being.

The fisherman replaced the stone in its box and tucked it back inside his shirt pocket. Forcing three last heavy breaths of the humid air, he steadied his legs, reached up towards the door above and began to climb. Unwrapping the rope, he lifted the hatch and peered out across a perfectly still and pleasant land, etched in early morning sunlight. A gentle radiance crossed his face, bathing his icy skin with a soothing autumnal warmth. He emerged from the bunker calmed with relief.

Ahead, the scene was dishevelled but recognisable, the silence peaceful rather than menacing, still absent of the cries from hungry gulls and the boom of rolling waves. The receding tide was now uncharacteristically quiet, as if in recovery, lulling itself back to sleep. The land too seemed in slumber, tucked up within itself, nestled in hibernation. The trees and tall grasses swayed gently, playfully, the air carrying the softest scent of salt. Emil raised his face to the sunlight, tracing his lips with his tongue to taste the land and sky and sea all around him. It was over. Now he could breathe again.

Walking round to the back of the cottage, the fisherman saw that he was not the only survivor. The outbuilding was untouched, while his boat remained happily bobbling in the bay. Having heard the vicious tumult that had resonated underground, he had pictured her body breaking – chewed up, spat out, engulfed by water. Shipwrecked, vanished, leaving only a few floating splinters among the other craft. But now he could peer down from his garden and see her there, hushed and unharmed, her gleaming hull shimmering in the pale reflection on the water. They had both been saved.

Emil returned to the front, taking off his scarf and hat before beginning to lift the wooden barricades from the doors and windows. Once complete, he retrieved the chocolate bar from his pocket to appease the sudden moan from his stomach, munching contentedly as he walked out further towards the cliff edge. He cast his gaze across the view, noticing the tips of the abbey ruins, the twisted yew tree, the limestone pathway: all as normal, all unscathed. There were no fallen branches or uprooted shrubs, no damage to the land or to the town. The scene was perfectly ordinary, until he noticed the hundreds of dead herring littering the ground.

The fisherman walked towards them, nudging the nearest body with his foot. Lifeless and damp, the fish smelled only of the sea, their scales shimmering in the hazy sunlight, their eyes black orbs, oblivious to his footsteps as he began pacing between them. The herring were fully grown and seemed free of disease or decay, as if their watery world had simply evaporated. He could not be certain when or how they died, but he could tell they were fine specimens; they would fetch a fair price at the market and more than make up for the missed opportunity of a day at sea.

As he stepped among the corpses, Emil could not think of any rational explanation, no reason or logic to justify such death – and such good fortune. Despite the prayers down in the bunker, he did not believe in miracles or prophecies, karma or luck. This had to be either a trick played by a fellow fisherman with too much time on his hands, or else something had happened during the storm – he had fallen and suffered a head wound, or sunken into a dream so deep that he could not tell it from reality. He made a fist, digging the fingernails into the flesh of his palm. There was discomfort followed by pain, then a searing sensation like a burn. No, he was not dreaming, nor deranged. Whatever the solution, at least he would eat well.

Making his way through the sparse spaces between the herring, Emil headed further towards the edge of the land. Gradually, he could see another mysterious shape, one that was quite unlike the others. He moved in closer, leaning down, his eyes so wide that they stung. As he tilted lower, he suddenly realised – this was not a fish. This was a child.

The fisherman stood over the body, watching the side of the face, tracing the curve of the spine, noticing the bend of the legs, waiting for any movement. None came. Reaching down with the ends of his fingertips, he was relieved to feel a faint waft of warm air from between the pale parted lips. He gently pressed a hand against the child's arm, the thick brown jumper cool and slightly moist. His hands and cheek were flecked with mud, but otherwise he looked unharmed. He seemed merely to be sleeping.

Emil gently scooped the boy into his arms and headed back up the path towards the cottage, the fish momentarily forgotten. Once inside, he placed the slumbering body on the sofa and went to fetch some clean towels and blankets. He hastily unfolded them one by one with a single-handed flourish and adjusted each across the length of the child. Stepping back, he rubbed a hand against his chin, his mind spinning.

The fisherman was unsure of what to do next. He felt he should know, feel something instinctual to cope in such a situation. After all, he had grown up by the sea, had seen plenty of near drownings, received enough lectures on the principals of lifesaving by his elders. He had even seen the heroic deed in action, having watched one of his brothers pulling a younger boy up onto the sands, tilting back his head, thumping his fists into his chest before breathing into the tiny mouth. But the boy on Emil's sofa had not been in the water, he was sure. He did not look starved of breath or even unwell. Yet his arrival remained a mystery, like the fish, which would also need attending to. Not knowing what to do, think or say, Emil went to make up the fire.

After twenty minutes, the child opened his eyes, turning them on the seated stranger with an easy calm.

He seemed unafraid, even contented. Emil waited, wordlessly watching from the armchair as the boy fumbled with the coverings, pushing them aside as he coughed and struggled to a seated position. Still, he did not appear frightened, only curious as he looked about his new surroundings lit by the glow of the fire and the faint light of the two small windows.

The fisherman remained quiet, still hesitant of a suitable response. The boy was also silent, staring at the older man with indifference until both their gazes widened, noticing the similarity at the same moment. Their eyes. They were identical.

"What's your name?" Emil finally managed to muster, his voice hoarse and forced. He realised it had been ten days since he had spoken to anyone.

The boy tilted his head to one side as if trying to understand. Emil had lost his native accent years ago, though perhaps the child was unused to hearing someone without the local lilt. When the reply came, however, it was unlike anything Emil had ever heard. One word or two? Or just a series of sounds? He was finding it difficult to tell, even as the boy repeated himself. The first word rhymed with 'bay', rolling into the second as more of a hiss or a hush, but despite the ambiguity, there was a firmness and insistence to the sounds.

To Emil's ears, he seemed to be saying 'a fish'. His mind flitted between the few languages and dialects he had come across, but none seemed to provide a suitable translation. It must be English after all, he realised, wondering if perhaps the child's speech had been affected by the cold or by shock. The boy continued to repeat himself: three, four, five more times. With each instance, Emil listened closely.

"A fish, a fish!" The child tried again, tapping his chest with a fist. His lips curved and stretched as he spoke, as if they could not fit around the words.

Perhaps he was talking about the herrings, Emil thought.

"Fish," he nodded, "You are right. But what is your name?"

Surely the boy understood his question? He was small but seemed bright and old enough to be attending school, and had no doubt been made to stand at the front of a classroom and recite what he was called. Emil leaned forward, as if being closer would help him to understand. His eyes were fixed on the boy's mouth.

"A fish! A fish!" The child was growing impatient.

Emil nodded kindly, turning away to face the fire. Having moved on his own to a new country, he knew all too well how it felt to be misunderstood. He would not ask the boy again. He sat back in his seat, tucking his wrist into his sleeve.

The child watched but did not comment. Instead, he tugged at the point of his chin, as if there should be a foot-long white beard growing from it. He reminded Emil of a wizened old man – a prophet, perhaps. Was he the one responsible for the fish after all, conjured with a magic wand or wizardly finger? The fisherman could not help himself. He opened his mouth and laughed, a strange and unnatural sound that brought a rare colour to his cheeks and made his eyes shine. The boy seemed to share his humour and gave a little chuckle of his own, rubbing his ruddy cheeks with both hands as he rocked back and forth.

Having removed the rest of the blankets, the child shuffled off the sofa and edged his way forwards. His shoes were muddy, Emil noticed; they could be damp inside. He should show him to the bathroom and find some dry clothing. He might be uncomfortable, become ill. His anxieties were cut short as the boy came closer, standing against his seated legs. A chubby palm raised to cup around one knee. Still, he did not seem frightened. And neither did Emil. It almost felt as if they knew one another.

"I think we best find you something to wear," the elder man decided, though he did not feel able to move with the fingers still around his kneecap.

The boy seemed to sense this, stepping back and slumping down against the sofa before bringing his left foot into his hands to try to remove the shoe. Emil watched him struggle for a short while, then smiled as the child succeeded, swiftly taking off the second and setting them side by side against the nearest leg of the coffee table.

Emil rose and walked across to the sofa, selecting one of the smaller towels from the pile. He demonstrated the action to the boy, rubbing it across his own arm and a leg before handing it to him. The child nodded and repeated the movement, not only across his limbs but his stomach and back and the whole of his head. Casting the towel aside, he then tended to his sodden socks, reaching out for the low table to steady his quaking body as he peeled them from his feet. The boy shuffled off his burgundy cord trousers to reveal white long johns, then fumbled the dark woollen jumper over his head, a long-sleeved white vest underneath. No wonder the child was fit and healthy, Emil thought; he looked warm enough to survive a Norwegian winter.

The boy recommenced with the towel, though his undergarments looked quite dry, and Emil took the damp clothes and shoes into the kitchen to launder them. With the fire alight they would be dry by morning, but the night would likely grow cool, as it had done since the start of the new month. The child would need another layer or two, maybe some slippers, but apart from his workwear, Emil had few spare clothes in the worn walnut wardrobe of his bedroom. With the boy back on the sofa, humming and forming crab claw motions with his little hands, Emil crept off to the back room in search of suitable attire.

He managed to recover an old navy jumper that had become stretched out of shape, a cream ribbed top with excessively long sleeves and a pair of shearling-lined leather mittens that he no longer used. Returning to the kitchen, Emil took some scissors from a drawer and began cutting the garments into shape. Inside an old biscuit tin kept in one of the cupboards was a set of needles and some thick thread. He took them out, prepared his tool and began deftly refashioning the items into smaller sizes, including forming the gloves into makeshift boots.

The boy had come to the table to watch. Emil did not look up but could sense his presence as he worked. The fisherman was well practised in using his wrists, elbows and mouth to perform the task, having helped his mother when he was young with all manner of domestic chores. Once he had finished, the child willingly wriggled into the cream and navy tunics, though the sleeves of the former still had to be rolled up a little. The boots proved a more successful endeavour; despite their rustic appearance, they fitted surprisingly well and would make a suitable alternative while the boy's own shoes dried. Up and down he went, waddling as he tried to walk, chortling with mirth like an old ship's master. Emil looked on, lips twitching as the small form shuffled around the room.

Eventually, the boy made his way across to the softly flickering fire and settled onto the sofa in a crumpled mound, seemingly overcome with fatigue. Emil retrieved the thickest of the blankets and wrapped it around the child's shoulders, watching his heavy eyelids ripple as he fought against sleep. He could nap while Emil collected the fallen fish, then they would eat lunch together, he decided. He was sure there would be something in the cupboards to satisfy them both if the boy would not eat herring.

For now, he would leave the bigger question unanswered. The child was alive and safe. Where he came from, what he was called and why he was sat by the fire in a stranger's house, Emil could not answer. He could only do what he felt to be right. If this was retribution, then he would gladly atone.

The cottage fell silent once more. Emil washed and changed, then made a mug of strong black tea with sugar. Barely fifteen minutes, yet they had felt closer to fifty. He looked over the edge of the sofa, seeking reassurance. Yes, the boy remained. He had not imagined him. And what if he had? Would he feel any different? Though he could not explain it, the day had felt nearer to years, as if he had himself created this child, raised him, nurtured him, now watched him like a nesting bird with a hatchling. The storm had left neither ruin nor desolation – it had brought reward and hope.

The boy stirred and shifted a fraction further under the blankets, the fire having settled into its own slumbering heap. Tiny dots sparked and spat in the grate, growing brighter momentarily before fading again like stars. Emil felt lethargic, but there was work to be done.

On retrieving his jacket from the hook on the door, he noticed the slight bulges in the fabric either side – his bunker rations and matches, hastily stuffed there at the final signs of the imminent storm the night before. He removed the bread and cheese, sliding them onto the side, though he could still feel the ache of hunger inside – it would be worth the wait, he told himself. They would dine like kings once he had collected the fish, perhaps hung a dozen or so in the smoker beside the outbuilding to eat later. There would be plenty of woodchips in the store, dry enough for another day or so, at least. There was fresh brine too, he remembered, and some salt to dry brine a further large batch. He would not even have to worry about selling them with their number so plentiful.

The thought of such an unprecedented haul served to banish the niggling doubts of earlier. For the first time in years, the fisherman would be able to make it through the winter without worry. It was a rare feeling of relief.

Stepping out of the front door, Emil paused to retrieve the hat and scarf he had removed earlier, throwing them on as he walked. He was glad to find the mass of herring remained. In the outhouse, he quickly checked his former preparations – salt and jars, woodchips and empty hooks. His knife sat clean and eager on the side, ready for his return. He found the custom-made basket with straps in a darkened corner, only ever used for the occasional beachcombing and garden foraging in the lighter days of the year. He picked it up and slung it onto his back, the tight salted weave crackling with age as he adjusted its placement.

As Emil headed for the door, he was suddenly hit by the absurdity of the situation. To abandon a day on the water in favour of plucking his catch from the land instead of the sea – it seemed foolish, like a fairy tale, bound to end in failure and sorrow. What would the men down at the market say about his plans? Would their jeers be any louder, any more hurtful, than those he so often heard hissed behind clenched hands and stooped backs? Less thought and more action, he told himself sternly. There was fishing to be done.

Back outside, the silky sun dispersing through a blurry haze, Emil set to work. He bent down, raised a single fish by its tail and brought it close to his nose, expertly inspecting the skin, fins, gills and eyes for signs of illness or deterioration. There were none. No sight nor smell that disturbed him, nor any clue as to how they had come to litter his land.

As he paced among the bodies, flinging one after another into the basket, the fisherman returned to his musings. Perhaps as a younger man, he would have simply shrugged and accepted the story before him, but the new world did not serve dreamers. He had seen the scars that false hope could bring, had carried his own from the day he was born, his ailment a caution, an observable omen of nature's wrath – so they had said. But the boy sleeping in his cottage was not a blight or burden as he had been. The child was surely on the side of the angels, a message from a higher and purer being. Could he believe it possible? A fallen figure, and Emil his rescuer.

Forty-five, forty-six, forty-seven and still counting. After twenty minutes of labour, the fisherman made his way back up to the outbuilding, intending to place the first batch in his hand-built smoker. He was still learning to master the process and had not yet come close to the quality of the famed Fortune's Kippers down towards the town. Still, he would have to try. With conditions as they were, he could not afford to lose the opportunity. Winter was coming, and following the hardships of last year, he did not want to think how he would survive. The political tensions were growing ever more strained over ocean territories, the fishermen's livelihoods slipping away, relics of a soon to be forgotten age. It was all they talked about at the market, though Emil avoided joining the conversation. He had seen the newspaper headlines, heard snatches of the radio reports. Having enough herring to last him many months was not lucky. It was lifesaving.

With his basket emptied, his mind a hubbub of doubts and unmade decisions, Emil wandered back towards the remaining litter. The haul and the child were so improbable that he could only shake his head in bewilderment, tossing aside one theory after the next as easily as the fish tails slipping between his fingers.

After another thirty minutes back and forth, he had still only retrieved a small fraction. He had filled the chest freezer, then hastily gutted and brined twenty or so more ready for curing. Back outside, there were yet more bodies as far as his eyes could see. He stooped, grabbed and flung, again and again, returning to the house to wedge them into the kitchen fridge-freezer as best as he could. In the outbuilding, he took up his trusted knife, gutted and removed the heads and scales off a dozen, then packed three plastic grates edge to edge before covering them with salt. Job done, he returned to the land once more.

Time passed and still the fisherman worked. Once the brining was complete, he opened the lithe forms and carefully hung them on nails in the smoker, setting the oak sawdust aflame with a match. The kippers would be ready the following day, his mouth already salivating at the thought. His final task was to pack as many fish as would fit into the hauling containers and load them onto his van; he would have to hope that the market was still open, where the catch would make him a modest but welcomed profit for his first day off from fishing in years.

Using rough estimates, Emil calculated that he would be able to keep the remaining stock for five or six months, selling a little each week, as well as having enough produce for himself. It was not often he could consume such quality fish, usually relying on any imperfect or unwanted extras for his meals, but now he could afford to indulge in his own yield. They would make a pleasant change from the cheap cuts of meat from the butcher and the few vegetables he grew in the garden, along with the tins of peas and beans he bought from the local shop once a month. From now on, he would be able to look forward to mealtimes.

With his toil finished, the fisherman paused to observe the view. The tide had slowly seeped back in, the sedate water forming a sheet of glass so motionless it appeared solid, the sky flawlessly reflected in its surface. He raised his nose to the wind, eyes closed, ears pricked, just the way he had done in his youth on the shores of his homeland. Now as then, he pictured what he knew to be out there in the depths. The ones they said were the cause of the storms, the reason they had to be hunted. The whales. Devils to be slain.

Emil had never been able to align himself with such a notion, no matter how many stories he listened to or the number of ferocious tempests he shivered through. The creatures were exiles, yes, but not because of their malevolence – far from it. He believe them to be the sacred ones. He had seen them from the window of his cottage, the most recent a week ago. While surveying the conditions for his planned voyage, he had noticed something just below the horizon – a stony arc, rising then falling like a sickle slicing soundly through corn. And their voices; they were like nothing he had ever heard yet entirely comprehensible, wholly communicative – further proof, he believed, of their singularity. Not merely animals but blessed beings.

As a child, however, Emil had been taught that such sightings were omens, a reason to run, to return straight back home and enter the basement while his father and the other older men headed to the boats. He could not count the number of times he had hidden, his elderly grandfather roused with energy and excitement, his docile mother anxious and quiet, his older siblings an uncertain combination of the two, never quite sure what or who to believe.

In their community, fear and fantasy were tightly interwoven like threads of a fabric, and as children, they had been bound within the binds, comforted and concealed by the repetition of ancient narratives both desired and dreaded. While Emil's elder brothers seemed content to remain cossetted by their grandfather's tall tales, he had wanted to tug away at their edges, to peak underneath, to reveal the truth. Whenever the storms came, he felt a yearning to view the world in all its ugliness.

In Emil's former village, it was thought that when a whale was killed, its spirit remained on Earth to haunt the land in human form. His own father had seen one – a girl no more than six years old, which he had said was the soul of a young calf he had snared. At first, the old man had spoken openly of his sighting, recalling the precise details of her hair, her coat, even down to her mittens. The whale had also been described, though to Emil's ears, it resembled nothing like the graceful forms he had himself witnessed. His father made it out to be beastly, his mutilation justified and heroic.

When the real girl was found a week later frozen under the ice of a nearby lake, Pappa ceased in telling his tale of triumph. Emil sought to erase the story from his mind: he had seen the girl many times walking hand in hand with her mother after nursery school. They had been in the same class. Her name had been Karin. It was during the funeral when Emil had decided that if a whale could become a human spirit, then the opposite could also be true. He spent many months scouring the sea looking for Karin and the others who he knew had drowned, died or disappeared in the area. Even now, he could not watch the rolling waves without wondering.

One summer, the first born of the brothers, Tomas, began to accompany Pappa on the boat to help haul the daily catch. In the late autumn, he was taken to the forest and taught how to set traps for rabbits and birds for their dinner – Emil could still recall the sumptuous meat, shreds floating in rich gravy alongside woody roots and boiled grains, salty crackers and sips of golden liquor as sweet as honey. But when Tomas returned one evening with a cat hanging from a rope, his father took him outside and down to the river, making him throw the corpse into the current. He was sent to bed without food or even a blanket, never to hunt with Pappa again. The family did not speak of the incident, and Emil found himself forever confused by the impossible boundary between right and wrong, good and evil.

Now the fisherman stood outside the front door of his cottage, about to enter his kitchen and prepare fried herrings with bread and butter and cups of sweetened tea for a child he did not know. A little boy who was not his own. His moral compass span in endless circles. A part of him was waiting for the sirens, the burly men in their speeding vehicles and padded jackets, their rough fingers across his arms as they put him in cuffs, the familiar sniggers as they noticed his hand. It seemed the logical and inevitable outcome of what would surely be considered a crime by the local community.

But there was the other part of him, the small voice growing louder, the one that had been fed by fiction and sentiment – the possibility that this was all meant to be. That out there, one of the creatures had been slayed by the storm and its spirit had found its way home, to a place where it could belong. And somehow, deep within himself, the fisherman finally understood. He was ready to accept his duty, to welcome the lost soul into his life. As he turned the handle of the door, Emil knew this moment was fated.

Five

The sunless sky was unsettling. Dawn had risen but lacked any brightness or warmth, leaving an ever unfurling reel of blanched parchment ahead, not even a wisp of cloud breaking the monotonous grey. Despite the absence of sunshine, the land remained illuminated by a pale iridescence, as if the light still lingered from the day before, clinging to the vista, fighting against the thickly twisting mist that threatened to swallow the muted view. The train rocked and lurched over the aged tracks, the aching timbers and loose stones groaning beneath its weight. The sound and motion felt soothing to Noa, who was hushed to near slumber as her temple gently nudged the chilled windowpane.

At six o'clock that morning, Aunt Isobel had driven her to the train station and waited on the platform, just as Rosa had done the day before. Once more, Noa had stood clinging to her backpack and satchel, anticipating the final stage of her journey. Her great aunt had softly recited a checklist: phone, charger, a flask of herbal tea, peanut butter sandwich and a glossy green apple. Noa had nodded, letting go of her luggage to wrap her arms around her aunt, suddenly realising how much taller she was and how fragile her relative now seemed. They had held one another a moment longer, ignoring the growl of the train as it approached, Noa inhaling the musky perfume of her great aunt once more, so like her mother's. She missed her already.

Her arms were still positioned in an embrace half an hour later. Head bobbing against the window, Noa blinked open her eyes and observed the unfamiliar scenery slipping away. Soaring structures gave way to bands of subdued hues, loose layers of green, beige and brown merging into one another. Offices, homes, roads and cars were soon replaced by sprawling clusters of trees and bushes, grasslands and shrubs, a scattering already tinged with the first golden touches of the new season. She ran her hands up and down her arms as the view scurried past, the clouds thickening, darkening, before the misty drizzle turned to dense droplets, clustering on the glass. With the cuff of her jumper, she rubbed off the condensation and watched the bloated pools outside pause then fall.

In her satchel, Noa had also packed a small book of poetry, one of her travel journals from the summer, a blank notepad and a handful of pencils. In the last few weeks, she had started drawing again – simple doodles of the environments and the wildlife she had seen on her trip and which continued to inspire her, floating through her dreams like mirages rather than memories; reassuring reminders of why the planet was worth fighting for. She had planned to sketch on the journey but felt too distracted, too busy with her farewell to her old life, the urban giving way to the rural, the vertical replaced by the horizontal, the view, like her world, slowly turning upside-down.

Noa broke her gaze to rummage in her bag for a

mint, slipping one into her mouth as she looked at the packed lunch her great aunt had prepared with such consideration. The nearest her father had come to caring about her diet was to fill one of his kitchen cupboards with baked beans and crackers – the only vegan foods he could think of. She pulled out the sandwich wrapped in a reusable cloth and tied with string; as she turned it over, Noa noticed a piece of paper slipped into the bind. Unfolding it, she read Aunt Isobel's neat handwriting: 'You are strong enough to weather any storm.' For the first time in her life, she believed it.

The tap was gentle but firm enough to disturb Noa from her daydream. The air felt colder, the space quieter, the day outside looking just as dull and disappointing as it had the entire journey. She noticed with alarm that they had stopped and the carriage had emptied. Another tap on her shoulder made her jump. The ticket inspector stood over her, repeating his request tautly, his wiry blonde moustache wiggling with words spoken in an unfamiliar accent. Noa nodded and apologised, slipping the note into her bag before quickly shuffling out of her seat.

Her mind still misty, she shrugged on her jacket over her smaller bag, slung on the bulging backpack, then exited the train. The sudden gust of icy air across her face and bare hands made her gasp, but sufficiently revived her senses enough to know what she needed to do. She was about to head to her new home, to be reunited with her father, to start a fresh chapter of her life as an adult, but in that moment, she did not want to move. Only the sharp nudge of a disgruntled passenger boarding the train persuaded her towards the exit.

The breeze brought with it the whiffs of smoke and engine oil, browning bacon and fried onions, the noise of the early morning traffic and departing train interspersed with the caws of hundreds of seabirds speckling the sky like scattered grit. It would never change, it never had, in all the years Noa had visited her father for odd days and occasional weekends. Just a few miles of countryside between here and her home, yet it was a different world, one stuck firmly and proudly in its past. No more city living. The hum of the sea and the stretch of endless sky were to be her normality.

Noa clamped her eyes shut against the sharpness of the unrelenting sounds, scents and sensations, silently wishing away the fear and regret, the unexpectedly sudden loneliness, the image of her mother and her great aunt wishing her well, encouraging her to be the person she hoped to become. The smiles, the tears, standing on the train platforms, brave and alone, solitary figures becoming smaller, becoming forgotten, becoming missed as the engines built up speed. Noa could still feel the ache of her face as she had sat in the carriage with her mouth forced into a grin, looking outside, looking inside, waiting. Then going, going, gone. They had been so full of faith, making Noa feel strong and capable, but now that she had arrived in Whitby, she already felt lost.

Pausing for a moment beside a bench, she thought about calling just to hear their voices. She felt useless, insignificant and feeble, like a child. How could she be so anxious, so unsure, when she had only just arrived?

Clutching at her keyring, Noa still found herself rooted to the spot, wondering what to do. Maybe she should text her father, let him know of her early arrival instead of the 'surprise' she had planned. Or she could turn back altogether. Sit in the station, wait for the next train. Wake up tomorrow and realise what she had always feared; that there was no place like home when you no longer knew where you belonged. Her eyes began to sting.

A middle-aged man in a flat cap and threadbare jacket nudged past Noa's backpack, causing her to rock to one side and bang her shin on the wooden seat. The jolt snapped her back to reality, the one where she had a plan to follow and an ambition to pursue. Her eyes quickly dried as her legs suddenly lightened, taking her on and away as if of their own accord, reminding her of the journey ahead.

With two firm tugs, Noa tightened the straps of her backpack and continued walking towards the bay, taking in the huge sweep of sky she so seldom saw back home. She filled her lungs with the bracing air, finally remembering all the reasons she had loved this place as a young girl, in those early years when she had visited with her mother. Heading towards the bridge, she looked up to watch the frenzy of circling birds above, a faint buttery orb hovering over the horizon. To her right, the steady rhythm of the rocking vessels, the colourful hulls painting a rainbow across the water. And on the left, a group of chattering tourists amid a stream of locals, walking and smiling, making their ways to begin their days.

She came to a standstill beside the crusty white railings to take a photo on her phone, but the image seemed so lifeless, so static compared to the vibrant scene around her. She wanted to put into words everything she was experiencing at that moment, the water and sky and birds seeming to align themselves so perfectly, like a painting, looking and wondering where this stranger had come from, Noa herself barely remembering. She pocketed her phone, intending to send the photo to her loved ones later, at a time when she felt a little less vulnerable. She had new friends to make now.

Like the city centre of Leeds on a weekday morning, Whitby's harbour whirled with activity. Noa slowed her stride to a gentle meander, taking in the fishermen on their boats, the amassed gulls with their beady eyes, a band of burly bikers nursing giant breakfast baps, employees heading to their posts behind cafe counters, seafood stands, amusement arcades, gothic clothing parlours and Dracula-themed attractions. It was all so quaint, so accustomed; a town where time stood still. She had been visiting for so many years, yet not a single pebble or strand of seaweed seemed to have ever moved. She could not help but be fascinated by the clockwork rotation of life here.

During her most recent trips, Noa had sought escape among the eerie ruins of the ancient abbey above the Old Town, where she could permit her imagination to roam between the mystical mounds of slate-grey rock, the winding paths that were once sheltered and holy now laying exposed and isolated. It was hauntingly beautiful in sun, sleet, or even snow, the latter of which she had discovered a few years ago on a post-Christmas visit. There had been a handful of times when Hamish had accompanied her up the many steps, lagging like a surly child, as if intentionally, pausing to apparently peruse the scenery before reaching the graveyard at the top. There he would go no further, his eyes fixed to the horizon while Noa went on ahead, alone and bemused. The likes of vampires and ghosts were just stories, but from the look on her father's face, she could sense he felt haunted up there.

Once or twice, she had asked him about the history of the abbey, a tale he had told when she was younger, back when they had eaten ice-creams on a bench above the bay. But despite her interest, Hamish had remained silent, seeming to bristle at the very mention of the local landmark, as if it held some sinister association for him. No matter how many hours Noa spent wandering wistfully round the ruins, reading the exhibits, recalling the chilling prose of Bram Stoker before chatting to the volunteers in the visitor centre, Hamish would still be there when she left, standing outside the church beside the same weathered gravestone.

Then they would descend the steps side by side, neither speaking, before taking the sharp left-hand turn towards the café with the beam above the entrance. They would sit and order coffee, tea or hot chocolate, sipping in silence as they gazed out at the holidaymakers, all marching jovially either up or down the steps, enjoying their leisure time. Happy families, Noa would always think. Eventually, she took to visiting the abbey and many more of the town's landmarks on her own.

Perhaps now that they had a whole six months to spend together, things would be different between them. Maybe this time, Noa imagined, her father would feel able to share his secrets, to reveal whatever phantoms were hidden behind his ever-thickening skin. To finally tell his daughter the truth. As she neared her father's flat, Noa realised that she would soon find out.

It had taken less than fifteen minutes to walk from the station past the harbour, cross the bridge amid the moving crowd, wave good morning to the life-sized polar bear model, then slip her key into the doorway between the fish and chip shop and the newsagents. Both businesses were open, the odours of fresh batter and tangy vinegar mingling with newspaper ink and fusty cardboard. Thankfully, neither seemed to permeate up to the flat above. That had its own distinctive aroma instead, a certain 'father fragrance' that combined overcooked vegetables, dusty carpet and damp towels. Noa was glad she had remembered to bring a scented candle this time.

While the flat may have been old, the novelty of having her own key was entirely new. Hamish had promptly put it in the post, first class recorded delivery, the day after Noa had confirmed her visit. She had seen it as a sign, a symbol of welcome to their soon-to-be shared home, though it was more likely to be merely a practicality. Though she did not know him well, she could tell he was not the sentimental type. Still, she felt a hum of anticipation in her stomach at the prospect of her surprise, the eagerness causing her to fumble with the lock and scratch the paintwork of the door. She grew conscious of the people passing behind on the path, imagining their stares and whispers at the unfamiliar city girl letting herself into the local loner's home.

As soon as the door swung open, Noa lurched inside and soundlessly pushed it shut. Along with the whiff of fish and chips, whether from downstairs or last night's supper, there came the smell of burnt toast, bleach and furniture polish. The hall carpet, she noticed, was surprisingly clean. She gently slipped off her backpack, coat and shoes, keeping her small satchel slung across her body, pausing to listen for any sign of her father. She could not hear or see anything definitive, but something made her think he could be upstairs. She began to toe the thinly carpeted steps soundlessly.

Hamish had said very little on the phone to her suggestion of moving in with him. Her previous trips had been two days at the most, and Noa was almost certain he had never lived with someone else for much longer – even her own mother. Yet despite her misgivings, she was sure she had made the right choice, felt confident that she knew her father's quiet and curious ways well enough to establish some sort of comfort – if not familial then at least amiable. After all, who better than a coastal native, a born researcher, a regular writer and the person her mother described as 'Rebel Man' to be her personal tutor? She could feel her blood pulsing through her limbs, her cheeks flushing, her hands softly shaking as she walked up the stairs.

On reaching the first floor landing, Noa stopped, staring ahead in confusion. The narrow space was barred by a wooden staircase she had never seen before. She traced it with her eyes, wondering where it had come from, and saw that it led to the ceiling – an attic. Soft light shone from the open square. She peered up, hearing footsteps and the squeak of a chair. Nothing, then a gentle cough. She kept still, waiting, wanting Hamish to have heard the front door, to call her name, to rush down and begin showing his daughter round her new home. But there was no sign of him.

Minutes passed as Noa continued to wait, wondering what he was doing. She remained rooted at the foot of the attic stairs, stifling her greeting as the sense of unease increased. Her palms had become moist, her heartrate heightened. Hamish was up there, she knew, but up where exactly, and why? Of all the dream scenarios she had envisioned for her arrival, Noa could never have imagined this. She must have spent hours picturing this very moment, their reunion, the beginning of their new life together, but a mysterious room had not been part of the plan. Staring up into the hole, she suddenly felt unwelcomed. Unsafe.

Despite her anxiety, she knew she could not walk away. Not now. Not when she had come so far. The protestor from the television had changed everything. It had been a signal, she was sure. Learning more about her father – whatever that might entail – was one of the reasons she had come here. Fighting against uncertainty, she closed her eyes and remembered her mother's words a few days before her departure: 'Make your own decisions,' she had said, 'Take care of yourself.' Words of kindness, Noa now wondered, or words of warning? Either way, the choice was hers. Waiting would prolong the discomfort. She began to climb the stairs.

With each silent footstep, the fear became replaced by exhilaration – she had found a hidden attic, a new world of possibilities, just like in all those mystery stories she had loved as a child, or the pirate tales Hamish had told her during their meetings, sat side by side looking out across an enchanted ocean. There was more to discover, she was certain. Adventure lay ahead.

As she reached the opening to the attic, Noa fumbled for the keyring on her satchel, clutching its form in her palm. She took the final few steps slowly, her head twisting left and right as she scanned the space. It was a square room with a wooden floor and ceiling. The left side of the roof sloped at a sharp angle with what looked like a skylight covered in thick cloth, the faintest trace of early morning sun seeping in through the sides. There was just one wall with any furniture, as well as the only source of light – an Anglepoise lamp with an unnaturally bright bulb, setting the figure sat at the mahogany desk into relief.

A floorboard creaked as Noa edged closer, alerting the silent man to her presence. Hamish spun round in his swivel chair, his profile appearing angular and slightly menacing in the stark light. Whether it was the brightness or something else, Noa thought he looked different – older, frailer. His face seemed thin and grey, his shoulders slumped, the skin of his hands lined and flecked with dark spots. He wore his usual attire, but the garments looked badly laundered, creased and scruffy, the trousers too short, the socks bearing multiple holes, though the navy slippers were pristine. He would not look at her, gazing instead at a barren patch of floor. Noa stood waiting for his explanation.

Hamish was frozen by his daughter's presence, startled like a wild animal, making no attempt to mask his interrupted activity nor to greet his unexpectedly early guest. A yellow highlighter pen hovered in his right hand, the left slightly shaking against his knee, the fingers blackened with ink stains. Behind him, the antique desk was strewn with papers, two of its three drawers partially opened to reveal more files tucked haphazardly inside. On the floor were some cardboard boxes, neatly stacked and labelled with dates, with a well-worn wooden toy perched on top – a boat with animals inside and across its deck.

Shifting her vision to the wall behind the desk, Noa noticed the documents and images amassed there like makeshift wallpaper, far too numerous and chaotic for her to take in all at once, but she could see people and places, some familiar and others unknown. Quays and harbours with ships and sails, cottages and cabins with fishermen and their families. So many haunting faces, all now forgotten. She gave an involuntary shudder as the multiple sets of eyes seemed to glower at her warily, the uninvited outsider in their midst.

As she looked closer, Noa could begin to see that the papers were arranged in some sort of order – thematic, chronological, she could not be sure, but it made her think of the detective dramas her mother watched on her days off. The attic looked like the work of a crime scene investigator, not a part-time journalist in a seaside town. There were pages cut from newspapers and magazines, some in a different language, taped up alongside official-looking reports, data charts, scientific papers and notes scribbled by hand, the majority bearing coloured dots in their right-hand corners. A handful of photos were slipped in between, most black and white newsprint, though some looked like they had been processed, glossy with age spots and framed by ripped edges and bent corners.

There were drawings too, intricate sketches in pencil or black ink pen, some quite striking in their accuracy, almost works of art. Depictions of cliffs and the local coastline, outlines of boats and of birds, an image of a man's face, a child's profile, then endless examples of sea creatures – fish, lobsters, crabs, oysters, mussels, whelks, anemones, squids, dolphins and whales.

Noa crept closer, her eyes drawn to the central page from which all the other clippings seemed to radiate. It was a cutting from an old newspaper, the front page featuring a lengthy article with an image and the headline 'Found Alive and Well'. She was about to scan the copy, but the photograph and its characters hooked her interest. A man and boy stood hand in hand staring at the lens with the same indifferent expression, an undistinguishable building behind them. Though the digits at the top of the page told her it had been printed in the Seventies, the couple seemed older. Ancient. Victorian, Noa thought. Like those creepy daguerreotypes she had read about. Faces of the dead.

A sudden sharp whine made her jump. Snapping

her head in the direction of the sound, Noa watched as Hamish rolled his chair further forward towards his desk, emitting another series of creaks as he slotted his pen into a rusted baked bean tin filled with an assortment of stationery and a single gull's feather. A faint wash of colour spilled across his skin as he shuffled up the papers and placed them carefully inside a manilla envelope, nudging them into one of the drawers before quietly sliding it shut.

After rubbing his eyes with two ink-stained fists, Hamish looked up to where his daughter stood watching. He felt he should speak but did not know what to say. How could he even begin to explain?

"What is all this?" Noa broke the silence. No hello, no pleasantries.

Hamish stayed mute, his face unreadable, seemingly unemotional, turning to stare at the wall as if it held the answer. Noa moved closer.

"The boy in the picture… that's you?" she asked, her eyes trained on the image as she traced the words of the caption.

The photo showed her father, Hamish Shaw, and a man the reporter named as 'Lefty'. She began to read the article itself, taking her time, absorbing each bit of information in turn. She could feel her hands growing cold, her body becoming rigid, her eyes straining as she stared. It was impossible. She must be mistaken.

"Doesn't seem that long ago," Hamish said, spilling into Noa's thoughts with his muffled, slowly formed words.

She wanted to reply, to ask more questions, to

reach an understanding before the tumbling cascade of possibilities made her sick, but she was stopped by something unexpected. The feeling of panic.

Noa kept her eyes focused on the article so that he could not see her face. She repeated the discovery again in her mind – not a heroic rescue but a cowardly crime. The newspaper said that the child had been found by the fisherman alive and well three days after his disappearance, but Noa was old and wise enough to read between the lines. Her father had been staying at the cottage, living with him – with a grown man. Alone. Together. She could not put the revelation and its implication into words, least of all in front of her father, the boy it had happened to. All she could do was stare at the blur of text, the unsettling image, playing the story over in her head, hoping she was wrong. As if these sorts of things happened all the time.

But it was no use – the fact that the attic had been kept hidden said it all. Six-year-old Hamish had not been found. The child had been taken.

Six

Noa watched her father peering at the wall as if noticing its clutter for the first time. He leaned forward slowly, then poked an ink-smudged finger at the two people pictured in the newspaper clipping. Tenderly stroked their chests, one then the other. She watched silently, conflicted, confused, but also immensely curious. The collection showed a side of her father she had never expected to find. A man who had secrets. But surely only criminals and psychopaths stuck stuff to their study walls? The voices of her mother and her great aunt cried out agonisingly in her head. The more she looked and questioned, the fewer explanations she could find. Yet still she stood, waiting for answers. Not from her father, she realised, but from her own deductions.

She could sense something was out of place but fought the assumption that she was in danger. It was how she had been brought up, a young woman living in the city. But this was different. This was a part of her father that had been hidden for who knew how long, maybe even before she had first met him. A whole decade had passed since then, and he had lived in Whitby nearly all his life. According to the article, he had been with the fisherman almost fifty years ago. Who knew what kind of monsters he had been battling with in his mind for all that time? Noa had finally discovered her father's secret, but she was reluctant to believe it was a sinister one.

"You were taken?" she asked quietly, cautious to control voice. She did not want to reveal the uneasiness that coursed through her veins.

Hamish did not speak, did not even turn to look at her. His eyes had glazed over, his body sombre as a statue, like some strange gargoyle carved from stone.

Noa suddenly felt the screaming urge to flee, to go back down the stairs two at a time and turn out of the door, run to the station and board the next train. To head home or to her great aunt's – anywhere she could feel safe, anywhere that felt normal. She inhaled, counting to four, held the breath for another four beats, then let out a steady, inaudible sigh. Despite the voices in her head, she did not move.

After what seemed like hours, Hamish focused on the visitor stood in his private space. His daughter, earlier than expected, in a place she did not belong. There was no hiding the truth from her now. No explanation other than the facts. Nudging a lock of hair from his forehead, he looked back across to the wall, his lower eyelids lined with grey velvety folds from working through the night. His eyes settled on the image in the centre, the photo he had pinned there so many years ago. The one that had started his enquiries, had raised the hope that had sustained him ever since returning to his hometown. He traced his finger along the caption and turned to Noa.

"I wasn't taken," he replied with a deep, steady sigh. "I was rescued. By this man… by my father."

Relief flooded her lungs. At least now he was communicative. Noa peered across to compare the face of the boy with the man in the image; yes, she could see the similarities. Maybe that was what had unnerved her – their resemblance. Her father and, it seemed, her grandfather. She looked closer at the fisherman they had named Lefty. In one hand, he held the chubby digits of the little boy, and in the other… but there was no other. Just an elongated shape where five fingers should have been. She scowled at the nickname.

"This is my life's work," Hamish continued. "I never became a journalist to write about fish prices or jumble sales." He attempted a laugh, but it came out as a croak. He was as pale as dry sand. "I had to find him. To know what happened."

Noa expected him to continue but Hamish stayed silent, seemingly waiting, perhaps listening, as if the room and its contents would finally whisper back, offering the resolution he had spent almost his entire adult life seeking. She did not know what else to say or where to look, her eyes finally resting on the little ark, a harmless toy, now an unsettling reminder of her father's shadowy childhood. She felt the pinpricks of apprehension electrifying her skin once more.

"Hamish, what are you talking about?" One final plea before she escaped.

Her father pointed to the photo, to himself as a child, to the man he had held hands with on the cliffs outside a solitary cabin overlooking the sea. If only he could step inside the picture and return to that world, he thought. If only his life had been different. His reply came slowly, painfully, marred by the speech impediment he had not yet managed to fully overcome.

"The night of the storm, I went missing. I don't remember how, but I ended up on the East Cliff outside his cottage." He paused to inspect the image once more, possessed by its potency. "He took care of me for three days. Three days and I was the happiest I'd ever been. Looked after. Wanted. Maybe even loved." The word fell away, fragile, forbidden, its speaker momentarily lost in its sound. "I never forgot him. He was my father, always will be. Wherever he is."

Despite the delicacy with which Hamish retold the tale, the obvious anguish in his eyes and his voice, the way his hands moved constantly as if he held a magic talisman between his fingertips, Noa could not believe it was all that simple. Like a modern-day fairy tale. It seemed improbable, almost impossible – how could a little boy just disappear then turn up three days later holding the hand of a solitary fisherman? A stranger, an outsider? And what did her father mean by 'wherever he is'? Unwanted thoughts willed their way forward, rising into her throat, waiting to leap from her lips and bring her father back to reality. But her reply was quickly muted.

"I know, it doesn't sound possible. Right, even. A man and a boy."

Noa tried to catch his gaze, expecting his eyes to reveal his lies, but her father's face remained as solemn and soft as before.

"Of course, there were rumours. Terrible things, they said. But I know the truth. I was there. And I was rescued, saved, by the only father I've ever known. His name was Emil Kleve. He disappeared on the twelfth of September 1973, one week after he found me. I never saw him again, but I will never give up searching." Silence as he slipped into memories once more.

Hamish had talked with such conviction, such power, his eyes still staring at the pages pinned to his wall with longing. What had happened to him, Noa wondered. What could the fisherman named Emil have done to earn such a place in her father's heart? Three days trapped in an odd house with an odd man. Three days without his mother or father, no family or friends or neighbours, and probably the whole town out looking for him. Local police, even reporters, all searching for the lost little soul, fearing the worst. He could have drowned. Fallen to his death from a cliff. Been snatched and sold into child labour. Unimaginable possibilities, each more horrific than the next.

Noa knew there must be more to the story. Hamish was not damaged, just delirious. He had clearly loved this man and continued to. Loved him enough to keep searching, enough to spend hours poring over documents and details in a hidden space of his home. Enough to forget his own daughter. His own flesh and blood. She moved across to the far side of the wall, reading as quickly as she could, even the documents in a different language, a few words of which seemed strangely familiar. There must be something else, she told herself, a part of the story she was missing. Something that would make sense.

The assortment spanned days, months, years, all the

way up to the present. The more Noa read, the more she understood that the fisherman had not been Hamish's father after all – not biologically, at least – and so the union had been cut short, the very day of that hand-holding photograph. And now here he was, a middle-aged man, riveted by the remnants of an experience that had not even lasted a week, that were potentially criminal, damnable – to Noa's mind, at least. Hamish had been little older than a toddler – how could he even remember? She began to wonder if his imagination had spiralled into fantasy, not due to madness but grief. Her father was not a liar, she realised. He was the one who had been lied to.

Noa stood back from the display and looked around for a second seat, but there was nothing except three bare walls coated in thick paint that had discoloured to a dull beige. She crossed then unfolded her arms, letting them hang by her sides, realising they were tingling painfully. The room felt like a mausoleum, cold and lifeless. She was suddenly exhausted and hungry, wanted nothing more than a hot shower and a vegan hummus wrap with peppermint tea. Home comforts, normality. In the space of a few minutes, all her ideas and plans had fallen apart. What had she done? What had *he* done?

She cast her eyes to the floor, away from the confusion of the wall, away from the silence of her father, the potential of his secrets. She felt disorientated, as if she had woken up in someone else's skin or had slipped into a bad dream. This could not be her father. This was not the Rebel Man her mother remembered.

Maybe if she closed her eyes tightly enough, she could open them again and find herself back in the city, in her old room with her old things, hearing the click of the kettle and the hum of her mother's morning song. All the things she had taken for granted and which now seemed so very far away.

From the side of his sight, Hamish watched his daughter, her gaze still averted, perhaps wearied by his words. He felt almost jubilant that he had found someone to finally tell his story to, who could be trusted to keep his secret, but he could not be sure it was a confidence his daughter wanted to share. She had come to learn, to explore, to write and to rest. And here they were, entangled in a family saga she had known nothing about. Hamish had been inhabiting two different worlds, two separate lives, and Noa had unknowingly become the joining point. He had unintentionally trapped her. He was not sure she would ever understand, yet here she was, still in his house, still standing in front of his collection. She had not run away. When everyone else had left him, his daughter had stayed.

Blinking wearily, Hamish forced the conflicting thoughts away, eyes roaming the room before coming to rest on the wooden boat. He had adored the toy as an infant, had ached to touch it. The memory was still so clear – his outstretched fingertips as they hovered over the miniature deck, wishing he could stroke just one solitary creature, his whole body writhing with anticipation at the prospect of finally opening the working drawbridge and seeing all the other animals inside. But no matter which adult he had asked, the answer had always been no. A polite smile or a snapped command, a gentle headshake or a smack to the back of the hand. Always, it was no. Now, of course, he could play with it every day. Admire the craftmanship, the delicate flush of colour over each piece, the coupled-up shapes in their neat rows, except for one form that now stood alone. Much like him.

"I need to show you something," he said, as if emerging from a trance.

Turning sharply to his daughter, Hamish rose from the chair and began patting his palms against his pockets – wallet, keys, phone, he thought to himself. Noa in turn snapped to attention, her eyes alert, either revived by the suggestion or perhaps just keen to leave. He could not blame her. It must look strange, this private world, but he was sure she would come to understand soon. He gave the wall one last look then turned off the light, plunging the attic and his work into darkness.

Downstairs, Noa retrieved her coat and shoes and waited for her father by the front door. Hamish hurried into the kitchen to replace his slippers, slinging on an anorak and a misshapen knitted cap, wisps of hair sticking out at all angles from the rim. As he returned to the door, his eyes darted around, hands repeatedly tapping his clothing. Noa watched, intrigued, sensing the anxiety and anticipation emanating from his movements. Finally, he went back to the kitchen, slipped something into his pocket, then led the way out of the flat and onto the street.

The early morning light had brightened, the town now a steady tide of people moving in all directions, the roads locked with crawling traffic, the gulls screeching as the first chips of the day found their way from polystyrene plates onto the pavements. Hamish lifted his face to the breeze as they began walking, weaving along the cobbled paths and past the historic old yards going towards Tate Hill beach behind the old fishermen's cottages.

Noa knew the concealed cove and its little pier well, though she had only ever been alone. It had been the memory of one of her father's stories that had first taken her there, lured by the haunting imagery he had so vividly recreated of the evil vampire stumbling onto this very shore. She wondered if Hamish came back to the beach for the same reason. From the subtle change in his expression, she could tell that he too had a certain connection to the place. Now standing with the stretch of pale sand before them, she noticed his entire body had settled, his shoulders had dropped, his face gradually softening as they both faced the open sea.

Moving towards a vacant bench, Hamish pulled a crumpled tissue from his pocket and wiped it along the length of the wood before indicating for Noa to take a seat. He sat down at the opposite end close to the edge, wondering if the gap between them held significance. Too small and she would be made to feel uncomfortable. Too large and it would suggest she was already feeling awkward. Though they had seen one another briefly earlier that year, he felt as if she had changed once more. Something had altered in her presence, in her spirit – if he were to believe in such a thing. She had grown in some undefinable and mysterious way he could sense but not name; he knew the space between them had once again widened.

Their muteness hung like a cloud around them, the chill of the dawn still lingering, rolling off the water's surface to coolly caress their exposed faces and hands. Noa slipped hers into the pockets of her coat, Hamish rubbing his own against one another, smudging the ink stains further. Their eyes gazed, becoming glazed, the tension slowly easing, their bodies relaxing as they succumbed to the serenity of the scenery, the iridescent sea dotted by boats, the two distant piers curved like a claw. Specks of cars passing, tourists amassing. Locals idling, dogs bounding. A picture-perfect snapshot of a sleepy seaside town. But there was something Noa needed to look for, the reason Hamish had brought her here.

"Tell me," she began, her curiosity wavering into frustration again at the puzzle her father had presented, the game he had coaxed her into playing. The mystery of the missing man. "Tell me why we're here."

The words drew Hamish from his private musings. He turned towards her slightly, trying to remember the last time he had heard his daughter's voice, whether it had sounded the same. Furtively, he took in the short hair, the curve of her chin, the eyes like Whitby jet polished into pebbles. He knew that face well.

The sudden realisation caused his breath to catch, his throat to tighten. Now that she was older, Noa was no longer the mirror image of her mother but of someone else. Someone Hamish had tried so hard to forget. From her long fingers to the cadence of her speech, his daughter was the double of a person she had never known, who had once been as important to Hamish as the fisherman had. Another part of his past almost forgotten. A piece of the riddle he had yet to resolve. His head felt thick with resurrected memories.

Noa watched the gently rolling waves, the birds skimming the water before soaring into the buttermilk sky, the sun still shaded by scudded cloud. Centre stage stood the indomitable West Cliff with its shops and arcades, fish market and band stand, lighthouse and fishing boats, and the famous whalebone archway. The bones. She thought back to the attic, to the sketches on the wall. She had been attracted to the ones of whales in particular, for their accurate detail as well as their ethereal beauty. The doleful cries of their mysterious song echoed in her memory.

She had kept her own collection of drawings from her time in Norway, but none of the depictions had ever come near to resembling the spectacle of seeing such creatures in the wild. She still daydreamed of the sea safari they had taken in the summer and the exquisite thrill of that first sighting. She wished she could put into words how she had felt for her father, longed to tell him everything she had seen and heard, learned and become, during her travels. It felt like the right moment and the right story, but she could not find the words to begin. Besides, they were sat there for Hamish. It was his turn to talk.

Though Noa was sure she had not spoken, Hamish began nodding his head as if in reply, as if he already knew, could predict where her eyes would fall and where her thoughts would lead. The bones, Hamish thought to himself, hoping his daughter would be thinking of them too. That was where the story began.

Seven

The cottage door opened with its accustomed creek, the room darker and warmer than before, with a note of something new drifting through the air – a scent, a sensation, enveloping him like a consoling embrace. Before Emil could register its source, he found his knees clasped tightly together, preventing him from moving any further. The small form had flung his arms firmly around the fisherman's legs, his costume rumpled and slipping, his lower lip trembling as he looked up with wide eyes and flushed cheeks. His little nose wrinkled at the man's musty aroma – dust and mud, salt and herbs, faint traces of sweetness, foreign but comforting. Then the boy began to laugh.

Emil managed to remove his coat, scarf and hat, slipping them onto the door hook before turning and crouching to adjust the child's falling tabard and flapping boots. The boy stood splayed like a starfish, calmed by the stranger's return, his laughter abating as he quietly watched the older man's single hand correcting his clothing, carefully, patiently. There seemed an unspoken understanding between them, forged in the silence, crystalised through eye contact. A recognition, a relief, despite not even knowing one another's names.

"I am called Emil," the fisherman said softly.

"A fish," came the reply, his eyes still shining.

The unnamed boy took the older man's left hand and encouraged him toward the low table beside the fire, the embers still rosy. The fisherman placed another handful of kindling on top before sitting down to take off his boots. The child waited, rocking from foot to foot, wringing his hands in anticipation. Emil soon realised why. The once bare wood of the table was now covered in papers of all kinds – some plain, others patterned, all evidently collected from the various cupboards and shelves around his home. He spotted the remnants of leaflets that had been hastily shoved through the letter box, the faded floral surface of wallpaper once used to line a chest of drawers, plus several yellowed slips from a notebook he kept in the kitchen for occasional shopping lists. Each and every page had been covered in drawings, lines and shapes in a thick black marker (the one he also kept in the kitchen beside the notebook). The child rocked on his heels, whinnying again, this time with a wide grin. He sought approval, Emil understood. He scanned the collection.

The pieces had been arranged in a sort of gallery, he could see, with the more accomplished ones towards the front. He could make out many of the forms – plenty of fish, of course, and what might have been seaweed or even an octopus. A boat, a house, the sea, perhaps a lighthouse. But there was one image that recurred over and over, solid and unmistakable in its appearance, almost as if the boy had been compelled to create its shape. It was without question a whale. And in that moment, Emil happened on the boy's new name. He would call him Noah.

Emil pointed to the largest depiction on a crinkled sheet of brown paper. The detail was uncanny, as if Noah had been working from memory rather than fantasy. Despite the fierce flames that now licked against the grate, the fisherman shivered. He looked up and saw the child's shoulders do the same, the air in the room momentarily displaced as if a third person had passed through unseen.

He pointed to the drawing and named the being in the child's language, the swell of the vowel sound thick on his tongue. *Hval*, hissed the voice at the back of his mind in reply. No, he thought, pushing the translation aside. *Hval*, it whispered again, until Emil realised the word had slipped from his own lips. He repeated it, Noah copying him like a chirping bird, his diction perfect, his face beaming in understanding. Yes, he seemed to say – *hval*. The boy retrieved the pen from his sleeve, turned one of the fish-covered pages over and began drawing again.

"Whale," he repeated under his breath. "*Hval*."

Emil nodded, waited, watched for a while. The fire reflecting in Noah's eyes looked like waves. The sea was dancing in his soul.

After a few silent minutes, the fisherman rose and returned to the kitchen, taking five of the herring from the fridge and moving across to the sink. He raised the first and gave it a quick customary glance – pink gills, bright eyes, no marks, no signs of damage or disease. Then he picked out a suitable knife. He ran the steel blade firmly across the scales before slicing off the tail and fins. With a fingertip, he lifted the gill and slipped the tip of the knife under the chin, smoothly pulling out the gut, leaving the delicate roe inside. He wiped his hand on a cloth and removed the lid of the earthenware jar by the side of the cooker, quickly diving his fingers in to retrieve a generous pinch of plain flour with which to lightly coat the fish. He did the same with the other four, placing them side by side in a wide pan soon simmering with butter and a few crushed stalks of rosemary collected from the garden the previous week.

Emil fell easily into the familiar rhythm, his mind recalling his childhood at the sound of the scrape, slap and suck followed by the satisfying sizzle as he set them to fry. When he was a boy of Noah's age, it would be his mother at the stove, busily preparing a feast for nine with all the merriment of a doting housewife. Then as now, herring had been a staple, though they had coated theirs in oatmeal and a scattering of coarse salt crystals across the skins. After the meal, when his mother would wash the dishes and his father would leave the cabin to work, Emil's *bestefar* would beckon the children beside the fire for one of his infamous tales, which would often feature the brave seafarers of the village, especially when they had been called upon to go hunting.

Farfar would gather the youngsters around him, tucking the smallest ones, including Emil, under both his lengthy arms, the infants shaking with excitement, the old man's remaining fingers creeping round their skinny shoulders to bring them closer. Every knock, rap and strike from the wind outside seemed to be an echo of the men at sea, of their relentless battle as they fought against the elements in search of the monster. As he began to tell his story, their grandfather's glossy eyes would burn bright, like an owl in sight of prey, the timber spitting and crackling impatiently in the grate.

Emil could vividly remember staring into that wrinkled and pockmarked old face believing every word. The mighty *hval* – the devil's aid, they called it, with a body big enough to fill an entire lake with its spilled blood. There were the valiant warriors scouring the surf, bellowing into the storm with their booming voices, their eyes reduced to narrowed gashes as they tried to peer through the salted mist into the distant depths. Then there, finally, they would see it – the shape, the surge of water, the unmistakable sense of something otherworldly below. Emil could still picture every moment.

As Farfar continued his narration in a hoary whisper, the brothers would rise to their knees with yearning, arms mimicking those fearless men as they hoisted and strained at the ropes and pulleys, positioning the ship as they prepared the harpoon. That modern marvel of engineering – revolutionary, awe-inspiring – precisely aimed straight at the creature's heaving mass, readied by one last shout of the shipman before soaring, striking, splicing the monster open with an immense roar. 'Hurrah!' the siblings would exclaim, some on their feet, others rocking back and forth on bended knees, their arms in the air, even the gnarled fists of Farfar himself, their fleshy victory flags fluttering above their heads in the dim cabin light. 'Rejoice,' the old man would cry, 'The brute is slain!' But the best was yet to come.

Back on their bottoms but no less buoyant with anticipation, the brothers would chew at their fingernails waiting for the next chapter. Their grandfather would stretch forward his few fingers, as frail and crooked as kindling, and begin describing the butchery. Out would come the imaginary flensing knife, carved slowly and deftly into the invisible purple flesh, the youngsters riveted, envisioning the gargantuan cadaver strewn across the room. They would be spared no details – the ribcage so wide it might be the roof of a house, the hot red liquid flooding the men's boots, the weighty wedges of meat ready for freezing, the stench of its innards, fresh against seared flesh. And the noise – the howling, the moaning, despairing and frantic sounds, their pitch and volume incomparable, unforgettable, the call of the beast in its own peculiar idiom. Full of fright. Full of fear.

Unlike his siblings, Emil could never sleep after hearing such stories. He would lay awake, staring into the gloom, wondering how many times his grandfather had been on such a boat, if his father had managed to capture a creature that night, if he himself would one day join the expedition and hunt and slay an ocean being.

He wished to be brave like his brothers, to relish the tales and celebrate their heroes. He wanted to wave his father goodbye knowing he would return a king, could bring profit and pride to his household, to the village, to the history books they seemed so set on saving. For even at a young age, Emil had known the tide was turning, the times rapidly changing. Soon he too would have to make the choice between the old ways and the new, between preserving village life and seeking better prospects in the city. He could picture no other place on Earth he would call home, but how could he hope to survive there when he saw such horror whenever he closed his eyes?

The odour of charred fish skins drew Emil from his reverie and back to the cottage, the herring having turned from silver to gold, tempting treasures glistening side by side. He turned off the gas and slid the fish onto a serving dish, leaving them to rest while he cut thick slices of brown bread on a wooden board. He then retrieved the butter dish and some mustard, taking them to the table along with plates, cutlery, two cups of water and the salt and pepper pots. Another small smile emerged as he looked upon the feast.

Enticed by the smells from the kitchen, Noah had made his way from the fireplace to the table and was attempting to pull himself up onto one of the chairs. Emil helped him, wiggling the back of the chair to tuck him under as the boy helped himself to a paper serviette, tucking it into the neck of his woolly tunic as if he were attending the finest banquet. The fisherman walked to the other end of the table, sat and then served the fish. He realised that he had never before had a guest to dinner in his home. If felt pleasingly ordinary.

They ate without talking, though the air was punctuated with the congenial clatter of crunched crusts, scraped utensils, eager sips and the faint rumble of contented stomachs. Though his fingers fumbled,

Noah managed to remove the skin and bones from his carcass and peel away the soft flesh inside. Emil cast his eyes across the table in stolen moments, observing the boy and his hunger, noticing how he wiped his mouth against his sleeve after every bite, held the mug by the base and not the handle, using just one hand for every action. Almost like a mirror. The eyes, the expression, even the colouration of his skin and hair and lips. Perhaps the child was not a slain creature come to haunt him after all. Perhaps this was some other kind of vision. Something his grandfather had neglected to warn him of.

Emil resisted the urge to pull the cuff of his jumper across his face, fearing it would be improper, impolite. He had to take on the role of the adult now – guardian, protector – for the duration of Noah's stay. The question of how long that might be swam through his brain like a persistent fog. He could feel the tension across his shoulders and along his spine, similar to the way he had felt in the storm – the anticipation, the sense of impending threat. His muscles were tight in readiness, awaiting the noise. The knock. The pummelling of the door.

They would come for the boy soon, the voice reminded him over and over, yet still he made no effort to reply, no move towards the outside world, the real world, the world where Noah had a mother and a father who would both be terrified for their son, frantic over his wellbeing. But he was safe. He was wanted. And for now, that gave Emil a comfort he had seldom experienced. A selfish act, but harmless. That would be his answer. To Noah's family, to the police, to his own conscience. No harm would come to the boy here.

He rose to help Noah from his seat, watched as he toddled towards the coffee table once more. The child surveyed his drawings one by one then clambered onto the sofa, tucked himself under the bundle of blankets and closed his eyes. The fisherman walked quietly across the bare floorboards, threw a little more wood onto the fire, then turned to see if Noah was yet asleep. From the way his eyelids wavered, it seemed the child was already deep within a dream.

As he began quietly gathering the papers into a pile, Emil stopped, a movement catching his eye. Something small was rolling, falling, slipping down the drawing he held in his hand – an object of some kind. He managed to tilt the page just in time to prevent it dropping to the floor, picked up the tiny shape between finger and thumb. Returning the pile of pictures to the table, he ran the found form through his fingers. It was carved from wood and painted blue, with two dots either side for eyes. A whale, he realised. A small toy whale. He placed it back on the table, his body cold and slightly trembling.

The fisherman made his way steadily back to the kitchen, his legs feeling a little loose, his mind suddenly clouded. He placed the dishes in the sink, turned the tap on, then off. His eyes were drawn to the window, to the dusk outside, the curves and lines of the land now barely distinguishable, like a forgotten sketch left to fade in the sun. It was the same view he had witnessed that morning, the same he had seen every day for ten years of his life. Ten years, and not even a single tree had changed. Not the path nor the harbour, the recurring weather or the seasonal wildlife. Everything moved in its own circle. Light to dark, life to death. And here he was, somewhere between the two.

In that moment, Emil reached two possibilities to the mystery of the child. Either the storm had brought a phantom to his home, or he himself had passed over. One still alive, one now a spectre returned, but he could not yet tell which had become which.

For a moment, he locked his eyes on the strip of sea, now the grey of granite and seemingly just as solid. The subtle ripple of waves had settled into a flat floor of monotonous water; ideal conditions for whale watching. Once in a while, strangers would come within yards of the cottage and perch on the lip of the cliff, wielding binoculars and cameras, the size of which Emil had never seen – so large, he had at first thought they were stargazers. But as he had followed their eyes out to the depths beyond, he had seen them too. The creatures. Swift glimpses, small promises – a hump, a fin, a splash or merely a wrinkle. Not enough to keep the men and their equipment returning, but plenty to convince Emil he had been right all along.

Today, though, there were no signs. He turned to glance over his shoulder, could not see the boy but knew he was still there, sleeping, dreaming. He finished washing the dishes, drying himself with steady pats as he continued gazing out. The sun was slipping – he would need to get the fish to the market before they grew too warm and became worthless. He refilled a cup with water and placed two slices of bread on a plate, leaving them on the edge of the table where Noah would be able to reach. Retrieving his keys, the fisherman left the house, locking the door behind him. It felt easy enough to go. What scared him the most was what might await his return.

Emil climbed into the van and started the engine, his heartbeat an audible thud as he checked the time. Usually, he only drove the short distance into town to take his haul to the market. Sometimes he would visit one of the shops for supplies, items he could not make himself or live without. Teabags and canned food, sugar and soap. He would try to be both quick and inconspicuous, keeping his right wrist buried in a pocket, eyes down, lips mute, his visit complete within less than twenty minutes. But today the journey seemed to stretch, taking up valuable time when he should have been at home. While he knew the herring would help him financially, he was growing less interested in the future and more concerned with what today might bring.

As he drove, Emil's eyes combed the surrounding land for any sign of dead animals or unusual forms. He could see nothing out of the ordinary. By the time he reached the market, he was certain he had been the only one to have seen the fish, to have found a boy. He parked in a vacant bay then heaved the heaviest of the boxes inside, waiting as patiently as possible for Sarah to weigh the goods. She knew not to bother with small talk, but her eyes were as wide and clear as new moons. Emil pretended not to notice, glancing instead at the other fishermen still around, chatting, laughing. They rarely spoke to him now, only dipped their heads, sometimes using the nickname they had given him as a greeting. Most, however, no longer bothered. They knew he would never respond.

The locals had been intrigued at first, keen to hear the stranger's story. Every seaman had a tale to tell, after all. A few months after his arrival, Emil began joining them at the nearest pub, listening to them talk about what was in season and the enduring problems with pricing, the most lucrative spots and the various tricks and techniques they had mastered over the years. The tone and type of idle chatter not all that dissimilar from an evening with his brothers when they had been older. Even the police sergeant in the town seemed to take a shine to him during those early years; he had been one of the few to use Emil's first name.

Yet despite the warmth of the welcome and the readiness of the other fishermen to share their experiences, Emil could not partake in their discussions. His own secrets, he vowed, would have to remain hidden. Never did he speak of his past, of his hometown, nor his new cottage and his personal fishing preferences. He was a listener, not a speaker, but here among a population where neighbours were as close as kin, his cool reserve could not last for long.

They could forgive Emil for his shy nature, for his unusual accent and for his aged attire – commonplace in his old community, but archaic and awkward among the newly-clad seamen of this northern shore. Nor did they mind that he worked alone, lived alone, ate and washed and slept alone. They even shrugged off his absence in church, despite old Edith slipping her handwritten gospel verses into the newcomer's hand every time she spotted him passing. But what the townsfolk could not forget was his silence.

What at first had been deemed to be timidity soon bloomed into arrogance in the locals' eyes, and as the years wore on and the fishing industry – the sole source of survival for many families and generations in the town – began to wither without hope of revival, some began seeking a likely scapegoat on which to vent their anger, the mute and one-handed man becoming an easy target.

His eyes fixed firmly to the sodden floor of the fish market, it took Emil several moments to register the voice. Sarah clapped her hands sharply, finally bringing the fisherman to attention. A couple of the men buried stifled chuckles into swollen fists at something she said that Emil had not heard, though he blushed all the same. She smiled in sympathy, handing him the cash before returning to the crates she had been moving when he arrived. A simple business transaction, devoid of the good humour and jovial chatter that Emil remembered filling the cavernous space on his first day, and which he suspected had continued ever since, though only in his absence.

The frosty edge of his reception was softened by the solid roll of notes now nestled in his top pocket, raising another rare smile on his usually impassive face. Despite the discomfort, the trip had proved fruitful in more ways than one. Not only had Emil made enough profit from the fallen herring to see him through the next few weeks, but he had not seen another haul like his own, nor heard any of the other men mentioning storm damage, mystery fish or young children falling from the sky.

Exiting the market with an unaccustomed spring to his step, Emil took a detour to visit one of the nearby shops for some fresh milk, bread and eggs. As he queued to pay, he noticed a promotional display of homemade fruit preserves. He picked one up the colour of congealed blood and looked at the label; an illustration of a knife spreading hot buttered toast with the dark syrupy mixture. He imagined doing the same, Noah's eyes and smile widening with delight. The fisherman placed a jar in his basket, raising his chin as he headed to pay.

Eight

Father and daughter stared out towards the whalebone archway across the harbour, both lost in their own contemplations. Hamish could remember the girl in red as if she still stood there, silhouetted beside the Captain Cook memorial like a bright flame. Though many of the specifics had faded, he could still recall how the moment had felt – to suddenly think of himself as a father, in the company of a stranger who was his own flesh and blood. It had filled him with terror, with paralysing anxiety, but also with a unique kind of wonder. It was that final feeling that still burned the brightest.

For Noa, the memory had waned, eclipsed by other occasions spent with more familiar family members and friends, and no doubt by her mother's determination to make their seaside visits as perfunctory as possible. There had been no photographs, no small talk between parents, no tokens by which to remember their hurried holidays. Whenever the father-daughter reunions had ended, Rosa had taken Noa to play in the penny arcades, walk along the pier and saunter across the sandy beach, before returning to the same hotel they always stayed at for a light meal and early bedtime. On every visit, Noa would fall asleep listening to the crashing sea, the cawing gulls and her mother gently weeping.

Thinking back, Noa wondered if Rosa had cried on

every trip and whether she would do the same for the next six months. It was only now that she realised how much her decision to move to the coast would affect both of her parents, dragging their emotions to the surface, making them confront their choices and their regrets while trying to support their daughter and allow her the freedom she craved. Noa quietly mused over her situation as the stone-hued soup of the sea spewed thick clots of creamy foam onto the damp sand, two dog walkers pacing up and down, leaving faint prints in the moist surface, while an old man on a bench to the right worked his way through a paper bag of mini doughnuts, three eager herring gulls mewing at him from above.

Hamish was silent and disgruntled, shifting every so often in his seat, unsettled, unnerved. Coffee, he thought. It would have made their excursion much more tolerable, rather than the stifling stillness they now shared. He should have made a flask of instant, the posh stuff that had been on offer, like he usually did when he came to the beach to record any findings. He had been too preoccupied today, first with more cleaning, then with his research. And now Noa had arrived early. She had seen his secret world.

The call had come only last week, his daughter excitedly explaining the plan, her idea to stay with him for six whole months. She had later written that she would be arriving a few days later, around lunchtime – he had kept the messages, reviewed them word for word, yet here she was, a full three hours early. A surprise, indeed.

At least the rest of the flat had been ready. Hamish had

never paid much attention to his internal surroundings, but he assumed Noa – or rather, her mother – would have certain expectations. He had preened and polished every reachable and visible surface, using the bottles, sprays and tins that had sat in the cupboard under the stairs gathering the very dust and debris they were designed to prevent. He had made an additional trip to the nearest supermarket specifically to buy the meat- and dairy-free products he had read about online, along with enough packets of ginger biscuits to feed a small army. He was relieved to have remembered Noa's new dietary needs, hoping it would make amends for the previous few visits when he had been clueless to her veganism, the fridge full of his usual beef, pork, cheese and eggs.

There had been adjustments made to the spare room too, a small square with sparse furniture but the benefit of a window looking out across the water. He had purchased a new mattress and a second-hand lamp, while the brown woollen rug from the living room had come in handy to hide the stain in the centre of the carpet. Wishing to add a little personal touch, Hamish had hung an antique ink drawing he had found in one of the charity shops on the wall opposite the bed. It was a copy from a late Victorian edition of *Moby Dick* set in a varnished wooden frame. Wild crashing waves, the mound of a monster, a dot of a man in the middle with his mouth wide open. It had caught his eye, made him think of the tales they had once shared. If only she had gone to her bedroom that morning instead of climbing the stairs.

Lowering his gaze from the cliffs down to the water and the beach, Hamish caught sight of a plastic bag being animated by the wind. He watched it swell like a balloon before softly sinking down onto the sand again, like a sigh. One of hundreds of waste products he would see in his lifetime. A sign of the times. Warnings washed ashore. He narrowed his eyes as it fluttered and flapped, fighting against the breeze, toying with his sense of moral duty. Just as he was about to move, Noa stood, strode down the path and headed across the beach. With pincered fingers, she plucked up the bag and took it across to one of the bins before returning to her seat.

Hamish watched her, a patch of warmth flushing unexpectedly across his cheeks. Yesterday, he had done the exact same thing, had been moments away from doing the same again today. But he had not needed to – Noa was here. He opened his mouth to tell her about another of his shoreline finds but thought better of it. It had been a dead jellyfish, one of many that had begun appearing in the past few weeks. It had been an exceptional example, yet so easily reduced to rubbish. He was glad Noa had not seen it, though it would only be a matter of time. Dead wildlife had become a daily concern in the area.

Though he made regular visits to this particular spot in order to check, track and record the diminishing animal and bird populations, along with the increasingly unseasonal weather, Hamish had never taken Noa to this stretch of shore during her previous visits. She could well have already discovered it for herself, he now realised, perhaps during one of her afternoon strolls, but she had never mentioned it. She rarely told him where she had been, and he had not wanted to ask. The fact that she continued to visit him at all was enough. He was about to make a comment on the scene when Noa spoke.

"The archway," she said, raising a hand to point.

Of course, it had not taken her long to spot the reason why this vista was her father's favourite. She knew that the unimpeded view with its defining icon on the horizon would hold a special significance for him. This was his place, his personal viewpoint, providing the key to his history and his memories. Somehow, it always came back to the whales.

Noa already knew the story well, of the archway and its history, the symbol of Whitby's whaling heritage. The bones had witnessed the town's rise and fall, the turn of an ambitious and hopeful new century with the promise of greater industry to come. The archway had looked on during the trade's decline and the fallen fleets that followed, leaving only fishing and fieldwork for the former whalers. Now it had become a curiosity, a photo opportunity, a location to meet people – *Monday, midday, under the archway*. The previous glory was one the next generation would know of only in history books, barely able to imagine what such ships and voyages might have been like, so far removed from the eras that were to follow, from the world of today. But in this town, the place of her father's birth, the source of her paternal legacy, Noa knew that the breadcrumbs of a hidden past were still scattered everywhere, waiting for her to find and follow them.

"They're not original," Hamish began, stretching his arm out ahead to point needlessly at the view, just as he had done when Noa had first arrived.

He knew the story he wanted to tell, the beginning of the tale his daughter had unwittingly glimpsed on her arrival, but he did know where or how to begin. The archway seemed the only way. He would just have to hope she believed his story.

"Those are the jawbones of a whale caught in Alaska," he said, wondering if he had told Noa the story before, in their earlier, easier days. Times he now wished he had made the effort to remember. "The bones before were shipped over in the Sixties as replacements, the others having weathered. That was when he came too, that very same day."

There was a pause, an almost visible tension etched in the air. Noa did not speak, could only continue to stare ahead, hoping her father would keep talking, not only to find out his story but to save her from her own thoughts. While the mystery fisherman had captured her interest, she was now lost in notions of another kind. Hamish had taken her to see the whalebones where they had first met, where the fisherman had found his new home, but he did not know that Noa had her history with whales, her own encounters, enquiries and emotions. Her own demons to face.

As Noa fought with her conscience, the sight of a gull crossing in front of the archway caught her eye, its wide wings beating softly, serenely, lulling her into a state of calm. She turned to her father; he was watching the bird too, his amber eyes narrowed, his aged hands faintly shaking where they rested against his knees. How easy it would be to reach for one, she thought, to hold it, to tell him that she understood. He had his secrets and she had hers, just the same as any father and daughter. He was not what she had imagined her father to be like when her mother broke the news ten years ago, nor what she envisioned as she planned her six months with a so-called 'rebel man', but Noa could not blame him.

"You don't have to…" she began, trying to catch his eye.

Hamish clenched his hands but did not turn to look at her. He was still staring at the path the bird had taken – a black-headed gull, he realised, quite common but no less splendid than the other wildlife that visited this stretch of coast. He sighed, brought his hands together, ran the edge of one nail under another as he took a deep breath then forced himself to continue.

"The fisherman saw the whalebones when he arrived from Norway," he managed, turning to face Noa as his confidence grew. "A place where whaling was a part of everyday life. And he found himself here, so many miles away, and yet there they were – the locals, putting up the jaw of a whale."

Ever since he had realised the fisherman's most probable ancestral roots, Hamish had imagined the solitary figure making the long and tiring journey to an unknown coastal town, a battered leather case in one hand and a hand-drawn map in the other. He had pictured him finding his way to this same strip of sand, observing the curious sight across the water, standing, watching, wondering why all the commotion, the opposite cliffside packed with people. Then seeing the men with their machines, raising something higher and higher, until the fisherman could clearly see the familiar shape. An emblem of the very lands he had left. Hamish would often watch the moment unwind in his mind, wishing he had been there in person, to be the one who had reached out to the stranger and have said 'You are welcome here', with kindness in his voice and a smile across his face. Years later, the archway would take on a life-changing meaning for Hamish too. He coughed into his fist before continuing.

"When I was older, a teenager, the town held its annual summer regatta, much of it dedicated to our whaling heritage. I never paid much attention to local goings-on, but it was exciting, in a way. All those people, coming from near and far, to find out about our traditions and customs. All those forgotten memories being unearthed." Hamish paused, squinting his eyes as the sea breeze whipped against his face, stealing away the last few sounds of his sentence.

It was the first time he had told the story, Noa the first person whom he trusted enough to listen without judgment or insincere sympathy, but he still found it difficult. The words felt hot and thick in his mouth, as if he were a child again trying desperately to make himself understood, to muster some clarity and consistency to his speech. The fisherman had been the only one patient enough to hold his tongue for Hamish to speak, to have waited for the words to sound and settle without correction or chastisement.

Noa shuffled in her seat, shoes squeaking as she moved one foot over the other. The images from the attic wall floated through her mind at her father's words; there were a handful that had looked like some sort of festival, newspaper clippings and old photographs showing the town transformed. One had been a full page and in colour – bright bunting and fluorescent bulbs, street vendors and a brass band, residents paused in their daily business, tourists with their anoraks and bulging backpacks, all amassed beneath and around the famous archway on the cliffside, peering down into the bay. Noa could imagine the harbour itself, filled with boats of all shapes, sizes and colours, each rocking and rollicking in the choppy waters like children at a birthday party. A happy reminiscence for many, but a day of regret for her father.

"The regatta," Hamish sighed, before clearing his throat, "That was the day I knew I was alone. The fisherman, Emil… he became officially 'missing, presumed dead'. I knew that my mother was long gone. And that morning, as the crowd started to gather outside, I found my grandmother had left me too."

Hamish had only just turned sixteen; now, he had no one. Shuffling downstairs at just after nine o'clock, he had discovered his grandmother lying in front of the sofa in the centre of the rug. At first, he thought she had fallen. Then he told himself she was just sleeping, had been too tired to go to bed and had simply laid down for a nap. She looked peaceful, her face free of its usual scowl, the one she had worn for the past three years. He had wanted to leave her there, telling himself that she was perfectly alright, probably dreaming of strawberry bonbons and custard tarts, treats they had once enjoyed together when he was younger, after his mother had left and there had been nowhere else to go. Happier years. Normal, almost.

Now she was dead. Hamish knew this, deep down. Still, he went to the kitchen, made them both a cup of tea, milk with no sugar, and took the mugs back through to the room, setting them carefully on the three-legged plastic nesting table. Only then did he check for a pulse, feeling only cool flesh that rolled under his fingertips like putty. Finally, he called for an ambulance.

An hour later, Hamish was walking among the spectators that had gathered in anticipation of the regatta opening ceremony, everyone jostling for the best viewpoint from atop of West Cliff beside the whalebone archway. From up here, he could see the start of the street where he lived, where men in uniform were at that moment removing the dead body, having told him to go and enjoy the event. She had died of natural causes, the man with the bushy black eyebrows had said. He would be looked after, taken care of, another had reassured him. Was there anyone they could call, his mother or father, a third had asked. Hamish had nodded or shaken his head again and again, and the three strangers had each clasped his left shoulder so tightly that he was sure they had made a bruise. He had given a false telephone number, telling the officers he would stay with a family friend, before picking up his wallet and keys then leaving the house, strolling away contentedly, willingly abandoning his grandmother like he had always dreamed of. His freedom had been a long time coming.

Edging his way closer, Hamish found a suitable viewing point by the side of the road, eyes wide and ears pricked to the scene around him, his senses unused to so much activity, to so many people, creating a whirr of excitement under the vivid late-summer sun. He eyed the man in the fashionable leather jacket and light blue jeans clicking away at a huge camera. Beside him, another similarly dressed man with a shock of bleached blonde hair was speaking to the town mayor, a handheld recorder in one hand and a reporter's notebook in the other. What a thrill, thought Hamish, to be at the heart of such an occasion. How he would love to be like them.

Then came the announcement itself, the official beginning – the launch of the ships. Two huge upright speakers emitted a shrill squeal followed by a booming voice, echoing up and spilling out across the sloping sides of the landscape. Something akin to a cannon was shot and a cluster of bright balloons went soaring into the air. Clapping and cheers followed, small plastic flags fluttering over a sea of heads, while down in the water, imitation whaling vessels began their journey towards the ocean. Actors dressed in historical garb waved from their crow's nests like in the days of old, but they would not be going hunting – it was all a charade. A performance, a pantomime, a reminder of the long gone glory days of the town. The gathered grew louder, voicing their united pride.

As he moved around the crowd, Hamish looked across the calm waters dotted with tiny spots of colour. Boats sailing for nothing more than show and spectacle, bobbing about without purpose, like priceless jewels strung up and exhibited, dripping from the horizon. Among the elation and commemoration, he imagined himself to be the only one struck by doubt. He was handed a flag but could not find the strength to raise it. One of the journalists slithered to his side and asked a question, but he gave no reply. A lead weight of emotion weighed down his entire being.

Hamish was feeling both grief and aggrieved, he realised, but not because of his grandmother. It was the whalebone archway, the remnants of a creature that held a mystical power in his mind, that featured in the most intense of his dreams and in the pictures he loved to draw, had always drawn, for as long as he could remember. Their images were etched into his skull, along with the memory of the man who had inspired his artistry.

Pausing to squint through the archway, Hamish could see a speck beyond set back from the edge of the cliff across the bay. The cottage. His former home. The place he could remember in every detail – its scent, its shadows, the way the light would sneak in through the sides of the curtains and move from wall to wall, casting dancing shapes against surfaces as he tried to focus on his drawings or on a story. How many times might the fisherman have stood outside his door and looked across over the bay to the very place where Hamish now stood, seeing the harbour and the houses, the traffic and the whalebones. Perhaps even noticing the boy he had once rescued.

Straining his eyes harder, Hamish truly thought he could see a silhouette. A man, calm and poised, watching the waters just as he was, as he had done so many times over the years. He had often seen the fisherman in daytime mirages and nightly illusions, not merely figments of his imagination but a form of real and physical presence, a living human being. The glimpses had brought Hamish comfort at first, quiet reminders of his happiest memories, but now they were stained with sadness and regret, his hopes seeming both so near and so far. He tried to let the feelings pass with the ebb and flow of the tide, tipping his head in greeting to the distant outline beyond, his mind muting the hubbub around as he scanned the shore for whispers, for the sounds of others who had also seen the apparition, but the boats were too much of a distraction, the scene below too thrilling to ignore. Hamish knew his visions were his alone.

Crossing his arms and hunching his shoulders, he began to walk away from the revellers following the shallow decline of one of the narrow streets lined with old fishermen's cottages. Now mostly holiday lets, their doorways were painted in bright hues and decorated with used lobster pots and handmade driftwood signs, macrame decorations and suspended shells – a far cry from the former slums that had crammed dozens of families together down the slender alleys known as yards. More reminders of a forgotten past.

Though he did not enjoy the spectacle of the regatta,

Hamish had always been fascinated by the town's nautical history, still depicted in the street names and buildings as much as in his school syllabus. While the ships and their trade had ceased long ago, their legacy lived on, etched in every façade and slippery cobble, caught in the sea's depths and between each grain of sand. The previous year, he had done a school research project on William Scoresby junior in the early 1800s when he was a whaling captain and revered scientist. Hamish's meticulous work had earned a gold star and letter of commendation. He had proudly cradled the portfolio home then displayed each page in front of his grandmother, only for her to sniff and turn her head away without a single word. The folder, letter and star had all made their way to the bin. Hamish had hated History lessons ever since.

Following his feet, he found himself entering his preferred newsagents on the corner, taking in the musty smell of cardboard and newsprint as he scanned the displays for his favourite sweets (he had yet to develop a taste for cigarettes and alcohol). For the past few years, Hamish had managed to make a little money each week completing homework assignments and writing forged absence notes for boys at school, occasionally finding a few coppers to add to the kitty during his rambles around town. He promptly chose his snack, picked out the right amount from his wallet, then placed the money in front of Mr Marshall at the counter. The man smiled at his regular customer, chattering about the regatta and his lack of customers that day as he put the purchase through the till, his words falling on deaf ears as Hamish eyed the other confectionery and perused the news headlines.

The local paper detailed plans for the procession that would take place later that day, with a word of warning against potential rebels and incitements of riots by out-of-work fishermen and anti-whaling protestors from the cities. Hamish had already seen and understood enough about both causes, the headlines and images indelibly marked in his mind. He had thought often of their predicaments, had witnessed the struggle on the faces of the fishermen he passed each morning on the way to school, the endless furrowed brows and downturned mouths around the harbour, the unsettling silence with which they now went about their work. Then there had been the demonstrators. He sometimes watched the television when his grandmother had fallen asleep, the box no bigger than his head, the screen always fuzzy, but the picture still seemed larger than life – activists, they called themselves, travelling all over the world to fight for peace, for equality, for the very animals he had admired for so long. 'Save the Whales' their posters read. He had scrawled the mantra across the inside cover of every notebook he owned.

As he left the shop sucking the sour dusty coating from the tip of his liquorice wand, Hamish could taste something other than sherbet. He could taste rage, feel the bile rise, sense the apples of his cheeks flushing. He was not an angry young man – his grandmother had seen to that – but he felt drawn to the civil war bubbling underneath the surface of an idealised seaside town. Behind smiles pulled wide like spun sugar, the men who had earned their livelihoods from the sea cast daggered glances at the men set on its protection and conservation.

Even in the playground, the tension had been apparent. Fuelled by the frustration of their fathers, the schoolboys' childish taunts had quickly turned physical, with fights breaking out on the asphalt between seafarers' sons and potential future protestors. Only a few days ago, a boy called Michael had been pummelled into a broken bloodied heap by Daniel, whose father was well known for traipsing up and down the beaches counting dead birds. The youths had hollered with wild exhilaration as the duo fought, raising fists in the air as they chanted cries of encouragement, but when it came to a winner, no one quite knew which side to support. Even Hamish still had his doubts.

He screwed the empty sweet packet up with one hand and stuffed it into the pocket of his too-tight jeans. He had worn the same pair for several years, his grandmother ignorant of his rapid growth, oblivious to anything to do with her only grandchild. He would later learn that her condition was called dementia, but back then, he was just a boy, abandoned by the adults he had grown to love, left in the hands of a woman who could not even remember her own name, let alone how to care for a child.

The house was empty on his return, a crumple in the rug and a discarded newspaper the only signs of anyone having been there. Hamish made himself a cup of tea and sat to read the paper, skimming past the daily news and unwelcomed reminders of the regatta celebrations continuing outside. A small article captured his attention – 'Missing, presumed dead.' He read the few sentences over again and again, unwilling to believe the latest update on the lost fisherman. But he could not undo what his eyes had already seen. His dead grandmother, the fleshless jaws of a whale, and now Emil Kleve – all gone. His father, his only hope, his final chance at happiness, had finally perished.

The police had arrived a few days later and taken Hamish from the house. In the two years that followed, he never saw any of his other relatives, and attempts to track down his birth mother by the authorities failed. He was placed with a foster family on the other side of the town, a retired couple, both former teachers, with a bungalow and a small garden, plus two elderly Golden Retrievers and a tabby without its tail. It was not the family Hamish had imagined, but the couple were kind and he felt welcomed by them, secure for the first time in his young life.

During the period with his foster parents, Hamish kept to himself, absorbed by his studies and sketches. Ever since his mother had abandoned him, learning had been his solace. He relished the chance to escape into the depths of his mind, to puzzle out problems, toy with concepts. He loved to research cultures and communities, crossing centuries and continents in the timeless stories he discovered from the local library, dragging countless borrowed books home in a wonky-wheeled shopping trolley before stashing them away under his bed. At night, he would make a canopy of his bedcovers, switch on a torch and immerse himself in the pages, copying passages and making drawings in the notebooks he had been able to buy with his savings.

Wildlife and the natural environment became his salvation, though Hamish saw himself as different from the other easy targets on the school playground. He told no one of his newfound interest, taking solo adventures to find the rugged corners of Whitby where he could see birds of prey swooping to catch vermin, find fossilised specimens washed up on the shore, watch miniature mammals making nests in the grasses, and pluck all manner of flowers and foliage from the landscape. He would wander along the River Esk, gazing up at the viaduct, scanning the estuary for waders feeding, or else head to Kettleness where the rock-strewn beach felt desolate and wild, the sea and wind howling all around, the birds still managing to soar with such grace. From hidden coves and secluded sands to grassy meadows and clumps of woodland, Hamish would walk anywhere, to any place he could explore until the sky darkened or the tide returned, or his stomach began to ache with hunger. Anywhere he could be alone.

By the time he reached the age of eighteen, Hamish had secured the grades needed for university, much to the delight of his teachers and the pride of his foster family. The former gifted him a book token, which he spent on nature journals and notepads, while the latter bought him a second-hand leather satchel and filled it full of stationery and his favourite liquorice sweets. Before he left, they also gave him six jars of strawberry preserve – a shared jest, a reference to his daily lunch of jam sandwiches. His foster parents had laughed through their tears as they hugged him goodbye, and Hamish had smiled, once again feeling nothing.

He could still remember watching the scene slipping past the murky window of the train carriage as it rolled out of the station, taking him to his new life. He had clearly seen a figure outlined against the far bank, standing, waiting, as if watching him leave. Gone in a blink, the apparition had been the only thing he could think of for his first month of university. He told himself to forget, that the fisherman was long gone. There was even his name on a tombstone, mere yards from the cottage. The past had truly been buried. Never again would Hamish call a man 'Pappa'.

Six months later, the memory had finally faded. Outside his hometown and away from the waterside and the whalebones, the constant wondering and the endless 'what ifs', Hamish had become used to and appreciative of his independence, creating a persona and lifestyle that suited his quiet nature and his private obsessions. His strong knowledge of British wildlife, weather conditions and rural habitats also proved surprisingly useful for making friends. He was welcomed into clubs by fellow students equally fervent in their determination to preserve and protect, though through direct action rather than the cordial discussion and silent strolls Hamish preferred. After overcoming his initial anxieties – namely his reluctance to speak to strangers – he soon found himself caught up in their politics and protests, marches and manifestos, giving him a new sense of importance and purpose, a reason to get up each day.

During the second term of his first year, Hamish's world shifted once more. Holding a homemade placard aloft on the steps of City Hall alongside twenty other protestors, his gaze had locked with another's, two dark glossy eyes that reminded him of Whitby jet. Like two fish entangled in the same net, the pair instantly became bound to one another, their pasts disappearing to make way for a new joined future. With one look, Hamish changed. With one glance, he had felt chosen, wanted. Finally, he had met someone who made him feel less alone. He had fallen in love.

For eight months of his life, Hamish had found his beacon, his anchor, a lifesaving buoy in human form capable of easing the transition between childhood and manhood, the past and the future, the problematic and the possible. Student life had been a shock to his system, but with his new companion, the violent jolt against his senses and sensibilities became a blessing in disguise, a current that coaxed him along rather than threaten to pull him down. In the comforting arms of his lover, Hamish found he could lay the ghosts of his younger self to rest.

Two halves of a whole, two like minds combined, but all too soon the bond between them began to break. Swept up in student life and political campaigns, they each drifted apart, slipping away in different directions, fading from one another's lives like sand through parted fingers. It did not take long for Hamish's soulmate to become just another mirage on the horizon of his history, yet another phantom on the shoreline of his memories.

A decade later, the possibilities Hamish had naively anticipated in his youth had also disappeared, returning him to his former state of loneliness, confusion and unhappiness. He had hoped to live again, to love once more, but lacked the motivation to even try. The dreams soon returned, led by the hazy vision of a man on the cliffs looking across the bay towards the archway, silent and sullen, patiently waiting for his son. In the early hours of many a sleepless night, the image would tug away at Hamish's mind, whispering to him through the darkness. 'Go home,' it would say, 'Go back to the land you know.' Eventually, he conceded.

As the train rolled into Whitby station, Hamish had dared to glance up at the cliffs, searching for the distant silhouette of the man with the honey-coloured eyes. But there was no one, only the vista he had seen a hundred times, with not a single difference to mark the length of his absence. Once he had alighted, he reached the roadside and looked left and right, as if expecting to find a face he recognised. Again, he saw no one, just the familiar paraphernalia he had grown up with. The harbour with its colourful boats. The tourists ambling around. The gulls swooping and lunging in their cylindrical dance. All unchanged, as if the town had been waiting for him, unaware of the big wide world he had come from.

He hoped he would soon forget the city with its constant noise and activity, its busy schedule and frantic pace. He would forge a new identity, no longer the vanished six-year-old boy but a transformed and improved man, a distinguished English graduate who had seen and learned and lived. He would be able to share the town's stories in his role as a local press reporter, a fully-fledged journalist, a seeker of the truth. He would not be embroiled in the same antics that had seen him raise his voice, extend his fists and find himself in handcuffs the morning after, as it had been during his student years. No, this time it would be different. He would be able to bring about change without conflict or drama. Without a broken heart. Even missing presumed dead, he could make his long-lost father proud.

After a tray of fish and chips and a bottle of pop, Hamish had walked to the newsagents to collect the single box of his belongings. His foster parents had moved away the previous year, and with no other family or close friends nearby, they had asked Mr Marshall to take care of Hamish's possessions until he was able to return. The shopkeeper seemed pleased to see him, the shy lad who was now a grown man with his own flat and a new job. Hamish was equally glad to see at least one recognisable face but could not find the words to say so. Instead, he paid for a bag of liquorice comfits, picked up his box and walked away, reluctant to stay and chat. He was more than happy to leave his old life in the past.

Once outside, Hamish took a seat beside the whalebones, their looming presence casting a shadow as he pulled off the tape from the box resting on his knees. Most of the space inside was taken up with only one item: the wooden ark. He reached in to stroke its deck with a single finger, both welcoming and resisting the recollections it brought, the happiness and pain combined. There were some papers and books wedged in either side, along with bits of stationery and a ball of old socks. Things he had forgotten. Things he would still like to forget.

In the top left corner folded into a neat square was a newspaper article. He opened it carefully, the headline immediately catching his eye – 'Missing, presumed dead.' Hamish scanned the text, the memories building slowly before overwhelming him like a flood. The more he read, the more he began to feel something reawakening, an understanding that had not quite vanished. Not yet.

There had been no death, he realised. No proven demise. No body in a coffin buried deep within the earth – merely a carved stone memorial, empty in every way. His hope had not been abandoned, just displaced. He might still be alive, Hamish knew. He could still be out there. And now that his son had returned, the fisherman could finally be found.

Hamish blinked, realising with surprise that his face was damp and stiff. He looked to see why his knee felt strange and saw a foreign object rested there. A hand. Noa's. His daughter was still sat beside him, still listening to his sorry tale. Her expression was one of serenity, of compassion, a look he now only saw in the most fleeting of dreams and distant of memories. Without quite knowing his intentions, he reached out, briefly allowing his fingers to touch hers – warm and soft, so unlike his own, he thought – then let his hand quickly slip away. He wiped it across his cheeks, rosy with embarrassment, then gave a forced cough to mask the silence.

"My father," he mumbled. A mantra, a prayer. "I came back to Whitby to find him. I'd lost so many people, you see." It was the justification for his return, his excuse to stay, but not the only reason he had built the wall.

Ever since he had left the fisherman, Hamish had felt a space inside him, a cavity that no person or passion had ever been able to fill. Not his love for nature, his studies or degree, nor the few happy times he had spent with his mother and his grandparents, his university housemates and his friends in the city. Not even his lover and the laughter they shared had felt as real as those few days in the cottage. Even having met his daughter, his kin, the desire to find the lost fisherman had remained his priority, the collection growing with increased vigour, almost beyond his control, morphing into its own monster until it penetrated every aspect of his life. It had risen from a deep and dark place within, obsessively, relentlessly, like an ever-increasing echo he had found impossible to ignore. While he had the wall, he was safe. While he had the wall, Hamish was not alone.

Noa would never comprehend how her father's mind worked, or why he had chosen to share the story of his youth. The death of his grandmother, the absence of his mother, the first romance he had formed then forgotten during university, and of course, Emil Kleve. She noticed he rarely said his name, as if there had been two different people, leaving her feeling more confused about Hamish than ever. But at least he had tried to hold her hand.

Watching the waves in their continuous roll, Noa noticed her face had become numb from the wafts of coarse wind, and she was hungry too; she wished she could just walk away, return to the flat and have something comforting to eat while she messaged her loved ones. To start the day again as if the past few hours had never happened. As if her father was just a normal man enjoying his daughter's company.

Maybe that was why they were here, she realised. His secret collection, his mumbled explanation – they at least explained why he seemed so fearful of forming any kind of meaningful relationship. Perhaps this was his attempt at ordinariness, at making a connection. He had not rejected her, but nor had Noa ever felt wanted or welcomed. She had always been on the edge of his world – now, she was beginning to understand why. Not because of who she was but because of what Hamish had been through. His past, his heartbreak, his desperate need to keep everyone at a distance. To protect himself. To prevent the past from repeating. Now, though, they needed to think of the future. Noa needed to know how this might end.

"What will you do when you find him?" she asked, louder than she had intended, with an edge that made each word sound like a challenge.

Hamish stared ahead, as if he had not heard, though the sudden twitch of his hands betrayed his true response. He understood Noa's question but did not know how to answer. What would he do when he found his father? Had he even allowed himself to think that far ahead? To the day when he would finally face the man himself, right there, stood before him – a living, breathing form. The fisherman would have aged, Hamish knew, but beneath the white hair and the wrinkled mask, there would still be that impassive gaze through eyes identical to his own.

Perhaps he would have to face a corpse instead, Hamish thought, like his grandmother, stumbled on at an unforeseen moment. At least this time it would be a skeleton, all signs of the man he knew stripped away, saving him the savage sight of a fallen body. The bones may still be battered and broken, beaten by the tide and the cliffs, but at least he would have some closure. A real body to bury and mourn in the tomb by the church. There would finally be an answer to the question he had been asking for too long.

"If I find him…" Hamish began, his voice frail and faint as his thoughts clustered uncomfortably, "If I find him, then I'll know. I'll know why he never came back. Why he abandoned his son. The boy he called Noah."

Nine

'Why he abandoned his son,' Noa repeated to herself, her father's response echoing like a gunshot in her mind. 'The boy he called Noah.' She stayed silent, unable to think of a reply, thoughts reeling one after the other. Every time Hamish spoke, she felt she understood him less and less. And that word – her name – said as if it did not belong to her but to him. How could he be called Noah? It had shocked her, even made her feel angry, as if a part of her identity had been taken, damaged, hidden from her view. And by her own father. She had arrived less than an hour ago and already she felt different. Hamish felt different. They had both changed, becoming unfamiliar figures in a stage play created by someone else's hand. Here she was, side by side with a stranger, on the first day of six months with a man she thought could inspire her, whom she had begun to feel an affinity with – the researcher, the writer, the Rebel Man. But she had been wrong.

For years, Noa had tried to come to an understanding of Hamish, an idea of him as a person rather than just a father, slowly pieced together through snatched irregular conversation, sporadic text messages and the occasional card or gift in the post. She had not thought about the unknowns, the question marks hanging over her father's life and past, the information her mother would never share. Maybe that was what she had meant by Rebel Man? Noa had thought it simply a witty nickname, a comment on his previous character, a glimpse into his former world, but now she wondered if it had another meaning. If her mother had meant it to be a warning.

A rustle roused Noa from her reverie. She looked down to the source of the sound; Hamish's hand proffering a packet of ginger biscuits. Despite her anxiety, she smiled, slipped one of the sweet treats from its hateful plastic packaging and nibbled along its crumbly edge. The scent soothed her as it always had, recalling the aromatic curries cooked by her mother, the Sunday morning porridge laced with spices and honey, the homemade flapjacks studded with crystalised cubes that her best friend Rowan would bring whenever they had disagreed over something silly. Noa continued taking tiny bites, savouring the smell as she imagined herself back home, sure of herself and who she was.

There had to be something she could say. A way to end the torturous ticking of time between them, other than by eating snacks. The waves and the gulls and the gale shuttling towards them from across the North Sea would only prove distracting for so long. Noa knew this was a cry for help. Everything Hamish had told her – stories he had perhaps never shared with another soul – needed to be resolved. He had dug into the cavernous cavity of his chest and found the tiny heart that still beat there, reduced to the size of a seashell, unassuming and fragile.

Despite appearing as an adult, Noa could see that there was a part of Hamish that was still just a boy, a child waiting for his father to come home. The years of yearning were there etched in his face – the sagging jowl, the map of creases, the double bowing beds of blackening skin beneath his eyes. He was a battered wreck – emotionally, physically – saved only by the feeblest of anchors, by his belief that the fisherman he had loved as a boy, and who had perhaps once loved him too, was still alive.

Amid the screeching sirens of the herring gulls high above, Noa took a final bite, wiping the crumbs from her hands into the path of a solitary sparrow beneath the bench. The bigger birds swiftly moved in, Hamish cowering but closely watching, mumbling their Latin names, his words falling away with the wind. He finished eating, a few fragments of biscuit tumbling onto his coat. He brushed a hand along his chest then carefully folded the flaps of the packet inwards before tucking them back into his pocket. He had thought his purchase would be a welcomed treat, a moment of enjoyment, like the ice-creams had been. But there was now a bitter taste in his mouth. A feeling of regret, of having done something wrong. Noa was still beside him, but she had ceased to speak. He could not imagine what she might be thinking, what feelings she could be concealing. This was not the start to her trip that he had wanted. He was not the father she deserved.

Maybe soon she would simply walk away, he reasoned. Collect her bag from the flat, return to the station, take the first train out of town and go to a place where she would never have to see the wall or hear her father or be plagued by screaming gulls ever again. The signs were there, stirring around the space on the bench. The tumultuous knife-edge tension humming in the air between them, their hands both hovering, moving from thighs to stomachs to thighs again, each in their own bubble of malcontent. Uneasy. Unsettled. Like waiting for a storm to come.

"Thank you for the biscuits," Hamish heard his daughter say, her voice laced with kindness. She had turned to him, smiling with sincerity, her eyes on his.

"Maybe we should have an early lunch?" he suggested, his own gaze slipping away and across her shoulder, fearful of rejection.

Noa looked the other way and saw the man her father had spotted behind her, middle-aged and alone, wearing a grey winter coat, bright white trainers and a red baseball cap, perched on the corner of a bench. He was happily hunched over a plate of chips dripping in thick gravy, stabbing at them with a wooden fork, the birds above cawing madly. She and Hamish watched the stranger with envy – finally, a distraction capable of easing the friction between them, of raising their spirits. They rose from the bench, each taking a final inhalation of the crisp sea air as they eyed the whalebone archway across the bay. Noa led the way back to town, listening to the faint squeak of her father's shoes as he followed behind.

As they walked along the cobbled road past the cottages converted into gift shops, jewellers and eateries, Noa slowed to allow Hamish to lead while she assessed her thoughts. She wondered what her mother would think if she had been the one to blunder in on the collection in the attic, if she had been the one to have heard the stories, to discover his secret life. Perhaps Rosa already knew. Perhaps it was why her mother kept away, hoping her daughter would do the same. After all, she had chosen the name Noa. Maybe she knew his history after all.

Hamish paused beside a café called 'The Crow Nest', turning to his daughter for approval. Noa surveyed the menu in the window and spotted a surprising number of vegan options, nodding to her father before heading inside to a vacant table by one of the windows. Having shrugged off her bag and coat, she took a seat and reached for one of the laminated cards, Hamish hovering nervously beside the other chair, as if waiting to be told what to do.

Noa took in the view, feeling strangely excited – perhaps this was the fresh start she had hoped for. Sharing a meal with her father for the very first time, in an actual café rather than ordering takeaway food from a delivery service or shop counter. She felt oddly grown up and in charge, as if she were the parent and Hamish the child. She realised that was how she now thought of him – childlike, scared and scarred by his past, fearful for the future, cowering behind a collection that had allowed him to live in a fantasy world. No family photos, no worthwhile mementos, just a handful of articles, drawings and an old wooden ark.

She looked across. Hamish was frowning at the menu in his hands, no doubt annoyed by the name, she thought. She was tempted to get a pen from her bag and amend it, but her father would probably be equally disturbed by the graffiti as by the grammatical error.

"William Scoresby senior was said to have invented the crow's nest," he mumbled, pronouncing the last two words with a hissing clarity.

Noa hid a smile, keeping her opinions to herself. Accuracy aside, she quite liked the menu design, featuring a charming line drawing of a sailor looking through a telescope atop of a crow's nest, a creation said to have been designed by the elder Scoresby for an enhanced perspective during sea voyages. She had already learned about him online but waited patiently for Hamish to continue. It was still a novelty just to hear him speak.

"What about the drawings in your flat?" she asked, remembering a similar image of a fishing boat she had noticed pinned to the wall.

"I made them," Hamish replied, a faint blush crossing his cheeks. "I used to love to draw. It was something he encouraged."

Noa nodded, thinking of her own interest, wondering how many more secrets Hamish had. She really knew nothing about him, and he barely knew her either. She had brought some of her sketchbooks from Norway; perhaps he would be interested in seeing them, she wondered. He could even give her some tips.

"I used to draw a lot when I was a kid," she said quietly, "But I really want to be a writer, like you. A journalist. To tell the truth about the world." It felt a bold admission, but she was glad to have said it, hoping her father would be happy, proud of her ambition. Maybe there was something in her that craved his support, she now realised. A validation of her existence.

"That's very… noble," Hamish answered, leaning across the table to tuck the menu back into its holder, the logo positioned away from them.

Noa did the same, hoping he would continue, but her father was once more lost to his own thoughts, staring out of the window. A couple passed by with a tiny black dog, barely the size of a balloon and almost as buoyant, bouncing along in its little leather waistcoat and matching top hat. The man and woman both wore head-to-toe black in a mix of leathers, velvets and ruffles adorned with gold chains, their matching raven hair cascading down to their waists and topped with what looked like silver welding goggles.

"There's a steampunk event," Hamish explained, though Noa already knew. She had been following various social media accounts for the local area, looking for stories she might be able to write about. The steampunk, goth and vintage festivals and meet-ups were all top of her list, each bringing an electric energy to the otherwise ordinary seaside town. Perhaps she would join them, explore a new side to herself.

"Yeah, I thought I could write about it," she replied, the couple and their companion having turned the corner and disappeared from view. "Use it as one of my projects." Hamish studied his hands in silence.

A young man around Noa's age hurried across the room over to their table. After swiftly running a hand through his thick mass of hair, he pulled out a pen and pad of paper from the top pocket of his shirt and stood like a sentry ready for their order. Noa took in the stranger's attire, her eyes caught by the profusion of intricate tattoos across his hands, wrists and neck, along with several piercings in his ears, eyebrows and lower lip. She had not thought about the possibility of meeting people her own age here and now wished she had packed something a little more interesting than charity shop jumpers and leggings. The waiter looked between Noa and Hamish before breaking into a grin of recognition.

"Ah, Mr Shaw! How's it going? Anything coming up in the papers?"

Noa watched her father shuffling in his chair, his eyes drawn from his hands to the young man, his mouth morphing into a faint and unnatural smile.

"Just the usual, Finley," he replied with forced politeness, "Steampunk event. Another church fete. Something about the fish market."

His words sounded as flat as his face, Noa thought. At least she would be able to employ a little more enthusiasm as a journalist. Finley was undeterred.

"Ah, great! Plenty going on, eh? I'm sorry, we've never met – I'm Fin, short for Finley. I'm Woody's lad." He held out his hand to Noa, shaking the tips of her fingers daintily, like royalty.

Noa smiled, introduced herself, then hurriedly ordered the falafel salad and a camomile tea. Fin nodded, scribbling down the order word for word before drawing a smiley skull on his notepad. He jumped a little, as if remembering something, then began reeling off the daily specials in a well-rehearsed tone. Hamish looked across to the menus as if he had forgotten what he had chosen, then turned to listen to Fin. Noa watched her father pondering the selection before asking for the first option. She wondered if he was always this uncomfortable in public. When was the last time he had even been to a café? He seemed completely out of place, a fish out of water, though perhaps he was still recovering from their unexpected reunion. It had been a very long day.

Fin finished his notes, thanked them both and shuffled off, Noa noticing his knee-high black boots as he left, the heels customised with hand-drawn white crosses in what looked like correcting fluid.

"So, why did you want to be a writer?" Noa asked her father once they were alone again. Her earlier anxieties had settled, her mind more focused on her own narrative and why she had come to Whitby. In their secluded corner with only a couple of other patrons in the space, the café provided the perfect location to question her father, somewhere he could not evade her queries.

"To tell stories," Hamish replied. He looked across at Noa, a subtle twinkle in his eyes visible for the briefest of moments before he turned his attention back outside to the street. "Not fairy tales and fantasies, but real lives. Lived experiences. The truth, I suppose. Like you said before."

He would wait until later to clarify what he meant by 'the truth'. It was something that had kept him awake many a night, something that was never quite black and white. It needed to be controlled, contained, presented in whichever form the writer favoured. There was power in holding the pen, but responsibility and repercussions too. The road to the truth was paved with good intentions, he had always said. He should have it made into a t-shirt.

Noa remained oblivious to her father's thoughts, too busy reeling in the fact that he had remembered her words, had listened, had agreed.

"So that's why you went to university?" she answered, eager to know more. "You went to learn how to tell stories as a profession. What was it like? Leaving this little cosy place and going somewhere new?"

"It was… necessary. Change can affect you in extraordinary ways." His response was paired with that familiar look – glazed, gloomy, as if lost in a memory.

Before Noa could press her father for details, the food and drinks arrived. Fin had brought over a mug of tea for Hamish, as he had forgotten to order something, and a round of sliced brown bread with servings of butter wrapped in foil, including a plant-based variety, Noa noticed. Their drinks and the bread were 'on the house', Fin informed them, setting down napkins and cutlery.

"Oh, by the way, Mr Shaw," he added, sliding the plates carefully onto the table, "Woody says you can come and see the collection again whenever you want."

Noa felt her eyebrows shooting up her forehead. Another man with another collection? What was wrong with this place?

"Thanks, Finley," Hamish responded without looking up, his eyes intent on the dish before him. He poked a finger at the wedge of lemon and the sprig of parsley balanced on the side, pushing them to the edge like a fussy child. Fin watched him with concealed amusement, his hard work unappreciated once more.

"No problem. Enjoy your meals," he smiled, sloping off back to the counter.

Hamish had ordered the local speciality of kippers. Three plump, bronzed bodies stretched across the length of the dish, their lifeless eyes and withered tails still intact. A presentation, a curation, a display worthy of admiration. How anyone could dislike such perfection seemed madness to him. While smoked herring had been and remained the most popular form of preservation, pickled and salted fish had also been typical for a time. Though he had only been six years old when he had first tasted them, Hamish could remember their different flavours distinctly. He often wished he could create such a meal in his own kitchen, but he knew it would never be the same, would never match the expertise of the Norwegian native he had once dined with.

As Noa watched Fin walk away, her father left staring at his plate, her brain switched from one memory to another as her nostrils caught the distinct whiff of the fish. Herring – raw, poached, fried or salted, from jars or out of paper parcels, hot or cold, morning or evening, the same unmistakable smell pervading. She had loved and loathed it, both feelings now surging to the surface along with her recollections. The day her mother ordered kippers for breakfast when they were staying in the Whitby hotel, and the first time she walked past the little smokehouse on the East Cliff while out exploring. Then discovering the popularity of herring during her stay in Norway, a recent recollection already strengthened by nostalgia, linking her past to her present.

Hamish took up his utensils, grimacing at the squeak of the knife as it slid through the first carcass pinned in place with his fork. Noa watched from the corner of her vision, wondering if the fish meant as much to him as they did to her. She took a sip of her drink then made a start on her falafel, hoping she could resume the conversation.

"I guess you missed the kippers when you were away," she smiled, attempting to lighten the atmosphere, Hamish having already finished his first fillet. "But that's what going to university is about, isn't it? New experiences."

Noa paused to look over her shoulder, spotting Fin polishing glasses behind the counter. She wondered what he made of them, the daughter and father, sat side by side like two strangers. Hamish had still not answered her.

"All those people, living alone – the parties, the freedom," she ruminated, "And falling in love, of course. Like when you met my mum."

The fork clattered from Hamish's grasp onto the plate, then to the table, to his lap and down to the floor. It seemed to happen in slow motion, the sound reverberating like a series of thunderclaps, leaving the café in stunned silence. Flushing beetroot red, he stooped over to retrieve the fallen cutlery. He dipped a napkin in the cup of tea, wiped the fork, but did not continue eating. He felt even more nervous than usual, almost distressed. He had always known the issue would arise, but not today. He felt he had already opened his heart for all the world to see, for his daughter to examine and probe. He felt exposed, vulnerable, set on edge by too much history and all those stories. Noa's eyes watched him, a hawk sizing up its prey.

"How did you first meet?" she asked with innocence. Finally, the question she had always wanted to know. Trapped with half an uneaten meal in a public place, Hamish had nowhere to hide. Noa had already quizzed her mother time and again about their relationship but to no avail. The phrase 'Rebel Man' was the most she had learned, though she was still unsure what it really meant.

"Your uncle," Hamish answered, looking down into his greasy plate, a hand in his lap, the other tracing the handle of his drink, up and down, again and again. He felt cornered, unsure how to respond, scared to go where the conversation would inevitably lead. Another part of his past he had hoped to keep buried.

"He took me to a pub. Your mother was working behind the bar." He forced down the lump in his throat. It seemed such an innocent answer, such a simple explanation, yet the look on his face told Noa there was more to be revealed.

Growing up, she had only been able to speculate on the details of her parents' connection. Now here was her father revealing tiny truths and factual details, finally piecing together the real story for her, including about her Uncle Jonah. Noa did not know much about her mother's twin, was not even aware her father had met him. But from his current expression, she could guess Hamish and Jonah had been friends. Yet another man Rosa had kept to herself, her eyes having turned to thin slits whenever Noa asked, 'What was he like?' Those same words now rushed forwards from her lips before she could stop them.

Hamish turned to his daughter, then away towards the window again, sighing lightly as both his hands moved to grip his mug. "He was unlike anyone I'd ever met," he began, his voice low, almost a whisper. "Strong, defiant. Passionately political, as we all were in those days."

Noa nodded. He was talking about the Eighties, she understood, one of the country's most tumultuous decades. She had seen a documentary about freedom fighters at the time: rights for workers, rights for women, sexual liberation, racial equality, foreign conflicts, fallen walls, the environment, the economy, corrupt governments, immoral politicians... It had been a dark and dangerous era, a time of revolution, a place filled with rebels. A world her father and uncle had lived through.

"He showed me videos, printed out articles," Hamish continued, finally taking a sip of his lukewarm tea. "We went to meetings, then marches. Caught coaches and trains, travelled up and down the country. We'd make placards in the evenings, go on protests at the weekends. There was so much to fight for. So much at stake."

Here was the Rebel Man then, Noa realised. Her father *had* been a protestor, just like she had seen on the television, and her uncle had been involved too.

Together they had been activists, campaigners – the very people she and her friends now hoped to become. In the space of a few minutes, Noa had learned she was related to not one but two fellow fighters.

"So that's why you became a journalist," she replied, wondering what it must have been like – her father and her uncle, the best of friends, brothers in arms. Rebel Men.

Noa knew even little of her uncle than she did about Hamish, but the fact that they had been so close – that he had been the reason her father and mother had met – filled her with relief. She had made the right decision in coming here, she now knew. She did have something in common with her father after all, and she was sure he would help her to learn how to write. All that passion, all that promise – it had to still be inside of him somewhere. He had not only the skills but the experience. He would be on her side. Now it was time to tell her own reason for wanting to become a writer. She would share her story, the tale of Noa and the whale.

Ten

Emil drove back to the cottage with haste, parking the van and replacing the empty boxes in the outbuilding with a flurry of hurried movement. He slipped the key in the front door, pressing his fingertips against the weathered wood as he held his breath. What had seemed only a few minutes down in the town now felt like hours. Too long, a mistake too far. On the journey home, his mind had tormented him with visions of what he might find on his return, of the chaos he had caused by taking and then leaving a small child alone. He let the door swing open, expecting the worst, but saw and heard nothing of concern. Finally, he exhaled. Stepping inside, he was relieved to find his home untouched. No forced entry, no expectant policemen, no body or blood. The only thing missing was the food he had left on the table.

Beside the dying embers of the softly settling fire, the sofa bulged with blankets, Noah still nestled underneath. Not a vision or a ghost but a real boy. Sleeping. Snuffling. Could it be considered a snore? Emil had never thought children would do such a thing. It brought him another unexpected moment of wonder, another flush of warmth to his skin.

"Hush, *mitt barn*," he whispered into the silent room, "Hush."

He stood beside the sofa to listen a little longer,

thinking the sound as soothing as the sea. Surveying the barely lit room, his eyes came to rest on the blue wooden animal on the table. The sight of its innocent form set sparks dancing through his weary mind. He began thinking, remembering. He stole silently back across the room to the kitchen, seating himself at the furthest end of the table, fingering a knot in the wood as he pondered. He looked down, stopping his movements. The pattern on the table was uncanny. A hump and a tail, the smallest dot of an eye. Everywhere he looked, the fisherman saw whales.

Emil slipped his hand into the pocket of his shirt to find the tin, still there from his night spent in the bunker. He was usually disciplined about returning his belongings to their proper places, but somehow, after the storm and the finding of the fish and the boy, he had forgotten to replace it. He clicked open the lid and tipped the charm onto the table. If it made a sound, he did not hear it. His mind was elsewhere, lost in dreams.

She had been a girl when she had found the unusual pebble on the shore of their hometown but a woman when she had gifted it to his care. It had not come in the tobacco tin – that came later, when the need to keep the object both safe and hidden became important. Instead, she had wrapped it in cloth cut from her own dress. He had smiled at the missing patch pocket, clearly visible, its stitches having left a pathway of holes. Her mother would be livid, he thought. He loved that she did not care. Not about the dress, nor their love for one another, nor anything their parents said that they could or could not do. The future would be theirs. He was to remember that, she said, every time he looked at the gift. A pure white stone faintly marbled with grey, a miniature replica of a whale.

Emil slipped the talisman back into the tin, trapping the memories inside along with it. He walked across to the bookcase, replaced the box, then carefully set some more wood on the fire. The cottage had grown cold now that the sun had dimmed. He could feel the gentle draft from the old windows, their squares of light now faded, as if masked by smoke. He walked over to each and tugged the worn green velvet curtains across, trying not to pause too long, to listen too much to the outside world.

As he turned to make his way back to the fireplace, he bumped into the boy, stood beside his legs in his mismatched clothes, one hand clutched to the corner of a blanket trailing along behind him. With his other hand, Noah formed a fist and rubbed an eye, then extended his fingers to reach across the cool space between them. Take my hand, his gaze seemed to say.

Emil reached out, took the proffered fingers – warm and soft, so unlike his own, he thought – and allowed Noah to lead him back to the coffee table. On the left was the stack of drawings, on the right a pile of books, removed, he could now see, from the lower shelves of the bookcase. Bedtime stories.

The boy looked up, waiting patiently for him to understand, his hand still clasped tight. The fisherman stooped to look through the books one by one, glancing between the titles, trying to remember the last time he had read them, when he had been trying to learn English all those years ago. Some of the names felt familiar, others foreign to his tired eyes, but suddenly they each seemed interesting, promising. Yes, they would read.

Noah stayed on the sofa, swathed in his multiple cloaks while Emil fetched a light supper and two large mugs of milk from the kitchen. Then he seated himself, perching the first novel on his lap, and turned the first page.

Day passed into night without either realising. The food had long been eaten, the mugs drunk dry, and still they sat on the sofa side by side with the stories. The final book was tall and thin, with a glossy cover showing a photograph of a faraway land. A land Emil knew well. He had brought the book with him a decade ago, one of the few possessions to enter the new house with him. He could remember slipping it onto the shelf alongside the volumes already there, tales he would read and learn from, had once hoped to enjoy again. It seemed so long ago, yet the memory came back as easily as the tide.

Noah ran his fingers across the cover in awe, as if he could feel the texture of the pictured trees and their spindly branches beneath his fingertips. He used both hands to open the cover, carefully revealing the first page. The images there caused Emil's breath to catch painfully, like a sudden inhalation of ice-cold air. Another world. Another lifetime. The boy made appreciative noises at the undulating lush green valley before them, the stretch of silvery water snaking through, the quaint little fishing boats dotted across the paper.

"Is it home?" he asked.

"No," Emil sighed. "Yes. Well… this is my home. My old home."

"Is that the cottage?" Noah tapped a tiny fingernail into the distance of a shoreline next to a dense forest.

It was difficult to tell but, buried in the photograph, there did appear to be a dwelling, a wooden cabin with a porch and a low roof. Emil stared at the shape, leaned a little closer, shook his head. An odd gripping sensation slipped across his chest, like a menacing hand working towards his throat. He leaned back, resting his head, closing his eyes until the feeling passed. Noah waited silently for a few moments, then reached his hand across to turn the page.

Emil looked down, gasping as he surveyed the picture. Yes, there it was – a perfect recreation of his homeland. His origins, his roots, still thick and deep like vines, still clinging on despite the distance and the years. The boy poked a finger across the vista, mumbling to himself, then waited for the fisherman to speak. Emil was too lost for words to reply.

"Storytime," Noah said.

"What kind of a story?"

"A good one, with a boy… like me."

Emil nodded. He was beginning to understand the child more easily now, the stilted sounds forming recognisable words once he had given them time and space to breathe. He briefly thought of asking the boy's real name again but resisted. He was Noah, and he seemed happy. His new guardian needed to know nothing more.

The fisherman turned to the next page, hoping for inspiration for the narrative expected of him, rubbing his chin in thought. He was not imaginative and had long forgotten most of the tales of his childhood with their monsters and morals. He sought an idea from the sighing flames of the fire, from the gently curling smoke as it climbed the chimney, from the echo of the fading wind beyond the wooden front door. It was no good. The only thing he could think of was that morning. What he had found after the storm had seemed a work of fiction, after all. He could clearly recall how the scene had looked, the still stretch of land, the absence of birdsong, the sky the colour of wet shale, the same shade he had seen so often as a boy at home. Home. A sudden thought occurred. Emil cleared his throat and began.

There was once a young fisherman, shy but greatly skilled, who had been in love with a local girl. They had met as children and grown up together, living at either ends of the same street. When he had finished his schooling, he became an apprentice of her father, a prosperous seaman and the only elder in the village to have seen his capabilities. She was a dutiful daughter, an only child, beloved of her parents. She could cook and clean, darn and weave, having inherited the nimble fingers and diligent nature of her grandmother. They seemed the perfect union, and once they reached adulthood, the couple were permitted to marry. The fisherman and his wife moved to a wooden hut built facing a wide cove with many trees huddled behind, just like in the picture. Emil pointed at the book as

Noah nodded.

One day, the couple were blessed with a baby boy brought to them by an angel, and together the family enjoyed many adventures and much happiness. The end. Emil moved to close the book, but Noah placed a hand inside the pages.

"What happened next?" he asked, his face crumpled into a scowl.

Emil shrugged. There was nothing more to add; his tale had finished. There was, of course, a different turn of events, but he could not put the truth into words, would not reveal the reality of his woeful past. He glanced around for a distraction and noticed one of the drawings on the table – choppy waves, a head bobbing above, a hand waving hello. He thought a little then continued with his story.

"The beautiful wife went swimming."

"Did she come back?"

"Yes. Why would she not?"

"Maybe she drowned."

The fisherman stared, stunned at the boy's astuteness. He looked back to the picture he had used as inspiration, now noticing that the woman was upside-down, the bend severe across her face. What he had mistaken for a smile was instead a frown. Noah was right. She was not waving but drowning.

Emil swallowed. He realised his mistake but did not correct the story. It seemed that Noah already knew far more than he.

"What about their son?" he asked tentatively.

"Hmm. He's gone too," Noah explained.

"But he was too young to go in the water."

"No, the angel took him. Back to heaven."

"I see." Emil could say no more.

The boy nodded, the tale concluded, his eyelids slipping shut into slumber. The fisherman did not move, could not think, would not stop remembering. He sat there with the boy asleep by his side, the surrounding space becoming a barren vacuum as the fire began to die, the air growing even colder, the cottage plunging into its familiar silence once more.

An hour passed. The boy had turned several times and now lay in the opposite direction atop of the blankets. Emil carefully replaced the book on the table, shuffled off his seat and made his way blindly through the darkness to his bedroom. There he rested on the soft musty eiderdown, comforted by its cool surface and familiar scent, though he knew he would not sleep. They would not let him – the memories, the voices. The ever-present spectres seeping from the bunker through the floorboards and into his dreams.

At three o'clock, he could take no more. Emil rose from the bed, groggy and sore, the exertion of the day finally catching up with him. He stretched his arms, flexed his feet, felt his neck and knees clicking as he moved. Taking the torch by the bedside, he switched it on and tucked it under his jumper before making his way to the front room. Everything was as it should be, including the boy, still soundly sleeping. In a few hours, the sun would start to rise, the birds would begin to call, and his boat would be waiting for him. Emil thought about the job ahead – seeking out the most lucrative spot, casting and hauling in the nets, checking and making repairs, noting changes to the weather and the tides. But that day would not come, he knew. He needed to stay right here.

The fisherman walked silently across to the kitchen, opening a drawer to find a few sheets of blank paper and a ballpoint pen. He sat himself at the table, angling the torch towards him as he began to write in slow cursive motions, mostly in English, adding the odd word from his native tongue. It made telling the tale a little easier. More natural, even. Almost as if the story were writing itself.

He noted the narrative he had shared with Noah from its beginning, making adjustments as he went. When it came to the ending, he was forced to pause, biting the tip of the pen before finally urging himself to finish, writing the finale he had long tried to forget. Whatever misplaced nostalgia the boy had sparked, Emil knew that now was the time for his past to be revived. To put pen to paper, thoughts into forms, the swirling shadows into a rigid structure – to cage them word by word, line by line. Maybe he would find the courage to share his new story, he thought.

For the former part, he had at least spoken the truth. He had been sent to work with a local man at the age of thirteen, having been refused the opportunity to join his father and brothers on their seafaring voyages. Too slow, too clumsy, Pappa had argued over many consecutive suppers, despite grandfather's determination to continue the family tradition and mother's assurance that her youngest was just as capable as the others. Emil had had no say in the matter, his future soon settled for him. He would leave and live in another homestead, his father had announced, and find his own path in life. Little did Emil know that he would be welcomed as a son, finding a place in the hearts of his new family and a renewed warmth in his own.

With his foster parents and their only child, he finally felt he belonged. He revered the father, respected the mother and adored the daughter. He learned and grew, personally and professionally, soon realising his handicap could be no match for utter determination and resolute effort. Within a few years, Emil became a competent fisherman, a valued member of the community and worthy of a girl's hand. He had known for many years that he was in love with the daughter, assuming all along that she felt the same. It was written in all the stories she had shown him, all the fairy tales about finding one's true love.

As they enjoyed walks along the wet sands and jaunts into the forest hand in hand, Emil became infatuated with the daughter's longing looks and light laughter. The girl was playful in her courtship – tender notes folded into miniature squares squirrelled into his pockets, stolen whispers under sooty skies flecked with silver stars, and the many other little games that she loved, him always willing to follow. Then the gift, a pebble the colour of bone, wrapped in a piece of fabric – a round shape, a familiar curve, almost like that of a whale. Emil's most favourite creature.

Ever since he had taken the tiny token from her lithe fingers, he had reflected on the moment romantically, idealistically, inspired by the tales they had shared during their private encounters. He looked at its soft surface and saw not a stone but a symbol of their mutual desire, linking to both his love and to nature; a talisman taken from but still a part of the outside world, like the girl herself. With her fair hair like a running stream, her pale skin the shade of a winter sun and her name, Marna, meaning 'of the sea', he felt he had met a goddess in human form.

Emil had planned to propose to her, marry the following year, then buy a small cottage beside the water where they could start a family. It was a dream he intended to make a reality, but then they had found the body, and everything had changed.

Looking back, the fisherman now wondered if the gift had acted as an omen, a sign of what Marna knew was to come but had been too scared to speak of. Like the whale, her soul would never be tamed. Like the sea, she would always be both near and far, visible yet untouchable, something Emil could never call his own. Now all he had left of her was the charm.

He stared at the inked page, the words bobbing on the surface, calmed and contained by their neat sentences and subtle allegory. Yet below sunk the hidden and unfathomable truth, the unavoidable reality – his beloved had chosen to end her life. She had drowned, her body washed up on the shore a day later, her wet dress revealing a protruding stomach, taut with the unborn son he would never know.

She had understood the changes, of course, teasing her loved one until he guessed at her condition. There had been fear at first, then a feeling of thrill and exhilaration – he, a father, his future hopes finally coming true. Emil started picturing the colour of the child's eyes, the shape of his face, the length of his limbs, keeping his thoughts to himself as he begged his dearest one to rest, to stay beside him, to never ever leave. Yet he had driven her away. His adamant plans and insistent words had pushed her to despair.

After that day, Emil would sit on the beach opposite the spot where it had happened, rolling the stone between his fingers, wondering if his son had been the same size. Perhaps smaller, barely formed. A grain of sand in the womb. Waiting. Growing. Despite his eagerness, he had kept silent, planning his future in his private thoughts as he fished with the father of his bride-to-be, imagining their wedding, their home – even choosing the boy's name. Their happiness within his grasp. At last, he had found a way to make his own mother and father proud. No longer an embarrassment, a curse on their name. The new-born would symbolise his own rebirth, a way to start his life once more, alongside the woman he loved. But he had lost them both. He had lost everything.

The memory resurfaced despite his protest, surging up like a fierce wave, gathering momentum as the truth repeated itself in his mind. Even now, the emotion seemed to suffocate him. The stone no longer held any meaning, serving only as a plaything to while away the tiring hours after returning from a day at sea, when his limbs screamed with exertion, when he felt most alone.

Even now, with the written story finished and the

talisman hidden within the bookcase, Emil could still sense the imprint of its form ringing across his fingertips. The rest of his hand felt stiff from writing, his mind wearied by too many words and too much thought. He tried to read the paper but could not concentrate, the lines swimming into one another tauntingly, tempting him to remember more, to feel the wound afresh.

He folded the pages in half, rose carefully from his chair and strode in silence across the room to his books. He pulled one out at random and stuffed the pages inside, closing it again with a macabre satisfaction, as if sealing a tomb never again to be discovered. He returned it to the shelf alongside all the other stories he had read in those early days, the days when he had such high hopes, such promising dreams. Now that time too had faded, pushed to the recesses of his memory.

Emil returned to his bed, settled on the mattress and made himself a pledge. One more day. Forgetting the past and ignoring the future, he would spend the next dawn until dusk with the child, without worrying what he might be and where he may have come from. One day to escape his normality, to leave behind the expectation and repetition of his routine, to banish the ghouls and the guilt he had become so used to sharing his home with. He would have one day to live a little, to discover the life he had always imagined. A taste of happiness.

He turned over, pulled the covering higher, closed his eyes and repeated his vow one last time. For the first time in years, the fisherman slept peacefully.

Eleven

If there was one thing Noa shared with her father, it was a lifelong experience of loneliness. As a toddler, she had been thrust together with the next door neighbours' children and the daughters of distant relatives but never felt included in their games. When she started school, her new classmates all too quickly left her behind, followed by snubs from dance partners and swimming buddies, then a few casual chums met on holiday or at the local park, all swiftly forgotten. She fared no better at secondary school with a so-called best friend who, after two years of companionship, turned into Noa's worst enemy over an argument about a stolen lipstick. But despite her difficulties socialising, she had remained optimistic, always hoping to find someone whom she could connect with.

It had been during a Year Nine Geography trip when Noa had finally made real friends. A group of twenty students and teachers had taken a coach to a barren stretch of countryside to see how a wind farm worked. While most of the youngsters had stood scrolling on their phones or listening to music, Noa and four other students had been riveted by the tour guide and the makeshift museum, which was housed in an old shed surrounded by grazing sheep. Though they had rarely spoken in class, something about the trip gave each of them the courage to introduce themselves, and they were soon planning a joint research project for their return. The new friends earned not only A-grades but a solid bond that had strengthened year on year.

As the group grew older, they discovered new avenues for their shared love of learning. Living in Leeds, there were countless opportunities for them to expand their knowledge, from attractions and exhibitions to events and festivals, giving them causes to care about, reasons to share their voices and be heard. After school and on weekends, the friends would meet to work on various schemes, with Noa invariably being the chief writer for whichever blog post, journal article, campaign speech or protest song they wanted to create. Having spent most of her childhood alone, she was now surrounded by likeminded souls who made her feel a part of something, giving her the motivation to start each day with enthusiasm. By doing right, she felt right, as if she had discovered her truth, her true identity.

During the Easter holidays, the friends attended a documentary festival with the title 'Wonders of the World'. While they saw many great marvels from places they had never known existed, they also noticed a recurrent theme – a distinct sense of urgency, of the world under threat. The need to act was desperate, a warning light continuously blinking, an emergency underway at that very moment. They had left the cinema heartbroken but newly awoken to their precarious place on Earth, and even more determined to protect it. When one of the friends suggested they spend their summer travelling, Noa was the first to agree, seeing it as a chance to develop her awareness and gain the confidence she still desperately lacked.

With their final school year underway and one last summer of freedom ahead, they decided to plan a trip to Europe, a chance to escape their home city to see the reality of climate change for themselves. Despite their academic responsibilities, the friends met regularly to carefully organise their visit, further fuelling their collective drive and forging the belief that they were planning more than just a holiday.

Emboldened by her friends and their shared passion, Noa was unaware of her mother's growing apprehension. Spending multiple months literally locked indoors with her teenage daughter had been both a blessing and a curse for Rosa, and while they had grown closer than ever, she was beginning to realise that her daughter's priorities had changed. Noa was no longer a little girl but an eighteen-year-old woman, about to finish school and venture into the world. Though she had shared her concerns with the other parents and half-heartedly agreed to the trip, Rosa still believed that her daughter would not go. That no matter how much she yearned to explore, she would soon realise where she belonged.

The group had settled on traveling by rail as the most economical and ecological option, with overnight stays in hostels to minimise costs, but they were still concerned about wasted days spent on trains. With one member fluent in French and another with family in Norway, they decided to focus their route on the north, beginning in Paris and finishing in Narvik before taking the quickest way home again. Along with the allure of the unknown, the idea of escaping the busy British summer in favour of colder climes and new cultures sounded ever more appealing. Merely learning how to correctly pronounce their Norwegian destination had sent them all into a fit of hysterical giggling.

Noa had drawn a map of the countries and key destinations, adding the sights the group hoped to see: the iconic skyline of the City of Light safe from smog, the quaint canals of Amsterdam free from flooding, the historic harbour perfectly preserved in Copenhagen, the Swedish coastline yet to be engulfed by rising sea levels. Then there would be the crisp cool air of Oslo still able to hint at snow to come, culminating in the stunning sight of whales off the coast of Norway, effortlessly gliding in the serene sea. From the mundanity of home to the isolation of a permanent winter wonderland; Noa had dreamed of little else for weeks.

Of all the inspiring sights on their list, it was the whale watching that Noa had been looking forward to the most. A love of animals featured in her most vivid childhood memories, from her vast collection of animated films and cuddly toys to the rare trips she had taken outside of the city, visiting beaches and lakes, forests and mountains. She had been researching conservation drives and what the world would be like without them – 'Two-hundred species go extinct every single day,' she had heard, one of the many truths that now thundered through her thoughts, a frightening reality but one she was determined to help change. If only she could make her mother realise how much it meant to her.

One evening, she persuaded Rosa to join her in

watching one of her all-time favourite films, the story of a girl who befriends a young orca. As they sat either end of the sofa wrapped in blankets, Rosa had looked across and noticed the tears on her daughter's face. With her newly cropped hair, wide eyes and distinctive jawline, she had begun to look almost identical to her uncle. If only Noa knew, Rosa thought, how proud he would have been of his niece.

She had waited wordlessly for the end credits to begin before opening her arms, drawing her daughter into a gentle hold. 'Go,' she had whispered into her ear, 'Live.' Noa had cried even harder, wrapping her arms around her mother's waist as tightly as she could, as if she were a lifebuoy keeping her afloat. She felt so thankful for Rosa's words, so relieved by her reassuring embrace, but also scared to let go. It was going to be a summer that would change them both.

The friends had met at Leeds train station on a cloudless early morning of what would become the hottest day of the year, a heatwave their friends and family would later message about while they took their first tentative steps in a new city, a different country – first stop, Paris. Noa's mother had bought her a new backpack, a water bottle and a passport holder, all made from recycled plastics and found in a local charity shop. They were not only gifts, Noa knew, but a sign of her acceptance. No, she would not be the fashion model or elegant bride or television weather girl as her mother had secretly hoped – not yet, at least – but her accolades were far greater, went far deeper. Finally, Rosa understood.

Vaguely aware of his daughter's plans to travel, Hamish had sent a parcel containing a seaside postcard with his name scrawled on the reverse and a paperback book, which he hoped she would take for the journey. Its front cover featured a linocut print of a coastal scene in soothing blues, greys and greens, a dolphin broaching the water, gulls silhouetted against a Van Gogh inspired sky, a couple walking, tiny against the immense cliffs. Noa loved the image and the book's promise of adventure, beginning the first page before the train to London had even left the station. She had finished it by the time they reached the hostel on the outskirts of Paris, feeling inspired and humbled by its humour and honesty, its sense of hope against adversity. While her travel buddies tried to spot the Eiffel Tower from their window, Noa turned back to page one to begin again.

Though she picked up other novels along the way, swapping with her friends and downloading a few to her phone, Noa found herself returning to her father's gift. As they traversed from country to country, she followed the couple on their physical and emotional journey again and again, reflecting on her own adventure, sensing a camaraderie with both the characters and the coastline the writer described in such perfect detail. The marvel of the natural world captured between its pages mirrored her own sense of awe as she took in every possible inch of her new surroundings.

Noa felt as if she had floated through the first weeks of their tour, her footsteps always lagging behind those of her friends, eyes wide and mouth mute as she struggled with a riot of conflicted feelings: amazement and anger, wonder and worry. As they explored, she snapped countless picture-postcards for upload, yet their captions remained blank. Despite the constant inspiration, she could not bring herself to write the truth. Hashtag pollution. Hashtag endangered. Hashtag dying. Hashtag goodbye. Instead, she made notes in private, thumbing her thoughts into her phone and scribbling illegible stream-of-consciousness responses into her notebooks each evening as the others snacked on yet more pastries and worked on their own masterpieces – songs, drawings, sketches and plays. They delighted in the inspiration their discoveries had brought, but for Noa, the responsibility of writing felt too much, her words not nearly powerful enough to convey what she had seen.

Almost a month later and after an epic train journey from Bergen, the five finally found themselves in Narvik, a former mining town secreted beneath snow-tipped mountains beside the calm waters of Ofotfjord. As they each wearily stepped out of the train carriage wilting under their packs, Noa headed towards the natural light, emerging outdoors to take gasping breaths of the purest, cleanest air – so fresh, she imagined it as a white cloud filling her lungs, whistling into her blood, infusing her organs with life. The moment seemed to stretch into a long expanse; it felt like she had found her very own Eden.

The travellers' respite was short-lived as a beaming woman cloaked in an ankle-length padded coat enveloped each of them in her arms, followed by equally hearty hugs from a burly moustached man, his tree trunk biceps wrapping them up like presents – Al's grandparents, providing the familial comfort they had all been secretly craving. The couple introduced themselves as Mo and Hem before bundling the youngsters into their creaking old car, bags strapped to the roof flailing multicoloured streamers as they headed to their new home.

The house was much like its neighbours but seemed to have its own energy as they approached. A typical wood and slate-tiled abode, the horizontal panels were painted light grey with white borders and the pretty front porch featured a trio of metal lanterns each containing a thick white candle. Inside the property, the rooms felt both spacious and cosy, clad in various cool tones of wood and stone, sparsely decorated with natural fabrics and a few practical furnishings. Though it was summer, the hearth was still blazing, the dining table opposite ladened with food and drink. Noa loved her attic room at the very top, the only one in the group to have a space to herself.

After a hearty early dinner of meat-free *kjottkaker* (meatballs) with potatoes and cabbage, Al's grandfather took them on a drive around the local area. They spotted the bobbing boulders of seal's heads in the bay and sea eagles soaring above on unseen strings, the sky so vast that the friends could take photos of pure blue unmarred by the myriad high-rises they were used to. It was as if they had landed on the Moon. The day finally ended with them curled up around the fireplace, the light refusing to dim into dusk. They tugged fat marshmallows onto long twigs plucked from the garden's oak tree, blowing and sipping at brimming mugs of soya milk cocoa as they listened to Mo and Hem's stories, before each retiring to their rooms to indulge in deep and dreamless sleep.

Soothed by their surroundings, the group spent a few days rejuvenating with long walks, lingering showers and lengthy conversations, their phones forgotten, their minds minimising their usual daily to-do lists. Eat, walk, sleep, repeat – it was all they really needed. Sometimes they worked collectively or individually, Kaia on her sketches, Al on his latest play, Stefan with his lyrics and Rowan comparing the local atmospheric pressure to the daily-changing digits on an app. Noa had tried to write, daring to read a few samples to the group when they convened after supper, but they were not the protest pieces or calls to action her friends were used to. Instead, she had been writing about the land. The people. Their heritage and history. It had made her feel more a part of the world than she ever had before.

After a few days of recouperation, the group were ready to explore. Their physical and mental fatigue had abated, replaced by the buzz of excitement, the pleasure of passing the summer holidays with friends and in freedom. They visited the local war museum and the Polar Park zoo, took the bus to Stokmarknes to see the newly opened Hurtigruten Museum, then enjoyed a long and scenic drive with their hosts up to Andenes for the unmissable sea safari, the whole group bursting into applause as they spotted a sperm whale breaching the waves near the horizon, their eyes too stunned to have time to fumble for their phones and take a picture. The days slipped away seamlessly, until all too soon they were beginning to pack their bags again ready for the return home.

A few days before their departure, the group rose early, gorging on fresh bread, loganberry jam and *brunost* (brown cheese) before waving farewell to Mo and Hem to catch the bus heading towards one of the coastal towns for its annual arts festival. They eventually descended the vehicle amid a ruckus of calls, colours and costumes: musicians and artists, theatre troupes and crafters, food and drink stalls, circus displays and parades, all mingling in and around and through the slim streets, hiding behind the lopsided buildings nestled around the harbour. The friends drank it all in, thirsty for adventure, feeling young and alive. After almost two years of uncertainty and restrictions, the festival proved to be the celebration they never knew they needed, the final exhale of a long-held breath.

Noa could feel her skin rippling, her eyes gleaming, her senses ablaze as the marvels unravelled with every move of her head, every turn of their path. While the others went on ahead to join an impromptu street dance, she tried out her newfound language skills on a local craftswoman with a stall of souvenirs – bookmarks depicting the fjords in watercolours, colourful braided bracelets with beads, along with some carved wooden keyrings in the shapes of different regional animals. Rummaging through, Noa found one in wood so pale as to almost look translucent, its soft grain reminiscent of gently rippling water, perfectly honed into the shape of a whale's tale. She let it slip through her fingers, soothed by its softness, calmed by its curves. She bought a handful of the keyrings as gifts, but this one she would keep for herself, she decided. A memory of her life at that moment: content, fulfilled and at peace.

Having rediscovered how to dance and laugh, play and perform, the group reformed and made their way to a vacant picnic bench, sitting down as they eagerly surveyed the stall signs for lunch suggestions. Determined to stay vegetarian if not vegan, Noa had been surprised at the variety of options during their travels. Even Al's grandparents had been happy to accommodate her needs, offering at least one meat-free alternative with every meal, plus every kind of confectionery they could wish for, with Noa constantly nibbling on the homemade biscuits or gelatine-free liquorice that seemed to always be on the kitchen table.

Knowing more of the language than anyone else, Al did the honours and collected a variety of paper plates piled with hot and cold snacks, some familiar and others entirely new – sweet waffles, savoury pancakes, pickled herring, different dark chunks of meat, mince in gravy, boiled potatoes, green beans, some sort of stew, bread rolls and a bowl of sauces. Wooden forks were shared, hands crossed, morsels savoured, the only sound being appreciative hums and grateful groans.

The favourite among the group was one of the meat dishes, though Noa had stuck to the sugary options for safety. Al pointed to the stall behind him where he had purchased the plate, the friendly proprietor still serving a constant queue. The sign above the serving hatch swung in the soft breeze; a recognisable shape, one they had been admiring only a few days previously. The outline of a whale. The group watched it sway in silence, contemplating what they had just eaten, what they had just done. The remainder of the food went untouched, their appetites suddenly absent as they made their way back to the bus stop.

Noa paused in her recollection, lifting her head to take in the café surroundings once more. Even now, she could not think back to the day of the festival without feeling a solid lump rising in her throat, cold sweat creeping across her palms, unwanted images clouding her mind and unsettling her emotions. She looked up at a clock hanging on the opposite wall, realising with guilt that she had been speaking at Hamish continuously for well over half an hour. She turned to check if her father was still paying attention, if he was still even sat there.

His kind eyes and keen expression were instantly reassuring. He nodded in both understanding and encouragement, his fingers steepled as he finally looked his daughter in the eye, as if he now recognised this stranger, could see something in her that he knew within himself.

Dipping a hand into her satchel, Noa pulled out the notebook from her travels, turning to the page with the missing corner and smudge of dried tears. She pushed it across the table, letting her father scan the first few words, waiting for his response. His permission, his encouragement, his insistence, perhaps – not only that he wanted her to continue but that he would not judge her either, nor her friends or their hosts, or the place that had felt like a second home.

Hamish looked at the notebook, running his eyes over the letters and the drawings, taking in the raw emotion emptied onto the page. "Noa," he said softly, "Please… go on."

Flushed with an unexpected courage, Noa continued.

Twelve

A sullen gloom hung over the group of friends for the rest of that day. By late evening after the long bus ride back home, they each managed only a thin slice of bread and jam savoured without a sound before slumping on seats around the empty hearth, staring into the unlit stack of logs as if they were aflame. The dusk still refused to darken fully, leaving a mottled hue of black and blue above the horizon, like an inked brush rinsed in water, like their souls spilt into the sky. Mo and Hem had left them to their thoughts, promising a brighter day to come. Noa longed to believe it.

She slept fitfully, her imagination riotous with unwanted imagery from the many videos and photographs she had been watching on her phone before bed. The men on shore with binoculars pressed to their faces, watching the waves. The cry and call to action when a whale was spotted. The shallops chasing their prey, lancing its flesh until it succumbed, still alive but unable to fight. Tugged ashore to the station where more waited. Then the final scene. Butchery. Slaughter. Thick blood-sodden wedges of meat to be used as feed for fur farms, processed into pet food or shipped thousands of miles to sustain foreign diners.

When she awoke, she felt as if she had blood on her hands. She had not eaten the meat but she had been there, had been a part of its purchase, had not spoken out against the people in the shack or the others waiting for their turn to order. Did they know what was happening? Did they care? Did she?

The shower felt soothing after the lack of sleep, but Noa did not feel clean afterwards. The memory of her GCSE English project came to mind. 'Out, damned spot,' she whispered into the stream of steaming jets. She dried off and changed, taking a mug of herbal tea onto the porch so she could admire the view and breathe the fresh air, but everything now felt different. Her heaven had become tainted. She stood sipping her drink, letting the tears fall.

Recognising the group's subdued mood, Mo and Hem prepared an even bigger breakfast than usual. It was Sunday after all, and only a couple of days before their departure. Al quietly and carefully related their festival adventure through mouthfuls of mackerel, though he and the others stayed clear of the salami, pate and leftover cold cuts that usually adorned their knives and forks on a morning. He described their mistake, their horror at discovering what it was, the disbelief that it could be sold so easily to a queue of people their own age, knowing or unknowing of its source.

The grandparents listened diligently, nodding knowingly, then began to explain the situation to the confused faces around the table. Noa had her notebook beside her; as Mo began to speak, she turned to the next blank page, retrieved a pen and began recording their conversation. Despite how she was feeling, every drop of anger and fury burning inside her, she had to know. She needed to listen to the truth, the reality, to hold back her passion and condemnation until she had heard another side to the story. The group sat in pensive silence as Mo spoke.

"Whaling here is a part of the culture, a part of life," she explained, her face as serene as the fjord beyond, "So it's understandable that many would like it to continue. They made the law in eighty-six, yet Norway has always continued with whaling. Forty years later, why change? It's become rooted."

She paused and raised a finger, slipping of the stool to shuffle towards the bookcase in the corner of the adjoining room. Hem spoke while they waited.

"Did you hear of Svend Foyn? He was a whaler and an inventor. Created the harpoon cannon. Powerful, deadly. So because of him, Norway became the top country of whalers. And very proud. Of course, the government is happy to keep things this way. Many people are. Even the protestors are relaxed about it."

Mo resumed her seat, opened a book in front of her and showed it around the table. Before retirement, she had been an English teacher at the local school, the book still marked with coloured tabs between the pages. She turned to one of them.

"This picture here shows a little of the process in Foyn's day. When a whale was sighted, the shallops would launch and chase it. Harpoon and spear it. Pull it close." She placed the book down to better mime her actions. "Then to shore they would go, to the factory. More men, more work. Meat, blubber, bones, all of it was used. Some think it was hard labour, but the knives sliced as if through butter. It was an industry like any other."

"Now, it's all machines," Hem cut in, expanding and waving his hands either side like two great oars. "Fast, efficient. Perhaps we don't reach the quota, but still, other nations and industries want the meat. It's a business."

Noa was noting every detail, sketching the outlines of the images from the book. Her mind had conceived a thousand and one questions, but for now, she knew she needed to stay silent, to hold back her emotions, to give time to these two strangers who had become her friends, close enough to feel like family. Their hosts had never set down whale meat at the table. They were not like the others, she was sure.

"Times are hard; the government want to support the people," Mo continued, "So they help the whalers. Only one expert aboard is needed, they say, and at the festivals where the young go, they can sell the meat. It's the culture. And better than processed foods, for sure. After the pandemic, many want to eat local, so the consumption has risen. But just a little."

The friends looked at their hosts then at one another, still unsure, still disturbed by something that felt so different from what they were used to. Noa could only think of the drawings in the book, her hand sketching the outline of a harpoon. She finished the shape and set down her pen, feeling a sudden rage swelling inside.

"But what about the whales?" she said, her words and tone instantly creating an icy atmosphere. She hoped she had not sounded rude, or even accusatory, but the anger and the upset felt too much, too powerful to ignore.

Most of all, she was surprised with her friends, with their muteness. Could they not remember the sight, smell and taste of what they had eaten? Had they not been there in the boat when the incredible image of a whale emerging from the water had caused their hearts to swell and their eyes to water? What about the reports they had read, the data they had gathered, each of them tapping away and sending facts and figures to one another during the night?

Noa knew then that she was in love with these beings, admired all of nature and her wonders. She could no longer look at a slice of cheese or a lump of meat or one of the eagles high above the landscape without feeling both gratitude and guilt. They should be appreciated, protected, respected, yet they were being killed. Not even bred for death but actively hunted, in the wild, in their natural habitat. To Noa, there seemed no possible justification. She looked across the table, the faces around her remaining wordless.

"I understand," Mo nodded, gently smiling at her. She reached out to touch Noa's trembling hand, running her calloused fingers over the young flesh.

Noa's eyes were both dry and wet, her body hot and cold as she fought her feelings, as she tried to understand. Seated next to her, Rowan wrapped an arm round her shoulders, giving a soft squeeze. The others all smiled, kindly but with a shared sadness. They were silent because they could offer no answers, she realised. There was no simple explanation they could provide.

Hem was stroking his moustache, drawing out the long, white, wiry strands further, his eyes set into some unknown distance, glossed over with thought.

"The whalers are not the enemy," he began philosophically, his tone low, his words considered. "The animals are dying because of everyone. Me and you, all of us. For many years, pollution has been destroying these creatures from the inside, and yet we continue. Fossil fuels. Plastics. Fertilisers. Industrial processes. These are the causes. This is why they are dying. We are the reason for their deaths."

The group nodded firmly, their eyes widening, a moment of revelation igniting a tiny flame within each of them. Noa scrambled to pick up her pen and made her final written note carefully, circling the statement three times. *We are the reason.*

The table had been cleared and the bill paid. Noa had not noticed. As she finished her story and looked around, she spotted a small silver dish on the table with a few coins and two wrapped mints in its centre. The notebook lay open in front of her father where the plate of herring had been, the final notation seeming to glow with its four capitalised words. He was staring at them, his brow furrowed.

Hamish traced his eyes over the open page again, one of many his daughter had filled during her travels. It had been an adventure he still knew so little about, but he could clearly see how it had transformed her, knowingly or not. As he had flicked through, he had seen the smiley faces and multiple exclamation marks gradually replaced by delicate line drawings of seascapes and animals, accompanied by letters stained with tears from countless nights spent in heartbroken reflection. He knew the experience well, wished he could have somehow shared in her sorrow back then. But at least he could try to help now. Noa said she had come to discover the secrets of being a journalist, to learn his profession. It was a duty he had a better hope of performing than of being a good father, but only if he started now. He closed the notebook and pushed it across the table to her.

"To be a good writer," he began, "you need to know what you care about, the story that matters the most to you. You've found your story, Noa. Your truth. You have to write it in your own way, using your own voice." He tapped the top of the notebook before replacing his hands in his lap.

Noa nodded, both reluctant and relieved to have finished what still felt like a partly told tale. She put the book back into her bag, retrieved her purse and placed a few more coins on the tray. She would buy some liquorice later, she thought. For old times. Then she would write, put down the knowledge she now had, unburdened by the burning ache inside, sharing the sorrow she had kept quiet for so long. Her hand was almost itching for a pen.

"And what about you?" she replied, her throat feeling suddenly hoarse, her eyes not quite dry. "What about your truth?"

Hamish picked up one of the sweets and peeled open the wrapper, slipping the white sphere between his lips as he watched the people passing by outside. "I'm still searching," he said, lost again in his own thoughts.

Once he had finished his sweet, Hamish staggered to his feet, put on his coat and waved an awkward goodbye to Fin. Noa prepared to leave before hurrying across to the counter to swap numbers with her new friend, her bag clattering against the table as she went. It was then that Hamish noticed the pale familiar shape: the keyring of a whale's tail. The sight caused something to spark in his mind, tiny but noticeable. He waited until Noa returned, holding the door open for her.

"I think you can help me," he said, "We can help each other. With our stories and our writing." He looked up and caught her eye, resisting the urge to look away.

Noa paused, catching her father's gaze, her face brightening into a smile. "It's a deal," she nodded.

Thirteen

The cool glow shone in a loose square, a faintly formed halo against the wall. Emil blinked into the half-light, the dawn trying to peer through his bedroom window, still masked by the thick curtains, the morning paused for a moment longer. A chance to catch his breath, to come back to life. He was curled up in bed, head nestled on one stiff arm folded underneath, legs heavy and limp, every muscle feeling unable, unwilling. His body had slept so deeply as to become like the dead, passive and immobile, his mind just as motionless. He sensed he had been somewhere else, living another life, and that soon he would awaken with knowing and intent. Wake and move, then set sail and sell fish. Eat then sleep. Repeat and repeat. It was a rhythm he knew well, yet today his mind and body felt lost.

When the light had brightened to a steadily beaming band, Emil rose and headed into the living space. Opening the curtains with care, he could hear the soft sighs of the stranger on the sofa, still slumbering, still present. His thoughts on the boy remained muddied, swaying between one possibility and the next without conclusion. A soul from the sea or a crime case for the constable. A boy who was magical or simply missing. A fiction or a reality. All seemed equally probable and impossible, with Emil wavering between.

Then he remembered his promise, the one he had made to himself before falling asleep. *One more day*. He would wait one more day to decide, another few hours in his company, to reassure himself that the boy was fit and well before he left. To return. To go back home, wherever that might be. Emil was used to saying goodbye, but the thought of the word filled him with deep sadness, dragging up all the other moments of his life when he had been left behind. He stole another glance at Noah, his face softening, smiling. One more day… it would have to be enough.

After a strong cup of black coffee, Emil washed and shaved, changed his clothes and combed his hair. He tidied the kitchen and checked the child's garments – they were clean and dry, even the shoes. He folded them, placing the small pile in the bathroom beside the sink. He filled the basin with warm water and placed a bar of soap within easy reach, upturning a bucket so the boy could stand on it. Was this what life might have been like, he wondered, if the unthinkable had not happened? He could feel the uninvited imprint of the talisman on his fingers. Rubbing his hand fiercely against the coarse fabric of his trousers, he made his way to the kitchen.

Ever since he was young, food had always formed a distraction. Emil could still remember the meals his mother had once made, when all the family – even friends and neighbours on occasion – would crowd around the table and help themselves to the abundant selection she prepared. His own attempts were sparce in comparison but no less satisfying. He looked in his fridge for options, found himself taken aback by the number of herring he had collected. Heads and tails, fins and scales, packed one atop of the other, cold and dead, still faintly scented from the sea. Again, he felt awed and extremely lucky.

Still undecided, Emil remembered the outbuilding. The cured fish would be ready by now. He tugged on his boots, retrieved his coat and headed out, closing the door quietly behind him. He looked around, expecting to see the remnants he had been unable to collect the previous day, but the land was barren. Not a single sign of the hundreds of bodies showed in the surroundings. It was as if yesterday had never happened, as if he had emerged from the bunker to find nothing out of the ordinary. He leaned down to run a hand over the dew-dotted grass. No imprints, no remains. An illusion. A miracle.

He moved swiftly to the outhouse, hurried by anticipation, though he need not have worried – the fish were all there, including those he had set to salt and packed into pickling jars. He would prepare more later, but for now he wanted to check the kippers, to see if his invention still worked.

The smokehouse was little more than a cupboard of his own design, inspired by the fishermen he had once spoken with, both in his native lands and locally, who had learned the art of curing by smoke from a long generational line of experienced hands. Since moving into the cottage, Emil had tried and tested various methods over several months, finally finding the best solution for the small quantity of herring he could not sell fresh or did not want to salt. Though his device proved effective, the trade was slow, having already been so well established elsewhere, but he still received the odd interest from a handful of smaller cafés and shops. Now he had such a lucrative catch on his hands, he could smoke without fear of burning his precious winter earnings, and even have a steady supply for himself.

Edging the door open, Emil peered into the fogged and dusted interior of the smoker. The scent set his soul alight, his skin warming with the simple pleasure of what he knew would be succulently cured herring, hanging bony and bronzed from their hooks. He removed the pairs carefully, piling one on top of the other, wondering whether he had enough material to light a second fire, to smoke another dozen or so from the supplies in the fridge. Eyes watering, nose twitching, he closed the catch on the cupboard, picked up the small crate of fish and walked back towards the house. He would decide later about the others; for now, all he wanted was breakfast.

On re-entering the cottage, Emil saw that Noah had managed to seat himself at the kitchen table. His face beamed, small hands entwined, resting on the wooden surface. His cheeks glowed as if vigorously scrubbed, his fair hair brushed neatly to one side. He still wore the homemade tunic but with the belt fashioned into a bow on his hip, his expression one of regal tolerance, like a miniature medieval king awaiting his court in a banqueting hall. It took all Emil's might not to bend slowly before him in greeting.

He slid the crate onto the table in front of where the boy was sat, watching as Noah peered in to see what treasure it contained. The excited gasp mirrored Emil's own quiet enthusiasm, and soon they were dining on thickly buttered bread, mugs of sugary tea and six of the freshly cured fish, their flesh flaking off at the faintest touch of their fingertips, leaving only a few oily remnants scattering their plates.

While he washed the dishes and Noah, balanced on a chair beside him, tried to dry them with a tea-towel, Emil attempted to describe his boat. He could imagine her resting in the peace after the storm, pretty as a postcard or a watercolour painting. Yet as idyllic as the scene he spoke of sounded, he did not wish to be out there. Today, there was no longing to feel the wind twisting through his hair and the salt sandpapering his skin. He did not yearn for the anticipation of the catch or the reassuring release of hauling up filled nets. There was no reminiscing about the scent on the breeze or the sound of the gulls. As he talked, Emil found he could remember each element so distinctly that he did not need to be sailing to be smiling. Soothed and safe, he finally felt at home on the land.

The touch was unexpected, causing him to start, his elbow stabbing into his side as he flinched, pulling his arm away. Noah reached out to the fisherman again. He was trying to dry the man's hands with his cloth. He seemed not to notice the missing digits, two stumps of flesh where fingers should have been. The boy rubbed the corner of the damp fabric over the skin with care, his little face furrowed with concentration. Emil watched, spellbound.

Once satisfied with his toil, Noah rolled the soggy fabric up and placed it on the side before reaching his arms out for support. He grasped his pudgy fingers around Emil, circling a hand and a wrist. The fisherman did not move, conflicted in a way he had never experienced before. It was as if the boy had not noticed, did not even mind. Not even Emil's mother had been able to look without her face puckering. He remained speechless and immobile as Noah climbed down from the chair, giving a satisfied huff before walking across to the sofa. He took his place in front of the coffee table, sitting cross-legged as he retrieved his pen and papers again.

Emil watched him with curiosity, his own feet rooted to the kitchen floor. He felt the urge to run and to stay, to laugh and to cry, peculiar sensations but not wholly uncomfortable. He turned and plunged his dry limbs back into the soapy suds, as deep as they would go, his eyes returning to the scene outside. The sunlight was now pouring through the window, bathing his face in warmth, though it felt more like he was glowing from within. The birds sounded a cheerful chorus, the faint hum of the sea and the air making a melody of the moment. He swirled the water with abandon, the slosh and splash an accompanying instrument, before tipping away the lukewarm liquid and drying his softened skin. He felt as if something had been washed away. He was cleansed. Renewed.

"Let's go into the garden," he decided aloud, picturing the calmness of the bay, the perfection of an early autumn day, both ideal for tending to the abandoned patch of greenery with his new companion.

Noah looked up from his work, bouncing the end of his pen against his lower lip in thought. He placed the lid on top and ran to retrieve his boots, shuffling them on before going to stand like a loyal soldier by the front door.

The area at the back of the cottage was what Emil referred to as his garden, but the space was denser and wilder than much of the nearby land on the clifftop. A waist-height stonewall had been built by the previous owner to fend off the worse of the wind from the sea, and all manner of cloches and covers had been designed by the fisherman to further extend the life of what little managed to grow in the difficult conditions. Over the years, he had worked hard to experiment with various plants and soils, fertilisers and pesticides, all cooked up in his kitchen or in the outbuilding from a combination of local hearsay and faded memories.

She had loved to be outside. While her father fished and her mother darned or washed or cooked, she would be in the garden, no matter what the weather, caring for her crops. When Emil had arrived to live with his new family, it was the first thing Marna had showed him. Not the house and his bedroom, nor the fishing boat and where he should put his muddy footwear. The garden had been her haven, the neat rows and curated patches her passion, a place where she always felt at home.

While the young fisherman had been learning the trade out at sea, Marna would try new ways of producing larger and more delicious fruits and vegetables to place on the family's table. Apples and pears, spinach and onions, courgettes and potatoes, her hands manipulating tools with ease as she worked shells and seaweed into the gravelled ground, dreaming of her own plot and small hungry mouths to feed in the future. Emil would always know when they ate the produce she had grown, the flavour far richer than anything bought at the market, her smile too broad to hide her pride. It was one of the many reasons he had so easily, and hopelessly, fallen for her.

Once Emil had moved to England, there had been no time to see to his own garden – he had needed every waking minute to learn all he could about his new mistress, the sea. Those early months had been more challenging than he had anticipated. The local fishermen had not been especially open to his questions or helpful in their answers, leaving him to spend many sleepless nights listening to the radio, tirelessly translating the shipping forecasts word by word into a notebook. He had pored over maps and charts, books and papers, many too old or too archaic to be useful. There had been dangerous excursions by boat just to discover the ways of the water, an expanse so distant and distinct from the one he had known that he felt literally out of his depth, clinging onto hope with every day that passed.

Over time, he realised where the men would gather to drink on an evening and joined them to hear their stories as they boasted of their bountiful catches or bemoaned the state of the ongoing Cod Wars. Some shifted aside so that Emil could sit beside them, though they rarely spoke to him directly. Others were more hostile, at first ignoring the newcomer before turning to snide jibes and cruel jokes, taking their frustrations out on the stranger, the easy target, the one they knew would never fight back. It had not taken long for the nickname 'Lefty' to arise on account of his missing right hand, though worse taunts were uttered.

The police sergeant had even spoken out one night, having overheard their sneers as he tried to enjoy a celebratory pint with a colleague. A few of the men tutted and rolled their eyes. 'He's no fisherman, not like us,' they had replied with distain, but the others became more amiable, allowing Emil to sit as a mute member of their group. Grateful but nervous, he tried to follow their unusual words with the missing sounds and merged letters, his English skills still basic at best, but he persisted. A few months later, he had made a few friends and was earning a steady wage. The nightmares still came to him, and he had not raised a smile since her death, but finally, he felt he had found a home.

There had been women in the pubs too – 'young, free and single' they were fond of saying – dressed in gowns and heels, cackling with laughter as they lit cigarettes and ordered tiny glasses of liqueur, their perfumes lingering among the smells of salt, smoke and spilt ale. There was one woman, seemingly unattached to any of the men, who would often sit beside Emil, plugging the gap between him and the others. With bushy blonde hair the colour of bleached grass and eyes a hazy grey colour, she had a quiet confidence that seemed thoroughly modern to Emil, and he found himself increasingly interested in her conversation.

As the evenings out became a weekly occurrence, he would sit a little apart from the others with his pint of cider, looking around for his new friend. He could always spot her by the bulky fur coat and brightly coloured neckerchiefs, her shiny black handbag bouncing against one hip as she strolled in. She would order a drink then sit and listen to the rowdy group of men, casting glances at Emil, then finally raise her voice with her own contribution to the discussion, a cigarette bouncing between her painted lips. Emil would try to follow as best as he could, watching the timer on the table – a single shot of whisky, which would take her an entire night to drink, before she shrugged on her coat and disappeared back into the night.

They all called her Ivy, though it took Emil several months to realise that this was not her real name. 'Got to watch that one,' the others had grinned, 'Eyes like daggers and a brew like poison!' The joke had revealed itself slowly in his mind but did not deter him from the enjoyment of her company. She spoke readily of her lonely life in the town, her grand ambitions to move to the city – any city – and to reign like a queen. The fisherman admired the sentiment, but while he was content to keep his own life simple and subdued, Ivy seemed to revel in the excitement of the unknown. He had hoped to find out more about her plans, but they had not been in touch for years, not since Emil had stopped visiting the pubs. Perhaps she had moved away, he thought, finally gone to follow her dream.

Emil wiped a hand over his furrowed forehead, continuing his slow pace along the overgrown garden path. Noah was racing left and right behind him through the tall weeds, looking for hidden creatures. The fisherman still thought of Ivy on occasion, when the working day had ended and he was alone in the cottage, staring into the fire. He would sit and recall her stories, hoping she was now in some thrilling metropolis somewhere, a glittering success, a star reborn. He ran a hand along the crumbling wall, his movement slowing as another memory resurfaced, this time strange and foreign, gaining clarity now that he had the space and time to think.

It had been a Sunday morning several years ago. Emil had woken in his bed to find his head pulsating with pain, his mouth like a sewer and his skin stuck to the sheets. He had no recollection of the previous night. In the kitchen, he found vomit on the floor, an empty bottle of whisky on the table and a collection of cigarette ends in the sink, swimming in the remnants of dirty dishwater. He had been drinking heavily, he realised, and with someone else, but he could not remember who. Embarrassed, confused and scared by his lack of memory, he decided to never step foot in the town again, to forget the other fishermen, the kind police sergeant, the woman with eyes the shade of a storm. He could not risk his livelihood, his identity, the preservation of his past. The truth slipping from his lips. He had always known he would be better off alone.

Despite his resolve, it had still been a forlorn and melancholy transition, but one Emil was now used to. The experience of that night had forced him into sobriety and solitude, and it had suited him fine these past few years. He had carried on. He had survived. There was no need to consider whether it was enough. But now that he could remember, he could not help but wonder what had really happened on that night seven years ago...

The fisherman turned to see Noah tugging at his sleeve, eager and excited for what the day had in store. Emil set his thoughts aside and led the way to the plum tree, blooming with seasonal fruits, which he instructed the boy to squeeze one by one for ripeness. The tree had done well, growing up and into the wire he had set against the wall. Emil plucked the darkest, densest fruit he could find, wiping the white chalky surface against his trousers before biting into the softly yielding flesh. They were perfect. He took another for Noah, watching his face contorting with pleasure, but had to shake his head firmly when he then began pulling off and eating up more and more, one after the other. The fisherman suggested they gather them instead, have themselves a feast later for lunch. Then they set to work beside the vegetable patch.

The boy crouched and observed, listening intently as Emil explained what each of the sorry green stalks should be – baby kale and winter lettuce, chives and peppermint. The herbs had fared quite well; they picked a handful of each, adding them to the pile, then removed the weeds and unwanted debris from between the rest. They worked methodically across the rest of the haphazard rows, assessing and testing, pulling and replanting, each movement a happy toil to the fisherman and a world of learning for Noah. He seemed riveted by every activity Emil suggested, even pulling off the few slugs that had gathered around the marrows.

Soon the sun shone high in the sky, the garden looked much improved and the slim pickings had grown into an admirable collection, but they would need more. Leaving Noah to guard their goods from the beady-eyed seabirds, Emil returned to the cottage in search of additional fare.

In the kitchen, he retrieved the basket he had used for the kippers that morning and began to fill it with anything he could find. The last lump of bread that still smelled fresh, the jar of jam and the butter. Plates and glasses, knives and napkins. A large firm tomato, slim sticks of celery, a handful of late raspberries with only a few bruises. In the fridge among the fish, he spotted a wedge of corned beef wrapped in brown paper, a couple of boiled eggs and the nearly empty jar of pickled onions he had been meaning to replace. He took the salt and pepper pots from the kitchen table then remembered the cupboard beside the sink. The bottle of dandelion and burdock was still there, along with a paper bag that rustled with its meagre contents. He added both to the basket, feeling pleased. He hoped Noah would be too.

Heading back outside, Emil found the boy in the same spot gazing out to sea, his hands still cupping the few gems they had foraged from the garden. He took them from him, dusted off any remaining dirt then set them down on a plate. The second dish he handed to Noah, along with the dullest knife and cleanest napkin, watching as the boy picked his lunch from the assortment, humming a cheerful tune.

Emil opted for the same selection, the pair then taking their time to consume the morsels in varying combinations, the sound of their eager chewing punctuated by complimentary murmurs. Emil discovered that the fresh chives worked well with the boiled egg he had shelled, while Noah took to topping the plums with a dollop of jam before ramming each one into his mouth, working them round with his tongue before plucking out the stone with his dainty fingers, like newly discovered nuggets of gold.

After dining like royalty, they lay in the grass side by side, silently observing the shifting billows of cloud above, hands rested on their pleasantly bulging stomachs. A few gulls passed by, one swooping low only to soar back upwards again, having decided the covered basket between the two dozing humans not worth the effort. There was little left to take anyway. Emil would need to go shopping again soon with an extra mouth to feed, he realised, before stopping and chastising his absurd idea, the belief that the boy was here to stay. His guest, the fallen miracle. No. They could not continue for much longer, could not hide from the truth or the town, as much as Emil wished otherwise. Just one more day.

Propping themselves up on their elbows, the pair watched the water for a while, lulled and at peace. The surface was completely serene with not a boat, wave or animal to mar its perfection, a flawless reflection of the tranquil sky above. Emil, of course, could sense what lay beyond, what the eye could never see nor know; the torrent that would be raging beneath the polished plane.

It was why he had decided not to take Noah on the boat with him, why he had chosen to stay on land with the small stranger rather than weather the seas with his usual travel companion. The breeze had whispered its warning that morning – 'Wind in the east, fishing least. Wind to the west, fishing best.' A local mantra that had never failed him.

"Can you swim?" Emil wondered aloud, realising how long it had been since he himself had left the safety of the boat and enjoyed splashing around in the water.

The boy slowly shook his head, as if ashamed.

"That's ok," Emil replied calmly, "Nor can I."

The child turned, eyes wide, mouth agape, like a character from a comic book. "But you're a fisherman!" he exclaimed, flailing a hand in the air.

Emil smiled, tilting his head upwards to focus on a spiral of barely-there cloud that was gradually disappearing, the white unravelling into the blue.

"Yes, that is true. But I'm more man than fish," he shrugged.

Noah exploded into laughter, doubling over, both arms clutched across his belly as he kicked his legs in delight. The seabirds cawed in confusion. Emil broke his gaze to observe the unusual behaviour beside him. After a few minutes, the boy settled, laying back down, his body and expression grown wearied, a cavernous yawn escaping his lips as he stared up at the sky.

"Like the beautiful wife," he said thoughtfully.

Emil made no reply.

The warm dry grass made a comfortable bed on which to rest, the vista above providing an endless stream of interest. Noah reached up and pointed, quietly babbling, the words incoherent to Emil's ear, either too fast or too peculiar for him to comprehend. He listened closely, following the boy's finger as it swooped and curved in time with the acrobatic forms above. 'Birds' and 'wings', Emil thought he could make out; perhaps 'feathers' and 'gulls'.

"Yes," the fisherman confirmed, "Those are herring gulls above."

But there was something else in the boy's repeated words, a sentence Emil could hear but not quite understand, echoed as readily as the birds' cries until it became unmistakable.

"They are my friends," Noah said again.

The notion seemed strange to the fisherman, but he soon realised why it had stirred him. It was envy – the idea of needing nothing more on earth than the beauty of nature, to be able to form friendships not with people but with places and all the wonders they contained. How simple life would be if the only friend he had ever needed to seek was the sea. How happy his former years might have been. Another winged companion came into view.

"A common gull," Emil mumbled sleepily.

"Tell me more," the boy replied.

There was a book in Emil's collection that was filled with detailed illustrations of British wildlife, including the birds that could be spotted off this stretch of coastline. There were many types of gulls, he told Noah, trying to remember back to the pages he had read so long ago. Black-headed gulls he often saw, and sometimes the great and lesser black-backed varieties. Kittiwakes were common, and a few little terns might pass by. There was the odd fulmar, and he had recently seen a Northern gannet from the window. The boy hummed and sighed in awed reverence. The fisherman too felt an unexpected admiration for his many sightings. He had not quite realised his privilege, the friends all around him.

If only he knew a story about birds, Emil mused, or even one about the other creatures of the sky, land and sea. There were a few Farfar had shared when the brothers were small, old Norwegian sagas with their sinister characters and twisted narratives, elaborated with gory details and dramatic gestures. Those stories still haunted him. They would not do now. Not for Noah. The bookcase – there must be more stories he could read aloud with some confidence, he thought. Emil rose animatedly, taking the basket with him, reassuring the boy over his shoulder that he would only be gone for a few moments.

Soon enough, he had returned with a bundle of books nestled safely in his arms. He sat back down, the pale sun still warming their sheltered spot, Noah shuffling up beside him, wringing his small hands in eagerness. Emil opened the first and flicked through a few pages, trying to choose a suitable passage. The child leaned over and tapped a finger at the start of a sentence. The fisherman looked, nodded, then began to read.

"'There I heard nothing except the thrumming sea, the ice-cold waves'," Emil began, his words slow as he tried to feel the rhythm of what he could see was an old poem and to improve upon his dubious pronunciation. "'The cry of the gannet and the curlew's voice for the laughter of men.'" He paused to describe the two birds to Noah then continued.

"'The seagull's singing for the drinking of mead. Storms beat the stony cliffs there, where the tern calls him with icy feathers. Very often the eagle screeches with wet feathers. No sheltering kinsfolk could comfort this impoverished spirit.'"

Noah held his head in his hands, his elbows braced against Emil's leg. His eyes looked out across the plateau of the clifftop and away to sea, as if he were imagining the seafarer sailing across the silvered waves, whispering his ruminations into the mist, unaware that a man and a boy were listening to his tale.

After four further poems, they moved onto a second book of short stories, selecting one by Hans Christian Anderson. As he read aloud, Emil realised he had heard it many times before in various guises but never in English. He was surprised by how poetic and atmospheric the words sounded when spoken, the ambience they created, in addition to the evocative imagery that flourished through the mind. Noah seemed mesmerised by the story, his mouth an open hollow, his eyes glued to the pages as he listened.

Finally, with the sun having sunk lower towards the horizon and the air significantly cooler, they picked their way through a few choice chapters of the final book, one of only a handful that Emil had purchased himself. He had been told about the author and had liked the sound of the title, but had only read it once before it had been placed on the bookshelf and forgotten. He regretted his abandonment of such an interesting tale for so long but now relished being able to reunite with its intriguing central character once more. His companion seemed equally entertained, having curled onto his side, running his fingertips back and forth over the coarse grass as he listened.

The sun had almost set, casting its honeyed rays across the sea, land and sky, bands of gold reaching out like tendrils, touching, soothing, sliding across the two motionless forms on the ground. Feeling peckish, Emil remembered the paper parcel he had put in his pocket when they had unpacked the picnic. He pulled it out and ripped it open along one edge, revealing the contents inside: five shiny black discs, their aniseed scent wafting up from the wrinkled packaging. Noah jumped onto his knees, leaning his face closer, his eyes almost as wide as the sweets. He let out an appreciative coo, picked up a round and slipped it into his mouth. Emil smiled, his own childhood joy reflected in the face before him. They had been his favourites as a boy too. He took one, savouring the taste as he watched the final remnants of sunlight fading.

In that moment, the fisherman knew that this day would be among his most precious memories, that he would always remember the boy and their time together. And afterwards, in the days to come, he would try to lead a better and happier life for himself; for tomorrow, he would take Noah back to where he belonged. Tomorrow, they would say goodbye.

Fourteen

The night had stretched on, pulling his mind along in different routes, new directions, endless beginnings without ever reaching their conclusions. But Hamish had not been thinking of the missing fisherman or of his long-gone mother, his student days or his former lover. The tales from his daughter's summer travels or the afternoon they had spent together did not enter his mind either. For a reason he could not comprehend, he had been thinking only of whales. Seen, imagined, drawn or set in stories. Blue whales and humpbacks, minkes and belugas, sperms and orcas, their distinct forms and echoing cries radiating through his thoughts, dragging him in and out of consciousness, as if attempting communication. Guiding. Consoling. Like returned spirits of the dead.

In the dream, Hamish had tried to replicate their language, to share in their secrets, but each time, he had found his throat caught, his voice empty. He had watched them swim further and wider until the bow of a boat emerged on the horizon, as if materialising from the mist, and then he had woken up, sweating and nauseous, searching his mind for a deeper meaning.

As he lay in bed listening to the clock slowly ticking its way to a more respectable waking hour, Hamish remembered the print he had left in his daughter's room. He wondered if it had been a poor choice, distasteful even, particularly now he knew about her feelings on whaling. He was glad not to have been quizzed on his own perspectives, conflicted as they were, as they had always been. If only he had known about Noa's trip to Norway before she had arrived. If only he had taken the time to ask.

The discussion in the café the previous afternoon had been the longest and most personal conversation they had ever shared, leaving Hamish with the smallest hope that perhaps he was finally beginning to understand his only child. Noa had opened her heart, revealing her memories and sensitivities, choosing her words with a thoughtfulness and maturity he had not expected. As she had talked, he had found himself ever more curious about her world and her mind, the way she was trying to navigate life and its complexities. He had begun to feel like a valued confidant. Now, he even wished to reciprocate that trust, to describe his own history, his own truth. He decided that he would agree to his daughter's suggestion; they would go to the attic, to the collection. He would explain what it all meant.

Once the clock had reached seven-thirty, Hamish washed and changed into his customary Monday morning outfit of brown trousers, a beige shirt and a mustard woollen jumper. Even though he had booked the day off work, he still liked to feel smart, prepared, ready for the latest story at the shortest moment. He would tell this to Noa when she was finished in the bathroom – it would be lesson number one in his guide to becoming a journalist. He had no idea what lesson number two might be, nor of the other advice she was expecting from him, but they did have six months together. He was sure he would think of something.

Refreshed after a comfortable sleep, a quick shower and a few minutes of meditation, Noa felt the calmest she had in days. She unpacked the rest of her belongings (including the forgotten provisions from Aunt Isobel, now soggy and stale), placed a few choice items onto the bedside table, then turned to admire the framed drawing on the wall. She had been surprised to see it in her room, the only item in the flat without a practical purpose – and it was hers. A gift from her father, other than his books and postcards. A symbol of the local town and its heritage, of the sea and its mysteries, of a new chapter in her life. 'Welcome home,' she told herself. With great care, she unhooked the image, took it across to the window and propped it against the glass, the light illuminating the detail of the lines and the depth of the depiction. She wondered what other surprises her father might have in store.

Before going to bed the previous night, nursing a mug of chai tea and another ginger biscuit, Noa had suggested to Hamish that they could look over his findings in the attic the following day. If she was to become a writer, then perhaps it would be the perfect place to start. She could learn how to conduct research, to piece all the parts of a puzzle together, like a proper journalist, assisting him in finally solving the mystery as well as advancing her own education. In between the confusion and suspicion, the rejection and frustration, Noa still felt compelled to help. Their visit to the beach, the lunch in the café, followed by the hours of walking around the town then a light supper of beans on toast, had left her with only one certainty – that she would stay, for now. If she could start to understand her father and his strange ways, then maybe she could survive for six months.

In the kitchen, Hamish had prepared breakfast. Noa shuffled in to see a rack of barely browned wholemeal toast, pots and packets of jam and butter, two oranges, a bunch of grapes, a carton of soya milk and two mugs of black instant coffee. He stood awkwardly beside the table as she entered, an uneasy smile stretched across his freshly shaven face. Noa grinned in thanks, sitting down and helping herself to toast, hoping her newfound serenity would radiate into the room and absorb into her father before his rigid shoulders reached above his ears. She watched him sit down sheepishly and unpeel an orange, though he usually had toast, before they both attempted to make small talk about the weather and how well they had slept.

Soon enough they were finished, Noa helpfully clearing the table before departing to her room – perhaps a little too eager to leave, Hamish thought, but he tried to cast the worry aside. It was only when he had finished washing and drying the dishes that he remembered the raspberries he had bought from the market, grown on a local allotment and packed in a recyclable cardboard tray. He mentioned them when Noa returned, dressed and carrying a notebook and pen. She promised she would enjoy them later, but for the time being, there was work to be done.

Having climbed into the attic with her father, Noa

stood before the collection once more. She had peeled back a corner of the cover from the skylight to allow some natural light through, but while the rest of the room did feel a little brighter, the stretch of collaged wall seemed even more imposing. The brilliance of the late morning sun lent the mood of a medical facility or police investigation room, and Noa found herself stood stiffly, one hand on her chin, wondering whether she was really ready to face her father's past, to discover his secrets.

Though he had gazed at its contents for hours on his own, Hamish was now struck by its power, its ability to confuse and fascinate with its myriad layers and intricate organisation. He watched his daughter assessing his findings, her face unreadable, keeping his own thoughts and theories muted. He was intrigued by the idea that she might spot something he himself had missed, that she might finally find a solution.

But Noa did not know where to begin. The process of slowly deciphering the many articles, images, sketches and details littered across the surface seemed somehow intrusive. This was not just a trivial mystery – it was her father's childhood, some of his fondest memories. She could only imagine the time he had spent trying to look for an answer, the countless nights disturbed by a new and better theory, only to find it discredited by the wall the morning after. It seemed an endless and unforgiving battle. This was the disappearance of a man, a possible crime case, a detective story where each strand was not so much woven as laid side by side, with no obvious points of intersection between them.

Noa sat at the desk and began jotting down names, places and dates, drawing lines between the possible links. Though her mind was puzzled, she could sense something else stirring her – exhilaration. And as heartbroken as Hamish must be, she knew this was how he felt too. The same restlessness, the anticipation of finding an answer, of discovering the final piece that would allow all the others to slip into place. The mystery had not been a burden for Hamish. It had given him a reason to live.

Standing by her side, arms behind his back, face forward and eyes locked on the central image, Hamish waited. There were more documents in his drawers, more references filling over thirty A4 notebooks. The colour coding, the handmade drawings. The boxes of books and the rolled-up maps. The letters, emails, printouts and postcards. And the wooden ark. All of it a treasure trove of information, of investigation, yet amounting to nought. He was still no closer to knowing.

"An impossible task," he confessed aloud, though he knew he was not quite willing to believe it yet. So long as he kept looking, there would be hope.

"Nothing's impossible," Noa shrugged, tapping the end of her pen against her temple, her eyes tracing a row of three handwritten notes on headed paper from the University of Tromsø in Norway.

During and after her visit to the country, Noa had been trying to teach herself Norwegian and found herself able to decipher a few of the words and phrases across each page. They were penned by someone called Ivan Michel Olsen who, despite the surname, had confirmed himself to be Emil's brother.

"So he was from Norway? Somewhere in the north…" Noa surveyed the map, noticing the trail of familiar names, places she had seen with her own eyes – Narvik and the Ofotfjord, Stokmarknes and Andenes, the Lofoten Islands and the site of the festival. Her mind cast back to the group sat around the picnic table, tucking into their dishes. 'Cultural cuisine' Al had called it. Her skin prickled with cold.

"Most probably, yes," Hamish nodded, "Though that particular brother wasn't too keen to speak with me. From my research, I'd guess around the Lofoten area."

Research, Noa thought. A veiled reference to using his job as a journalist to uncover so much secret information. He had risked his profession and his credibility to discover the name and address of the fisherman's family members. She studied the picture of the man they called Emil, wondering what he might look like now.

"There was another brother you spoke to, then?" she asked.

"Yes. In English, thankfully. I have the recordings."

Noa looked to her father, expecting him to produce one of those old-fashioned cassette players she had seen on television shows from the Nineties. Instead, he pulled his phone from his pocket, swiped the screen a few times, then held it between them as the deep tones of two male voices, one recognisable, the other unfamiliar, began echoing around the room. With her hand darting left to right across the page of her notebook, Noa struggled to transcribe the recording quickly enough.

The second brother, the eldest of the family, confirmed that Emil had departed from their hometown in northern Norway (precise location unspecified) to a place called Whitby in England during the early 1960s. He had kept in contact with his brother sending letters once a year, though they had never contained more than a few lines of basic factual detail. He had settled in a cottage atop of the cliffs, was working as a lone fisherman and had learned how to smoke herring – kippers, as they called them locally. No mention of a wife or children. No mention of a mother or father. No word of how he had come to make a success of himself, 'the youngest and least able' of the siblings, in his own words. The brother knew about the disappearance, the declaration of assumed death, the emptying of the cottage's contents and its subsequent condemnation. The surrounding land had been surveyed, deemed extremely hazardous on account of potential landslides, and the house and area cordoned off. A curt 'Will that be all?' followed before the call abruptly ended, the screen fading to black.

Noa looked over her notes then glanced across to the wall, trying to decipher the recording and its meaning, but her mind was still trapped in her own memories, the recurrent image of the festival food stall with its carved wooden sign swinging on chains. Its shape was mirrored by the many sketches drawn by Hamish's own hand, both beautiful and unsettling.

"Maybe he was a whaler," she wondered quietly, her

eyes coming to rest on the weathered old toy with its lonely-looking animals. "And something happened in Norway. Perhaps the business failed, or another brother took over, so he came here."

Hamish slowly folded his arms across his chest, his brow furrowed. It had been something he had already considered time and again, though had yet to find any proof of, and it still did not explain why the fisherman would have disappeared.

"The link between Norway and Whitby is mere coincidence," he reasoned, regretting his tone almost at once. Noa was here to help, he reminded himself. A fresh perspective in an ever thickening fog. "But I know he loved whales as much as I did. Hence the drawings." He motioned to the wall, a curator taking pride in his own private gallery. "He told me stories, captured my imagination. That never left me."

"But wouldn't it make sense that he returned to Norway?" Noa thought. She did not wish to burst the comfortable bubble her father had created, but it seemed the most obvious solution. Perhaps meeting the little boy had made Emil pine for his own family. Convinced him to forgive whatever had happened in the past. To move on, to start anew. "He was still in touch with his brother, after all."

Hamish opened and shut his mouth like a fish gasping for breath, his arms suddenly stiff against his elevated chest, his stance grown rigid, defensive, like a determined toddler. He wanted to shout at the top of his voice, to discredit the possibility with the one fact that he believed held the whole mystery together, yet the one certainty he would never be able to prove. *My father would never have left me.*

The thought screamed and flailed inside his mind, but he was now well versed in battling with his emotions. He kept his gaze averted, slowly counting to ten in his head while willing his breathing into a steadier state. Forcing his shoulders to slither a fraction downwards, he reminded himself that she was not like the others. She was not here to condemn an innocent man. She would not think him a criminal.

"I checked the records," he finally replied, hoping he sounded neutral despite the twinge of irritation still coursing across his skin. "No evidence of him leaving the country, nor of him settling in a nearby village or town."

The fisherman was unlikely to have gone to a bigger place to live, but still, Hamish had searched. He had tried alternative spellings of the name and had scoured news articles, both in the UK and from abroad. There had been nothing conclusive. Nothing insightful. The only piece he had found of any interest had been about the drowning of a young woman in the early Fifties. She was from Andøya in Norway, the only child of a fisherman and his wife. Her name was Marna.

Sensing Hamish's growing frustration, Noa knew she would need to try a different direction. Running a hand across the back of her neck, she shuffled the chair closer to the wooden ark perched on top of the cardboard boxes, almost as if it were stranded on a cliff. She raised her eyebrows at her father questioningly; he nodded his permission. Down the little door came, revealing more of the coupled animals inside. Giraffes and cows, lions and horses. Zebras, crocodiles, parrots and pigs. Two by two by two – except the final creature. She looked around the rest of the ship, all pairs in perfectly neat rows, apart from this one. Its mate was missing.

"I stole it," Hamish muttered, his mouth creeping into the smallest of smiles. His posture slackened, arms returning to his sides, face softening as he bent down to peer into the belly of the boat.

Yes, there they were – the only friends from his childhood, objects he remembered so well yet had been forbidden to touch. Maybe when he was younger, a toddler, he had been allowed to play with them by his once-kind grandparents, but he could not recall the occasion. Instead, it was always the stomach-clenching fear of being caught within touching distance of the ark, his grandfather deceased and his grandmother deteriorating daily. 'It's not for you,' his mother had always said.

There had been something about that day. Perhaps the coming of the storm or the sudden departure of his mother as he slept. The fact that she had not made him breakfast or that the front door had been left unlocked. Whatever the reason, six-year-old Hamish had seen his chance. He had climbed out of bed, washed and dressed himself, found fruit and bread to eat, then had planned his escape. He would go to his favourite place, brave and alone, like a real explorer, but he would need a companion to help. He had seen the wooden toy, felt the keen longing for its inhabitants and had done the deed. Swift as a seabird, he had swooped into the innards and plucked his most beloved of beasts – the blue whale. It had taken him twenty years to remember that he had done such a thing, but looking back, he felt a certain pride in that moment. The very first instance when he had chosen his own path in life. Hamish could not help himself; he let out a chuckle.

Noa watched her father stooped over the little boat laughing to himself, a child once more. Every time she began to feel closer to understanding who he was, she sensed him slipping away again, like the tide, like the weather. Ever present yet always changing. There had been no mystery to Hamish's disappearance, she now realised. The fisherman had not stolen the child and kept him captive, as some of the more lurid reports on the wall surmised. If her father's memory could be believed – and this she still doubted – then he had willingly walked from his home on one side of the town and made it all the way across to the other, up to the cliffs and to Emil's cottage. No crime had been committed. Unless, of course, Hamish was mistaken.

"And where's the whale now?" Noa asked, hoping the conversation would deter her thoughts from journeying down more sinister paths.

Hamish righted himself, knees clicking in unison, bending backwards a little with a grimace on his face. An old man still searching for his stolen childhood.

"It's a mystery," he whispered into the ever-brightening light, his eyes fixed once more on the central photograph, the little boy holding hands with his hero.

"Maybe you left it in his house," Noa suggested.

It could still be there, she thought. The pair of them could go back during the night, take torches and dress in black to escape detection from the authorities. There might be other items of interest too – papers, clothing, things Hamish would recall from his visit. Then Noa remembered the recording. The house had been emptied. There would be nothing left to find.

"No. These were all I managed to retrieve," Hamish sighed, tapping a toe against the bottom box below the ark. "The books. I had to find them, to have them safe with me, though the most important ones are still missing."

"Can I take a look?" Noa was intrigued now.

She watched her father move the toy with the care of a conservator, not one of the animals shifting inside. He then removed the strip of tape from the first box, releasing the unmistakable odour of old paper gone damp and dusty. He moved it to one side then opened the second box below. Together they unpacked the contents, lining them side by side across the floorboards, from William Shakespeare and Jane Austen to Charles Dickens and the Brontës, through to Agatha Christie and Jules Verne, H G Wells and Arthur Conan Doyle. There were two copies of the Bible, several nautical guides filled with charts and maps, an illustrated book of birds, another on farming, some encyclopaedias and a collection of poetry with a navy leather cover and deeply creased spine.

"This was how he improved his English," Hamish explained, flicking through a well-preserved copy of Homer's *The Odyssey* clad in a green dust jacket.

"Did you know back then? That he wasn't English, I mean?" Noa asked.

"No," he mumbled, lost in another tome with a maroon cover, "I just thought he was like me... different."

He placed the book down then began unpacking the second box. Five books in, he realised Noa had grown silent, still waiting for an explanation.

"What I mean is..." Where could he begin? It was something he never talked about, tried not to remember. "As a child I... I had difficulties... a speech impediment. The other boys would always make fun of me. Even Mother and Grandma sometimes. But he never did. He was patient. Kind. I never felt ashamed when I spoke to him."

Noa nodded, remained quiet, subdued by her father's experience. She knew how it felt to be bullied, but thankfully never by her own family or friends. There was much she still had to learn about the man she had moved in with.

The final book completed the eighth row. Father and daughter stood side by side surveying their work. Nearly the entire contents of the bookcase from the cottage now covered the attic floor, close to every copy Emil Kleve had owned. A fine collection, many would argue, but for Hamish – and perhaps for the fisherman too – they had been more than just revered authors and helpful non-fictions. They were links to the outside world, to places and people and times otherwise unknown or forgotten. They had been the only items in his home that had held any meaning, that had a kind of soul or substance. And like the fisherman himself, Hamish would keep searching for the others.

He tried to identify the missing books for Noa, but his words felt inferior and empty. How could he explain what they had meant to him, the delight of sitting with a kindred spirit discovering the world together? He described the vast folio that had been spread open across their legs, the one with the vivid imagery depicting what he now knew to have been the fisherman's homeland. Then there were the two filled with nautical poetry and short stories, tales of sea voyagers and their adventures complete with ink illustrations, and a paperback novel about an old brave sailor and his struggle with a colossus sea creature. Hamish had listened to them all. It had sparked his passion for reading as a youngster, though he had never found a book to match those he had heard during his time at the cottage.

Over the years, Hamish had been able to recall odd details about the missing books, sudden memories coming in bright flashes. He had spent hours rummaging in charity shops and antique centres for them, scouring online sales sites and leaving messages in the local paper, but still they evaded his reach. They were out there somewhere, he knew; he needed to find them, to keep them, to preserve the pages for when the fisherman returned, for the day they would be reunited and could finally read stories again together.

"The missing books," Noa began, "What if Emil took them with him?"

The thought seemed so obvious, yet Hamish had never considered it. If the fisherman was still alive, then perhaps he had kept a few possessions. And if he still cared for the boy he had named Noah, then the books would almost certainly be among the few items from his home that he would want to keep. It was a possibility both probable and reassuring.

While Hamish paced the perimeter of the collection on the floor, picking up copies to flick through their pages and place them carefully back down again, Noa had returned to the wall. A small newspaper clipping with 'September 1980' written in pencil on the top reported on the Declaration of Presumed Death for the missing fisherman. Plans had been made to erect a commemorative stone in the graveyard of St Mary's Church later that month, its monetary donor unknown. Just two short paragraphs for a decision that must have hit Hamish like a bullet to the chest. The wound must have been his reason for leaving, Noa thought, remembering the story he had told her the previous day. It had been the push he needed to escape his hometown and lose himself in academia, hoping to forget the past, longing for a better future. Yet despite his exemplar grades and career prospects, his passion for politics and newfound friendships, despite falling in love, Hamish had still come home. He had left his new life behind for this – a dead man he had hardly known yet still loved, immortalised by a handful of faded and outdated documents pinned to an attic wall.

As much as Noa wanted to help her father find the missing man, she was confused and concerned by the seeming lack of interest he had in her own life. She watched him ambling around the dusty tomes, absorbed in memories that did not include her, that he had intentionally hidden, while she, his daughter, had been overlooked, undervalued, largely ignored apart from the odd parcel and short text. Her entire existence lay dormant, with not a single reference to their relationship in the whole house. No framed photos, no fingerpainted pictures behind magnets on the fridge. None of the gifts she had bought him on display, nor her letters stacked neatly in a box of their own. Only the endless files on Emil Kleve, a stranger, a nobody, a forgotten fisherman no different than the thousands of others lost at sea. He was dead, Noa was sure of it, but she could not bring herself to say so out loud. Hamish might not have been the father she wanted or deserved, but he was still human. He was still hurting.

Perhaps somewhere in the house there was another space with her childhood memorabilia cluttering the walls in ornate gold frames or propped on meticulously dusted shelves. Noa allowed the thought to fill her, to infuse her cold limbs with life again. There was always hope.

"Do you have pictures of our family?" she asked her father softly, a chance for redemption, a willingness to forgive, if Hamish could provide a single sign of caring for someone other than his six-year-old self.

He lifted his gaze from the rows of books on the floor to his daughter, though he still avoided her eyes. Instead, he noticed her jawline, its sharpness even more pronounced in the attic's harsh light. Yes, she looked just like him. Just like the man he remembered. A flush of colour ran up the length of his throat, spreading across his chin and cheeks. He moved a hand across the back of his head in deliberation then walked cautiously over to the desk.

In the bottom drawer was an envelope Hamish never opened – not because he was uncomfortable with its contents but because he had memorised them so well that there was never any need to look. Perhaps now was the time to pass them on, he thought, just as he had always intended. He reached to pull out the drawer, cringing at the guttural groan of wood against wood before retrieving the package and handing it to his daughter. Noa took it wordlessly, turning it over in her hand. No writing, no coloured dots; just a sealed plain brown envelope from a barely used desk drawer. She had no idea what she would find inside, but the possibilities made the pulse in her neck radiate, the hairs across her arms tingle and burn.

As she began to peel back the flap, she felt pulled from one extreme to the other. Her father as selfish and cold-hearted, abandoning his daughter in favour of finding a man he barely knew. Her father as kind though quiet, keeping his heart hidden, his true feelings disguised, and here could be the proof. Another concealed collection finally shared with someone he cared for. Someone he trusted.

Maybe she would find something other than old photographs, she wondered. There could be those early Christmas letters she had written, eagerly describing everything she had done and received during the holidays, decorated with hand-drawn stars and snowmen in the corners. Or maybe copies of her school results and rare achievements, sent by her proud mother. Drawings perhaps, or simply pictures after all. She would not mind; she just needed something, anything – just one symbol of his only child's existence, distanced but never neglected. The hope felt enormous, swelling in her chest, thumping in time with her heart.

As Noa was about to pull out the contents, a loud rap from below made her start, the packet floating from her hand, coming to rest by her feet. Hamish stood frozen, a copy of Hans Christian Andersen's stories open in his palms, his forehead rumpled with fine lines. They both waited in silence, as if they had been caught, then the knocking resumed – louder and more insistent. Hamish stooped to replace the book on the floor with a measured delicacy before retrieving the fallen envelope.

The thumping continued, followed by a voice calling their names, though Noa noticed it was 'Mr Shaw' rather than 'Hamish'. The tone was familiar, someone they knew. She forgot the envelope and hurriedly headed downstairs to answer the door, sighing with relief as she saw who was standing there – Fin. Both hands were pressed either side of the door surround as he struggled for breath, Noa waiting patiently as she took in his outfit: a flowing black faux leather jacket, shiny military boots and a pair of brass-rimmed circular goggles on top of his heavily tousled hair. She tried to think of something funny to say but felt her features slip as she looked into Fin's eyes, wide and alert with something other than a friendly welcome. Something that seemed more like fear.

Fin ducked his head to remove his goggles, as if

he were taking off a hat in greeting, then stood for a few moments trying to find the right words. If he had run in those shoes, Noa thought, then there must be an emergency. She tried to offer him water, opening the door wider to encourage him in, but Fin shook his head.

"No time," he replied, still trying to breathe, "Need Mr Shaw."

As if conjured by an incantation, Hamish appeared at his daughter's side, his face even paler than usual as he stared at the visitor, wondering what could have happened. Noa was still trying to help, offering Fin tea or coffee, which were both declined. After what seemed like hours, he finally spoke, the words hitting Noa and Hamish like a tidal wave.

"You better come to the beach. They've found a body."

Fifteen

The lifeless form lay along the same stretch of beach Hamish and Noa had visited the day before. The opalescent skin was dusted with damp sand, the open eyes glaring at nothing. A faint smile played across the lips, as if it were merely resting, dreaming of another time and place somewhere out at sea. The air hummed with a pungent stench, the drone of mumbling voices from the gathered crowd mingling with the constant calling of seagulls desperate to sample the still fresh meat.

The body was not the tangle of bones Hamish had been expecting to find when he had heard Fin's words, had raced to retrieve his shoes and coat, rushing down the cobbled streets without a thought to the people he pushed aside in his passing nor the daughter and neighbour he had left behind. As he had sprinted, heart pummelling, breath rasping, he had thought only of the body. The fisherman found. The fisherman dead. The fisherman gone for good.

Now they were stood in silence facing the sorrowful spectacle alongside at least forty other locals and tourists, their faces partially obscured by cameras and phones masking wrinkled brows and downturned mouths. The body was not a skeleton. It was not even human. They were witness to a stranded white whale, an adult beluga. An exemplar specimen just over four metres long, Hamish guessed, with its characteristic short beak, absent dorsal fin, rounded pectoral flippers and small tail flukes. He could recall the last time the same species had been seen in British waters a few years earlier – alive, swimming and feeding in a stretch of urban river, of all places, somewhere close to the capital. He could remember following the story on the news, then writing his own report for the town press on historic cetacean strandings along the North Yorkshire coast. The task had captivated and appalled him, rare instances but no less distressing to research.

This example had died at sea, Hamish was told, seemingly of natural causes. Bearing no external signs of injury or disease, the whale had simply washed up on the shore a little under an hour ago. Hamish thanked the man beside him – Adrian, the local vet and the most experienced of the town's self-appointed conservationists – as he completed his detailed update to the journalist. The taller man clapped him warmly on the shoulder, confirmed once more that everything was well in hand, and suggested that Hamish give a hopeful tone to his article, reassuring the public that the situation would be taken care of. Adrian walked away, leaving Hamish nodding dumbly.

His mouth dry and stale, his eyes transfixed by the pale mass with its haunting grin, Hamish had not even thought of having to write up the event until the vet had mentioned it. His mind was elsewhere, swimming in a deep, dark, turbulent current. He could only look at the motionless form, solid skin the colour of clotted cream, black eyes blank but shining, with an expression that seemed to lull the crowd into a state of reverent calm. While his head repeated Adrian's information – the importance of noting the precise details of the specimen and its location, contacting the Cetacean Strandings Investigation Programme hotline, ensuring members of the public did not try to intervene or touch the finding – Hamish felt himself held captive by the thick thud of his heartbeat, rendering him as inert as the beluga's body while the tides of water and watchers continued to ebb and flow around him.

He noticed Noa and Fin had sat together on one of the benches above the bay, their faces etched with shock and pity. No matter how many reports there were on television or in articles and videos online, the reality of seeing a stranded whale was far removed from the excitement suggested by the media. Despite their ever-increasing numbers and the numerous recordings and images being created and shared by the surrounding semi-circle, everyone on the beach knew they were witness to an unnecessary death. A murder of sorts. The destruction of an innocent creature, with no solution to its demise, no culprit to shame. A hopeless waste of life. Hamish hung his head helplessly.

Looking away across the water, he recalled the beluga illustration pinned in the left-hand corner of his attic collection, a relatively recent creation compared to the others, sketched from a library book he had discovered a few years ago. The allure of the white whale had been with him for years, ever since he had met the fisherman. Hamish could remember the moment he had produced the rusted tin from his pocket, the one with the dent in the discoloured lid, and had removed the intriguing object from within. A pale pebble, no larger than a walnut, softly curved in the shape of a beluga.

Even at the age of six, he had known how much the token had meant to his rescuer, how important it had been to share in the secret of its existence. Unlike his own wooden whale, he could tell this one held a long and secretive history, an age-old mystery now lost, like the fisherman himself. Hamish had never known what had happened to the stone in the metal box, nor to his own stolen toy. Those days in Emil's cottage on the cliffs had been the last time he could remember holding it. When he had arrived home with his mother that evening, hoping to slip it back into the ark, he had found the whale had vanished.

During his investigations, Hamish had discovered a number of stories online about animism – souls residing in places, objects and animals. From ancient folkloric tales to contemporary cultural accounts, he had narrowed the array of search results down to a few chosen narratives associated with Norwegian, Sami or north British coastal traditions. One told of the bodies of drowned fishermen floating further and further out to sea until they were drifting in the vast oceans, turning somersaults with great shoals of fish, becoming embedded in nets of stringy seaweed until finally being swallowed by a whale. Their bodies dissolved, slowly feeding the creatures, the men's souls absorbing into their thickening skin. Realising their rejuvenation, the lost fishermen would then try to swim back to shore, to their homelands, without realising the danger. The lucky ones would merely be seen before forlornly resolving themselves to a life at sea. For those less fortunate, their bodies would become stranded, on the beaches or atop of rocks, their deaths absolute as they succumbed to their fate on the once familiar shores.

Hamish turned to the crowd. A young girl no older than seven was reaching out a hand to the whale, her fingers covered by a woollen mitten despite the reasonable warmth of the early September morning. Her hair in ribboned pigtails, she beamed as her father took a photo then another, her little paw creating a bright pink blemish against the beluga's milky skin. A sudden band of blue appeared between the two, Adrian holding his arms out wide, blocking the man's view, causing the girl to run round his legs to the safety of her father. Another local stepped in, then a third, only for one of the other children waiting by the side to run forward and take his turn with the newest seaside novelty. A shout, a shove, the raising of multiple voices and a distinct shift in the atmosphere finally managed to persuade Hamish to move from his position and head towards his daughter, still seated with Fin on the bench, her head rested wearily on the boy's shoulder.

She smiled in greeting, though Hamish wondered if she had been crying. Her eyes seemed heavy and sunken, her mouth quivering as she sat up and shuffled awkwardly in her seat, one hand toying with the ornament on her bag. She too was plagued by recollection. Their shadows were everywhere.

Hamish stood beside the bench, soundless and subdued, their faces three clay masks of indifference betraying the raging emotions they shared within. It was a circus, a cabaret; tragedy turned into entertainment. More people arrived than left, jostling closer for the best snapshot. There were tears and head shakes, parents sheltering the view from their children, others on their phones, calling and texting, wondering how they could help this poor creature, who would come to save the day. Surely wild animals could not die and decay on a public beach, they thought. But like Hamish, Noa and Fin, the gathered remained rooted, stranded alongside the whale, paralysed by the knowledge that any hope had been lost; its life was already over.

Hamish knew he had work to do. He needed to go into the office, type up the article, send it over to Alan then call a couple of other colleagues. Noa nodded lightly as he explained, working the whale tail keyring through her fingers absentmindedly. Fin would stay with her, she announced. They would go over to his house for a couple of hours. Neither Hamish nor Fin replied, so Noa stood up and turned her back to the scene, ready to leave – somewhere, anywhere – but not to the flat, not to where she would be alone, abandoned once more.

Fin nodded, mustering a cheery tone as he replied. He would make them tea and snacks, then show Noa the 'cabinet of curiosities' upstairs. Hamish gave a hum of agreement, knowing the appeal of Woody's collection would far outshine his own in the attic. Noa tucked her hands into her coat and began walking towards the town, Fin soon following behind. Hamish watched his daughter and her new friend leave, his body loosening with relief – the wrong reaction, he knew, but one he could not help. He cast a last glance at the motionless corpse and murmuring crowd before heading towards his office.

The comforting sight of the town brought Fin and Noa back to normality. He led the way at a gentle pace, his brow softly burrowed, features pensive, pausing to greet the odd passer-by that he recognised, lingering a little longer to shake an elderly man's hand. Noa noticed that Fin was well known and liked by the locals. She stayed by his side, matching his steps, her body moving robotically while her mind remained at the beach, left behind beside the beluga whale. She wanted to console the creature, to soothe its soul, even though it was now just a mass of rotting flesh. Despite the sight and the smell, the cacophony and the chaos, she had sensed something on the beach. It was as if she could feel its fear.

Noa had known what Hamish thought when Fin turned up at their door, the words simple but weighted with meaning. It had sprung to her mind too. The image of a skeleton. The sensation, the hysteria. There would have been even more onlookers, their gossip louder, their sorrows etched with fascination. Would the shock of seeing a different kind of corpse beside the water have been different? Would it have been any less heartbreaking than what she had already seen? She would never know, hoped never to find out. But perhaps for her father, it was not quite the same. Maybe for him, a human body would have been a welcomed sight. A final resolution to the mystery.

Slowing his pace, Fin took a sharp left down an

alleyway that led through to the back of his house, where he unlocked and opened the door leading to the kitchen. He called 'hello' into the darkened space but there was no reply. Noa followed him inside, unable to resist looking around the charming room with its net curtains, rustic enamel sink and a tall wooden dresser filled with crockery against one wall. There was a circular table in the middle covered with different sizes and designs of lace doilies, each surrounding a dish or stand full of sweet treats – an iced carrot cake, a lemon drizzle loaf, a glass plate with chocolate butterfly buns and bowls of bite-sized bakes and confectionery.

The past hour was momentarily forgotten, Noa's hunger revealing itself in a fierce, audible grumble. They both laughed, feeling at ease as they took off their jackets. Noa continued to look at the table of delights while Fin filled the kettle and picked out two matching cups and saucers of vintage porcelain, perching silver teaspoons on their sides. They would have fairtrade oolong in one of his favourite teapots, he decided, and a slice each of his latest creation – a vegan spinach, pea and mint tart with homemade pastry and vegetables sourced from the garden.

With their coats and shoes placed in the hallway cupboard, Fin carried the ladened tea-tray and led Noa upstairs to what he called the front room. She stepped inside and took in the décor, wondering how many decades old the room might be, how many more identical others were dotted around the old-fashioned town. Her father's flat would no doubt be the plainest and dullest among them. In contrast to his drab beige walls, this interior was papered in a faded floral of pinks and purples, with a brown swirly carpet and a colourful round rug woven from thick strips of fabric. The fireplace appeared to be original, neatly tiled with a gleaming gold grill, a coal bucket and a set of tools hanging from a stand. It was flanked by two floor-to-ceiling bookcases and a glass-fronted mahogany display case on the opposite wall.

Noa looked for somewhere to sit, noticing a decaying armchair in the corner, its cushions sagging and stained, its owner obviously absent – the man called Woody. She wondered where he might be and what he might look like, taking a seat on the equally dishevelled sofa opposite. She slunk into its worn padding with a contented sigh, wishing Hamish's home felt even half as comfortable. Fin slid into the space beside her, carefully balancing the tray as he handed across the meals and mugs. Soon they were sipping and chewing in companionable silence, happy to do something so normal. For half an hour they ate and drank and talked of trivial things, glad to have escaped the turmoil of the beach, though neither could stop thinking of the whale.

Once the plates were clean and the teapot empty, Fin took the dishes back to the kitchen and returned with a small key. He stood before the glass-fronted cabinet that stretched across nearly the entire length of the back wall, motioning for Noa to join him. She stood by his side, eyeing the contents through the polished panes as he carefully unlocked the door, noticing ever more interesting items the closer she looked. Fin began talking about some of his best-loved pieces, repeating the many tales Woody had shared with him over the years. The old man adored accumulating all kinds of objects, he said, and had done so ever since his youth. Most of what he found or purchased now went towards their monthly market stall at the Pavilion, but in the cabinet, Woody showcased his rarest findings – his 'keepers' – many dating back to the eighteenth and nineteenth centuries. These were the pieces that meant the most, either to his ancestors or to the coastline he called home.

Noa slowly took in each shelf, the faintly dusty wood crammed with items: miniature replicas of sailing ships stuffed impossibly into glass bottles, taxidermy mice mounted onto wooden pews, shards of rock sliced open to reveal glistening gems within, fossils of flora and fauna, plus shells in unusual shapes and colours. Steel medical implements sat alongside miniature ceramic bells, and behind them, jet mourning pendants and brooches glistened on individual stands. At the back were photographs and postcards, scenic images mostly in monochrome and sepia tones, old holiday snaps of a familiar seaside town. Donkey rides and sandcastles, striped deckchairs and stalls selling sticks of rock, adults and children of all ages and classes standing, posing or caught mid-run in their excitement. Happy faces, cherished memories.

Fin reached a hand to the top shelf, tentatively retrieving an object from the back. It was pale and smooth, about the length and width of a man's finger. Etched on the surface in grey lines was a topless woman, her cascading hair covering her modesty, her legs conjoined and patterned, finished with fins. A mermaid, crudely drawn but full of character and charm.

"Scrimshaw," he smiled, rocking the piece in his hands to make the most of the dim light from the single bulb above. "The whalers used to scratch images into bits of spare baleen – whale bone – using their surroundings as inspiration."

Noa leaned in to look closer, trying to feel as enthusiastic as her friend sounded, but she could not ignore the wave of discomfort washing over her. Fin sensed her distress, quickly placing the scrimshaw back in its place before pushing the glass pane gently shut. With the door locked, he slipped the key into his pocket and sat back down on the sofa. His face had lost its cheerful demeanour and now looked thoughtful, perhaps even a little hurt.

Noa joined him, unsure of what to say, her eyes fixed on the empty fire and the stack of tinder at one side, a promise of colder days to come. She imagined the flames burning, the heady smell of smoke warming her, calming her, as it had during the summer when she had listened to her kind Norwegian hosts telling yet another story about their culture and community, their memories and heritage. She wanted to speak as easily and as considerately as Mo and Hem had done, to tell Fin her own tale, but she was mute. How could she hope to be a journalist when she struggled to express how seeing a beached whale made her feel?

A patterned hand appeared by her side. Noa pretended not to notice. She had never been the kind of person to fall for someone at first sight, and with her emotions still burning, raw and frayed, she could think of nothing worse than a romantic interlude. But the hand remained. She kept her own determinedly in her lap and watched as Fin's upturned fist unfurled the fingers, revealing a palm etched with black ink, the lines blurred with time. A circle the size of a satsuma appeared, outlined across his skin, the detailed marks and shading depicting a nautical compass rendered with such precision as to almost look real, apart from one detail. The compass held no needle.

"People talk about moral direction, knowing the right thing to do," Fin began, gazing into his hand as if looking for movement, waiting for guidance. "We can sense in our hearts which way to go, the best path to take, but we only know when we get there if we've chosen well." He fell silent, closed his hand and tucked it inside the pocket of his hooded top.

Above the fireplace hung a mirror, reflecting the cabinet across the room. They could both just about see the scrimshaw mermaid within the glass case, watching them both, an enchanting temptress imprinted onto skeletal remains.

"I went to Norway," Noa replied, trying to control her emotions. "I saw whales. In the ocean and on a plate. I know what happens. What used to happen here in Whitby too." She paused, blinking fiercely. "Death and slaughter, the same old story." She could say no more as she shifted her eyes back to the empty fireplace.

The atmosphere in the room took on an uncomfortable edge. Fin sighed. "There's no way I could ever go out there, shoot an animal from a boat. Haul it, slice it, freeze it. Tuck into its flesh for dinner." He spoke candidly and with clarity, providing an unexpected balm to Noa's entangled nerves.

Fin clenched his hands into fists, his toes curling into the carpet under his socks. He swallowed the discomfort aside. "But I've never known what it's like to rely on my surroundings for food, for fuel, for everything. To have a family to feed, people relying on me for their survival." He kept his eyes averted, wondering if he made any sense, if Noa understood.

"I've never had to choose sailing or tilling the land or lugging coal to earn a living. Never needed oil to keep the streets lit at night or to make soap to stay clean, strong bone to make fishing rods or to grease and ease cotton threads. They say Whitby was built on whaling and it's true. It wasn't just an industry; it was a whole community, a way of life."

He paused, waiting for a response: rage or resentment, hurt or confusion. He had already encountered them all. It was the same discussion he had faced ever since he was old enough to understand and form his own opinion, shared and sometimes shouted during school debates and playground scuffles, evenings at the pub or on protest marches. No, he could not agree with the violence and needless killing, the spilled blood and inactive bystanders. But his home and its history felt different.

Since he was a boy, Fin had wavered between the two sides, fighting endlessly with his internal moral compass, hoping it would guide him to the right attitude, the better belief. But like his tattoo, the needle and its direction remained elusive. He could only hope that Noa would know how that felt. After all, she had chosen to come to Whitby, and she would be used to her father's interest in ecology what with all the articles he had written and had published.

Noa continued to consider Fin's words in silence, her mind swaying from one idea to another, her feelings stirred, though they were not as extreme or upsetting as they had been before. There were many questions, but for now, she did not need to know the answers, nor did she want to pick a fight with her new friend. Like the roll of the tide, she was happy to let the thoughts fade away. But she was curious about something.

"What's in your other hand?" she asked, pointing at Fin's hidden fist within his hoody, relieved to see a broad beam emerge across his face.

"Beat me at a boardgame and you'll find out!" he replied.

Springing to his feet, Fin walked to the bookshelf and opened the cupboard at the bottom, revealing a chaotic stack of battered boxes. From the top he pulled out a yellow fabric bag shaped like a banana, which rattled on his return.

"Let's see whether you've inherited your dad's way with words."

Noa laughed as Fin emptied the bag of lettered tiles onto the sofa cushion between them, turning each one over with the glee of a child. She did not correct his turn of phrase – in fact, it had felt strangely normal to hear the word 'dad'. Could she say it herself now? Had they finally reached that point? The thought quickly passed as she became engrossed in Fin's instructions, soon too consumed by spellings and definitions to think of anything or anyone else.

An hour and three rounds later, all of which Noa had won, the friends heard the thud of the front door below and a series of sharp barks. Woody had returned. Checking her phone, Noa saw that the afternoon had become evening, with two new emails from her aunt, several messages from her friends and eight missed calls from her mother. Nothing from Hamish, of course. She wondered what might have happened to the whale by now, whether it would still be there on the beach, waiting for night to fall. Were animals afraid of the dark? She could feel its loneliness like a dull ache deep inside her. Perhaps her father had found an answer, a way to somehow save the whale, doing more than simply writing a report of facts devoid of feeling or opinion. That was his job, after all – to capture the truth. Would she be able to do the same?

She blinked again at Fin standing over her, waiting for a reply. She had not heard a word, but there were footsteps on the stairs – heavy, laboured, then the scuffle of paws and the creak of the door. Woody ambled in, older and frailer than Noa expected, grey-haired and red-cheeked, a pair of dog leads in one hand and a walking stick in the other. He gave a wide smile to the young couple, setting the leads on the side before making his way to his chair.

Noa gave each of the energetic dogs a ruffle on their heads and greeted the older gentleman politely, bashfully, realising only too late the scattering of pastry crumbs across her lap and her scruffy socks, one with a small hole in the left toe. The two black spaniels sniffed at the offending items, quickly clearing up the fallen morsels from the floor before taking their places either side of the armchair where Woody was seated. Fin had put the game away and offered a round of tea, which Noa declined, hugging the strap of her bag, her hand reaching for the talisman hanging from the metal hoop. The old man smiled, gummy and gleeful, then gave a gasp as if in pain.

"The bag!" he cried out, having had a moment of sudden recollection. He pointed towards the door.

Fin nodded, seemingly to humour him – perhaps his grandfather or an uncle, Noa thought – then commanded the dogs to sit and stay before leading his friend to the door. She gave a little wave to the already slumbering trio slouched in and around the old armchair before taking one last look at the room and its collection. She wondered if and when she would return, what other stories she might be told, whether Fin would take her hand and share any more of his ideas and memories. At the sound of her name, Noa hurried from the room, nodding a final goodbye to its inhabitants.

She retrieved and slipped on her shoes and coat, lingering over the movement as she realised that she would need to head straight home, to see Hamish and find out what had happened to the whale, with the attic groaning above them under the weight of all its secrets. And what were they going to do before each bedtime for the next six months? It would soon be winter, with fewer excuses and opportunities to take her usual nightly strolls and moonlit ambles. Did her father like boardgames or films, television or reading? She briefly wondered if Fin and Woody might have a spare room to rent; she had felt much more comfortable in their cluttered cosy front room than she had in Hamish's house so far.

As they entered the kitchen, Fin found the bag Woody had mentioned on the table. Noa noticed it was one of the fold-up reusable kinds, pale blue with tiny white boats on one side. He handed it over to her along with a wooden bento box wrapped in a pink elastic band.

"Dairy-free fruit scones – a gift from your new neighbours," he smiled.

Noa gave a whispered thank you then slipped the box into the already heavy bag, their mutual grins wavering as they hovered by the front door.

"If our beluga had washed up two centuries ago, everyone'd be full of praise, not pity," Fin mused, "It'd be a blessing, a gift from God, every single part cut up and used. Nothing going to waste." He had to try, to put his blurred thoughts into words that might mean something. "But now, today, in this world? Just a toxic timebomb. A tabloid headline. A viral video. Tomorrow, he'll be old news. He'll be gone."

Noa could see the sentiment in Fin's eyes, then felt a sting in her own. She nodded, muttered another thanks and goodbye, then ducked out of the door and began walking before it was too late. Only when she reached the exit to the street did she look back, spotting Fin at the end of the alleyway, one hand raised in a wave with a distinctive shape in its centre. She would know that outline anywhere.

Under his long fingers, each ringed with silver, tattooed in the very heart of his palm, Fin had shown where his allegiance lay. It was the tail of a whale.

Noa walked home in a heady state of astonishment, recalling the many unexpected events of the day and the promise of further adventures to come, the mysteries this place and its population, human or otherwise, might still have to share with her. She passed couples and groups clad in sensational costumes full of frills and feathers, lace and leather, with goggles or fascinators, some carrying canes while others wore contraptions that looked both ancient and futuristic. The event was in full flow, showing yet another side to the seaside town she could now call home.

On entering the flat, Noa found the lights off and received no reply to her shouted greeting. In the kitchen, she found Hamish had left a note on the table under a nautical-themed paperweight: 'Back later, food in fridge'. Noa sighed, briefly stung by disappointment before releasing a breath of relief. She was alone but not yet lonely, the novelty of the new still stirring her senses. She found dinner, a bowl of pasta, which she reheated in the microwave while preparing a herbal tea. She laid the table before seating herself to enjoy her solo meal with the soft smugness of a newly independent teenager. She could get used to this. The silence, the solitude. Not even a gull to disturb her thoughts. A fork in one hand and a pencil in the other, she ate and sketched, trying to perfect the inked outline she had seen in Fin's hand.

By ten o'clock, the dishes and kitchen had been cleaned, the television had grown tiresome, and the drawing had been abandoned as the shape wiggled and waned out of form. It had been another long day and Hamish had still not returned. Noa wanted to tell him about Woody's collection and the homemade vegan tart, to thank him for the pasta and find out what had become of the stranded whale, but her questions would have to wait. Having read through the stream of messages on her phone, she sent her family and friends a photo of the print from her room with the caption 'Smooth Sailing'. Now all she had to do was to climb into bed and ponder over what the following day might bring.

All was well, all was calm, Noa thought, settling under the duvet. Finally, she felt relaxed and content, her new beginning finally begun. Closing her eyes, she found her head filled with Fin's words about whaling. Even though her feelings remained conflicted, she felt glad to have been able to talk to someone who shared her anxieties, who was still trying to come to terms with the truth, past and present. She realised that she was no longer worried by her father's attic and his odd behaviour; the thought of spending six months with him seemed a lot less daunting now that she had a new friend to spend her time with.

Though she knew a good night's sleep would help ease her mind, Noa could not stop her imagination from spinning. Whenever this happened at home, she would open a window or go out into the garden – but here, she felt safe enough to be able to go for a walk, to take in the cool night air. Clambering out of bed, she pulled on some baggy trousers and a jumper over her pyjamas, then retrieved her shoes, coat and bag before heading out of the door, hoping Hamish might be back by the time she returned. The street was still thrumming with a mixture of middle-aged men, tourist couples, weary workers, glamorous goths and steampunk enthusiasts, as well as a few evening seagulls, none of whom were either rushing or idling. She eased past, heading for the wall beside the bridge that overlooked the bay.

It was a wonderful sight. A scattering of twinkling lights, sleepily nodding boats, rhythmically rippling water and an enormous stretch of midnight blue with the most flawless full moon perched high above. Noa loved being able to see the night sky from a new place; it always made her feel grateful to witness a different side to life on Earth. Her mind floated back to the scene she had admired from the bedroom window at Aunt Isobel's, the silvered crescent reflected in the Seine in Paris, the blanket of blue she and her friends had gazed up at during their stay in Norway. Such simple scenes, yet each memory felt powerful and magical, as if the world above was somehow sending a message, trying to communicate with the people below, with Noa herself.

As her eyes adjusted to the light, she could make out a few glowing flecks above the silhouetted buildings on the other side of the water – planets, perhaps, or important stars. If only she knew what they were called. Maybe Hamish knew something about astronomy, she wondered. Perhaps he could teach her. No doubt her would have taught himself how to use a telescope or read a star chart in the past. She would be with him for nearly two hundred days and nights, during which time he would have the opportunity to tell her more about the world and its wonders than she could ever learn online or from a documentary. But that would all depend on Hamish.

Yawning into a chilled fist, Noa headed back to the flat, finally feeling ready for slumber. Her father had still not returned. She knocked against his bedroom door and tentatively peeked inside, but it was empty. The room had even fewer furnishings than the rest of the flat with no decorations or personal items, as if he were simply lodging there temporarily, a guest in his own home. Having now been into the attic and Hamish's bedroom, Noa realised she had seen the place in its entirety, and still there was not a single sign of his only daughter anywhere.

Pausing to check the kitchen, Noa noticed the blue bag on the table with Fin's homemade scones inside. She pulled them out, opening the box to inhale the freshly baked scent, memories of her own mother's cooking floating to the surface. Still too full and too tired to eat anything, she replaced the lid and slid them onto the counter. As she turned to leave, Noa noticed that the bag still bulged with other items, the ones Woody had put in there. She took them out, turning each one in her hands. Four books. Four somehow familiar books.

She laid them out on the table, flicking through a few pages. The largest contained photographs of a lush landscape with wide open waters, tiny wooden houses and endless trees. The second was a novel by an author she knew but had not yet read, its title suggesting a nautical narrative. The other two were collections of poems and stories, the odd page featuring quaint illustrations similar to the drawing on display in her room.

Where had she seen them before? she wondered. It felt recent, sometime since her arrival. Maybe on a television programme she had flicked through or somewhere in the flat. A shop window she had passed by or in the cabinet at Fin's house. Then it struck her. The books. The ones they had arranged on the attic floor apart from the handful that remained missing, that Hamish had spent years searching for. The copies that had alluded him for years, turning his childhood dream into a lifelong quest to find a forgotten fisherman. And Woody had found them. The books from Emil Kleve's cottage.

Sixteen

After the foraging and the feasting, the bird-spotting and storytelling, Emil and Noah had returned to the cool interior of the cottage to find it filled with shadows, the daylight having almost completely dimmed. While Emil cleaned the dishes and tidied the kitchen, the boy washed and changed in the bathroom, putting on a 'nightshirt' that the fisherman had fashioned from an old pillowcase with holes cut into three of its sides. As always, Noah seemed content with the creation, and once ready for bed, sat himself in his now customary position at the coffee table to sketch some of the birds they had seen earlier that day.

Lulled by the gentle babble of his companion, Emil scrubbed and skewered some large potatoes to roast in the oven before cleaning his face, hair and hands in the kitchen sink. He set a gentle fire aflame in the grate and settled down into the armchair, watching the young artist at work. It still seemed surreal that soon the boy would be gone, that he might never see Noah again. He played the scenario over in his mind, trying to define his narrative, to still his anxieties. He did not fear going to the police station itself, despite the questioning and the accusations, the blame and the hatred he might receive. He knew it would be difficult, distressing, but he would survive. It was the part when he returned to an empty home that he could not bear to think about, did not know how he would feel, how he might go on. Alone.

He feigned calm contentment as they ate, both sat cross-legged on the floor in front of the low table, digging through the crispy potato skins with spoons and greasy fingers, pounding knobs of butter into the soft crumbly mash within. They sipped the rest of the dandelion and burdock drink before finishing with a plum each, soon fatigued by their ample meal. While Emil stoked the fire, Noah stared into the embers, reciting the new words he had learned, his pronunciation improving with each repetition. The fisherman remained silent but gave attentive nods whenever the boy wavered, watching as his eyelids slowly closed and the sentences became slurred with sleep.

He helped the child up onto the sofa, noticing how he arranged the blankets around himself, murmuring something before falling into a dream. Deeply, soundly, Noah's thoughts soon filled with sea breeze and liquorice treats, flying forms and courageous characters; everything he had seen and tasted, heard and imagined during the afternoon, the fisherman's words whispering through his memory. But there was to be no such slumber for Emil.

The fisherman continued to sit by the small blaze, preoccupied with his plans for the following day, for the future, the version of the truth he would decide to tell and then live by. Once more, the night stretched out before him, chilled and gloomy, languid and restless. The spectres quickly returned.

Emil woke to a warm, tight sensation across his

legs. He had somehow managed to sleep, slumped in the armchair still in his clothes and boots. He blinked, adjusted his vision and focused on the form before him – two fleshy hands wrapped round his kneecaps, tapping out a rhythm as the boy hummed, very much awake. The light through the curtains was barely visible – either it was still early, or the bad weather had returned. For a moment, the fisherman wondered if it might be another storm, but he could feel no signs of warning on his skin or in his blood. His fears of the outside world came from something other than his environment.

Dressed in his own clothes, Noah looked like a stranger, both to himself and to the fisherman. An other, an outsider, back to the missing boy he had been when Emil had first found him. It felt like a lifetime ago. They dined once more on remnants from the fridge and garden, but there was a sullenness to their breakfast, an unspoken awareness that something was changing, the lingering smell of smoked fish and burned wood adding to the atmosphere. But this could not be how they would say goodbye, Emil thought, holding out his wrist to support Noah as he climbed onto the chair beside the sink, insistent on helping with the washing up. No, he would need one last memory, one final reminder of the time they had shared, the stories they had discovered in this house that now finally felt like a home.

With the dishes washed and dried, the pair returned to the fireside. As Noah settled himself on the sofa, Emil retrieved the box from the bookcase, gently turning out the treasure from inside. He held out the two talismans, one in each hand – the wooden whale and the shape set in stone. The boy took the objects with great care, cradling them both in his lap as the older man sat himself back down in the armchair. With a heavy exhalation, the fisherman began his next tale, the story of the beluga that had become a boy.

Word by word, Emil allowed his imagination to unravel, giving a voice to the thoughts and hopes he had dreamed up when he had discovered the child and a thousand or more fish strewn around his land. He had come to believe that the mystery was a sign, a symbol of the infinite powers of nature to give and to take, to inspire and to warn. Yes, he had been guilty, implicit in the choices of his homeland, the slaughter served on silver forks and family dinner tables, then and now, and perhaps forever more. But the boy was his blessing, an emblem of the blame absolved. A final end to his purgatory.

As the story reached its conclusion, Emil felt as though something had altered inside of him. There was a lightness, a freedom, a wave of relief washing over his entire being, body and soul; a feeling he had long wished for but never achieved. The boy looked at him silently, softly smiling. Perhaps he had been right all along, Emil thought. Maybe his fantasy had become a reality after all. But as Noah rose to place the two whales on the table, the spell was quickly broken. The child was not an animal spirit come to release the fisherman from the torments of his past – he was someone's lost child, someone's son. No longer part of Emil's private world. It was time to say goodbye.

The sea and sky were the same shade of palest grey,

a muted sphere of light scarcely visible above, the land still and sedate, as if still wounded by the recent tempest. Man and boy were mute, lost in dreams as Emil drove them down to the town in his van. He parked near the railway station and walked with the boy by his side towards the row of terrace buildings and the police station behind. He had not told him where they were going or why; he would understand in time. Besides, Emil did not think he would ever be able to say the right words, still found himself fighting the urge to remain in the cottage together for one more day. Just one last adventure. But it was too late. The time had come.

Sergeant Wright was stood at the door of the station, a mug of coffee in one hand and a sheet of paper in the other, a toothpick between his lips as he focused intently on reading the report. On hearing the crunch of footsteps, he looked up to see two figures advancing. It was Emil Kleve, he realised, breaking into a hazy smile of recognition. The man still had the same old-fashioned clothes, the same wearied expression, and those strange golden eyes, like an owl's. The sergeant could not remember the last time he had seen him – nearly ten years, he was sure. The fisherman nodded shyly in greeting.

Tucking the report under his armpit, Sergeant Wright threw the toothpick to the pavement and raised a hand. He was about to speak but paused as he noticed the small form ambling by the man's side. The sergeant's eyes grew wide as reality dawned – it was the missing boy. Emil Kleve had found him. Without a word, he led them both into the station.

The two officers inside sat up straight at their desks as the sergeant informed them of the situation, instructing the first to take care of the child and the second to make the necessary phone calls. Refilling his mug with instant coffee and topping up another for Emil, he then led the way to a small and stuffy room at the back of the building, lit by a single narrow window looking out onto a brick wall and a row of overfilled dustbins. The wooden table and chairs were scruffy and stained, the tiled linoleum flooring worn smooth with years of footfall. There was a smell of stale smoke, fried food and boot polish. Emil felt his heartbeat heighten.

The sergeant took a seat at one end of the table and indicated for Emil to sit in the empty chair opposite. After another slug of coffee, he began arranging an assortment of papers from a beige file, talking quickly, enthusiastically, his accent thicker than Emil remembered. He sat in silence listening, trying to take in Sergeant Wright's babble of words, grateful for the mug clenched too tightly in his hand, the sting of heat providing a welcome distraction. He kept the other wrist tucked into the sleeve of his coat, the memory of his former pub acquaintances resurfacing.

Sergeant Wright had known Emil since the day he arrived. He had been one of the few locals to help the newcomer settle in, showing him around the town and giving helpful advice on where to go and who to know. He had provided the contact number of the man with the boats for sale, letting Emil use the station phone to complete his purchase. Then there had been the incident in the pub that the sergeant had helped to resolve, though he had known it would not be the first or last time the fisherman would face conflict. Despite the distance that had grown between them, both physical and personal, there remained a mutual trust, an assurance that they were both the 'good guys'. Glancing over his notes, the sergeant already knew the interview would be merely a matter of formality. Emil Kleve was a hero, not a felon.

At first, the inquiries were straightforward and routine, and Emil felt a growing relief as he answered them one by one with as much clarity as he could muster. His mind began to shift to the boy, missing once more, buried somewhere in the building. Now that Noah had gone, the past few days seemed as thin and fleeting as a morning sea mist, threatening to drift from his memory completely. He wanted to ask where they had taken him, to make sure that he was safe and cared for, but there were still questions he had to answer, truths he had to reveal.

Five minutes soon became fifteen as the sergeant spoke and scribbled onto his notepad. The fisherman grew anxious as the enquiry continued. He did not wish to talk about the talismans or the drawings, the storybooks or the garden feast. Those moments felt too personal, too private, already imbued with a dreamlike quality that made them sacred and special. For him and Noah alone to reminisce. He found himself getting caught up, feeling caught out, his replies becoming stumbled and stupid, but he could not tell the truth. He knew what they did to men like him. He would not survive.

The sergeant, however, was more than happy to

complete the blank spaces in Emil's recollections and mumbled answers, assuming it to be a lack of confidence in his second language that was causing such constant hesitancy. Indeed, he was only too pleased to put words into the fisherman's mouth, to make the necessary alterations to the story and relate back what he had written on the report – that Emil had simply been in the right place at the right time. He had found the boy that morning, alone but unharmed, and after some breakfast and a wash – thus was his kind nature, the sergeant added – he had escorted the child to the local police station: an ideal law-abiding citizen. There were no suspicious circumstances, no evil deeds afoot, and the police would not be pressing any charges. The child would soon be with his family, then all would be well. The man had done the right thing.

In another room, an officer had tried asking Noah questions, but the boy had been unable to reply with any coherence. 'Something wrong with him up there,' the officer told his colleague when he went back through to the main office, tapping a finger against his forehead. He reached into the drawer of his desk and found a foil-wrapped toffee tucked in one corner. He walked across the room, holding it out to the boy, who snatched it between his fingers like a gull with a proffered chip. Noah stood with his head down, chewing slowly, stubbing the toe of his shoe against the curling corner of a floor tile.

The other officer was still on the phone – the headmaster at the local infant school had called that morning with concern for a missing boy called Hamish

Shaw, but neither he nor the police had been able to get in touch with any relatives. This was the fifth time the officer had rung the number of the mother with no reply, but just as he returned the receiver, the phone began bleating sharply. He picked it up, listened for a few seconds, then rose abruptly to his feet. The other officer raced to his side, both abandoning the boy to rush to the back room.

The interview was over. The sergeant and the fisherman sat supping their cold coffees, neither speaking, both pausing mid-sip as the two officers barrelled through the doorway. 'Good news,' they announced in unison. The missing boy's mother was on her way. It was over. Emil felt his body turn to stone.

The remainder of the morning was filled with the steady hubbub of voices and activity, the officers rising and returning to their seats, flicking through files, dialling more numbers, barking questions, repeating answers. This was a safe town, a strong community. Crimes were rare and minor. Emil had been a good man performing a good deed, and now the mother and child would be reunited. A local journalist and a photographer were on their way, and the sergeant anticipated more media interest to come. There were even a few locals outside, word having quickly spread down the cobbled streets and into nearby homes and businesses. This was a cause for celebration.

Emil sat alone in a corner of the station, observing the rising chaos with concealed concern. Somewhere else in the building was Noah, the boy he had come to think of as his companion, a new friend whom he would likely never see again. Soon he would walk away a free man, his record untainted, his actions ignored, but he could not feel relief nor gratitude. Instead, he was consumed by a distinct pain, a growing ache pervading his entire body and permeating his mind. He had known this feeling before, the indescribable dread. It was just the same as when they had told him about the body, so many years past. Now he was being submerged once more, washed under the waters of grief.

The crowd outside the station had multiplied, rows of eager faces grinning and whispering as they awaited the missing boy and the happy reunion. The journalist had arrived, poised with pen in hand, with a man and his camera beside him. Women in aprons and hairnets balanced on tiptoes for a better view, having abandoned their shops for the latest source of gossip. A few equally curious tourists had joined them, peering across their heads. The headmaster had turned up and positioned himself near the front, as well as the school receptionist, librarian and caretaker. Passers-by paused and hovered on the side-lines, vying for a view. Even the resident gulls seemed to ease their flights for a glimpse of the occasion.

The sergeant emerged from the station entrance, ceremonially announcing himself. He talked briefly of the success of his committed team and their strident hard work, as well as the diligence of one local man, who wished to remain nameless, who had found the boy alone up on the cliffs that very morning. His simple act of kindness was an inspiration to them all, he added. It had brought the town together, raising smiles, filling hearts with hope and joy. There was a round of applause, a few of the women bringing fresh handkerchiefs to their faces at his closing words, before he motioned to one of the officers to bring out the boy.

Emil watched from a distance, feeling tethered to the situation but longing to escape. He would wait until Noah had finally walked away before returning to his cottage, to the safety of his sanctuary. He would lock the doors, close the curtains, try once more to forget. Always, he hoped to forget.

After another few minutes, a car pulled up and parked on the opposite side of the road, a woman emerging from the passenger seat. She moved so quickly as to form almost a blur, but Emil could make out flashes of colour and texture – the bundle of blonde hair, almost the same shade as her matted fur coat, with a glimpse of green fabric at her throat. From her stumbling gait across the road, he imagined her to be in heels, and between the briefly parted bodies of the spectators he spotted a black handbag swinging frantically by her side as she hurried towards the station.

The crowd chattered excitedly as she made her way through, then an officer appeared among them holding Noah by the hand. The woman shouted a name, the boy moved forwards, and the applause began once more as the two figures collided.

"Hamish, my darling!" The mother took the child into her arms, gripping him fiercely like a bear with its cub, the boy burying his face into the matted pelt of her lapel. There were cheers and laughter, the flashing of a camera, the ever present squawk of birdcall.

People flocked towards the mother and the sergeant, shaking hands, patting shoulders, the cacophony continuing, the seagulls shrieking. Eventually, they began to peel away, those in uniform moving toward the station, standing tall, smiling wide. They each gave Emil a nod as they passed, a sign of confidence and completion, though the scene felt far from uplifting for the fisherman. Sergeant Wright joined him. The mother had been visiting a friend, he told Emil jovially, watching the woman posing for the camera, preening her hair. She had taken her only child to his grandmother's house up on West Cliff, and when the old dear discovered him gone the following morning, she assumed her daughter had simply taken him back home. He finished the tale with a low chuckle and an exaggerated shake of his head.

Emil nodded, his eyes still fixed on the boy and his mother. Sergeant Wright gave him a soft pat on the arm, thanked him for his assistance and wished him all the best as he headed back inside the station. The fisherman said nothing, eyes trained on the two figures now moving away before finding himself striding forward in their direction, quickening his pace, squeezing his way through the bodies, reaching the road just in time to see the woman and her bundle heading towards the parked car. She held the child in her arms, his face visible across her shoulder.

Noah looked straight at the fisherman, into those gentle eyes he had come to know so well, then raised a hand in his direction.

"Goodbye, Pappa!" he shouted, waving wildly.

"Hush, me bairn," the mother replied, opening the car door and climbing inside. The engine revved as the vehicle set off, gathering speed along the road until it was out of sight, leaving only a faint cloud of dust in its wake.

Emil stood on the pavement, unable to move, unwilling to speak. The throng had dispersed, striding past the stranger with indifference. Just another tourist, another face in the crowd. Forgettable and soon forgotten. They did not know, would never know, how the fisherman felt at that moment. How the final strength of his spirit had been stifled within a minute. A blighted beacon, a lighthouse unlit. Blackened, his existence now obsolete.

Seventeen

You better come to the beach. They've found a body. As soon as the sentence had slipped out from between Fin's breathy gasps, Hamish had felt his knees beginning to buckle and his body turn to ice. He had been sailing along in search of the fisherman for so many years that the discovery of a body had upturned his existence, shaken his core, like being plunged into the depths of the Arctic ocean. Man overboard. He had felt agony and ecstasy, disbelief and relief, running to the beach with his hope on a knife edge. But there had been no skeleton, no pile of bleached bones. Still no sign of the man he had once known.

Almost twenty-four hours later and with the cruel clarity of hindsight, Hamish could almost laugh at his stupidity. With every hurried step he had taken, never once had he considered that the body might be someone else, another lost soul dredged up by the tide. Then to find not a man but a beached whale – it seemed impossible. Absurd, even. The humiliation. He had set his heart and hopes alight for naught. He was a lonely old man without a father, without a chance. The same as always. Just as with every single clue he had managed to remember or reveal over the years, this one had also led him to a dead end – quite literally. He was no closer to solving the mystery, and now had a beached beluga and an upset daughter to deal with.

Standing on Tate Hill Pier observing the scene in a state of shock, Hamish had wanted to bury himself in the wet sand or else wade into the water and disappear. The constant disappointment and the gnawing despair had nearly driven him to insanity. He had managed a muffled goodbye to Noa and Fin as they had left the beach, then had made his way to the office to seek refuge, hoping the distraction of work would ease his thoughts.

Hamish had passed most of the afternoon staring at a blank screen in an empty room, listening to the clock ticking in time with the cursor's blink. He felt alone in every possible way, the sting of solitude burning in his palms, stretching across his skin. He picked up his mobile and searched for Adrian's number, then switched the screen off again. He thought of calling Andrew, the landlord of the pub next to the beach, with its windows overlooking the bay – a possible witness to the stranding. He could even have called Woody; perhaps Fin would have answered. Maybe even his daughter. But the phone remained unused and silent, his mind too preoccupied for conversation.

Flexing his fingers, Hamish manoeuvred the mouse to bring up the internal database and typed in the name, his fingers hurrying across the keyboard with the ease of repetition, the same words he had entered nearly every day for the past five, eight, maybe even ten years. He had lost track. Of course, accessing such files was an abuse of his position, not to mention a waste of company time, as his editor would likely say. Perks of the job, Hamish preferred to call it. It did not matter either way. He had never found anything other than a couple of irrelevant notes alongside the two news reports: one on the day he had been reunited with his mother, the other a few days after the fisherman had disappeared. Short-lived sensations, the talk of the town one moment before becoming obsolete and forgotten the next. Except for the one man that still cared.

The cursor continued to blink in the data field, displaying the same words as always: 'No new search results'. Leaning back in his chair with a sigh, Hamish flinched at the unexpected sound of his phone, its vibration making an unpleasant rattle against the wooden desk. He stooped over to peer at the number displayed, his eyes widening at the name, a name he had not heard from in years. Rosa Rivera. Noa's mother was calling. The noise continued, his musings evaporating as his body grew tense. Panic filled his lungs and clenched at his throat as the noise seemed to grow louder, echoing around the room. Hamish switched off his computer screen, scooped up the phone, span in his seat towards the window and then answered the call.

The voice on the other end was low and steady, the words carefully chosen, giving Hamish an even greater sense of unease. It was the first audible greeting he had received from Rosa in perhaps a decade. As always, she took the lead, her questions casual and conversational; no harm could have come to his daughter, he realised with relief, though he still felt extremely anxious. Yes, she had arrived safely, he told Rosa. No, she did not need anything. Yes, they had eaten. Then a pause followed by a heavy silence. No, he had not forgotten his promise. As much as the attic had uncovered about his past life to Noa, there were still secrets that he wished to keep buried. He had sworn to Rosa not to speak of it. He had promised never to betray that trust. But then he remembered the photos.

Hamish blanched, his posture becoming even stiffer in his seat, his eyes staring out of the window at the floating lights of the town and the bay beyond, the day beginning to settle into dusk. The photos in the attic, the ones Noa had asked for, the ones he had produced from his drawer without more than a passing thought to their contents, to the truth they would reveal. Stupid man, he thought. Pathetic fool.

He said a feeble goodbye to Rosa on the phone, placed it back on the table, then slowly ran his fingers through his hair. The sigh came long and slow. How had it all become so complicated? he wondered. He had not the strength nor the skills to cope with reality. He was not a father, had not been much of a son either, or a partner or even a friend. He had rebuffed everyone who had ever come close, had built barriers not for protection but of denial. He had led a life void of meaning, of purpose; an observer, confined to the shadows of his own stage.

Pushing away his sentiment, Hamish turned back to the screen, switched it on and began writing. The words came with practiced automation, a stream of deadened consciousness, his years of experience in detachment showing their worth. 'The beached beluga, a sad tale for our modern times' – the locals would lap it up, gasp and gossip over the details, before eating their greasy fish and chips from yesterday's news, smearing condiments all over the bleached-white carcass, the bloated body that had spoiled an otherwise idyllic tourist spot. Within fifteen minutes, Hamish had reached the wordcount, hastily submitting his work before switching off the computer. A single report had taken him five hours. Five hours he should have spent with his daughter.

Feeling ravenous, exhausted, conflicted and forlorn, Hamish packed up his belongings and locked the room. Leaving the office, he could see the door of his flat from the other side of the road and wondered whether Noa would be there. It was a strange thought, to have to consider someone else, someone he barely knew. He took a step back as a group of extravagantly costumed revellers made their way past, heading towards the pub beside the bridge. He watched them go, admiring their outfits, envying their laughter and light-heartedness.

Feet shuffling under the weight of his straining limbs, his overgrown hair prickling into his eyes, Hamish stumbled rather than walked across the road, his calves feeling as if he were striding through seaweed. Once the door had been opened and shut silently behind him, he felt an instant comfort from the cool and dark interior space of his home. He called out but there was no reply. He was alone. Knees buckling, legs sagging, he let himself slide to the floor at the base of the stairs, the random voices echoing from outside through the door, the festival now in full swing, the stranded whale already forgotten.

After ten minutes of immobility and anguish, Hamish felt better. He pulled himself up to his feet, resuming his 'keep calm and carry on' British mentality his grandparents had always spoke of. Switching on the lights, he swapped his shoes for slippers and shrugged off his coat. In the kitchen, he found some dried pasta and a pot of sauce in the cupboard, which he cooked inexpertly on the gas hob, making double his usual amount so there would be enough for Noa when she returned.

Perhaps she had met Woody by now, he thought, stirring the beige shapes around in the pan. No doubt the old man would be wanting to share his many tales with the youngsters – he did love an audience. Hamish had already been told plenty of his yarns over the years and agreed that Woody was a talented storyteller, though he had heard better. He often wished he could remember more about the fisherman and his conversation, not only the stories but the way he had told them too. The timbre of his voice, the mispronunciations, the lingering pauses after each full stop. Hamish could almost recall them, but not quite clearly enough.

Settling down in the living room after his meal, he sipped at a cup of milky tea and thought about what lay above. The books and the wall, the ark and the photos. The secrets and mysteries, alluring and unsettling, and what Noa would think of it all. Then came the sound of Rosa's voice in his mind, threatening to exhume the memories he had tried so hard to forget. Not now. Not while Noa was with him. There must be a way, he realised. He could hide the photos, replace them with others – surely there were some from Noa's childhood he had kept, ones Rosa had sent when she was feeling generous. He could burn the others, never have to worry about the damage they might cause. The tears and the anger. Yes, he could lie – he was good at that. He would evade the truth and protect the only people he loved, the only ones he had left now that the fisherman was gone.

As the soothing tones of the radio weather forecast lulled him towards sleep, Hamish thought of the little white whale he had seen between the older man's fingertips. The talisman, his lucky charm. How he wished he had stolen it too, like the wooden whale. He could have had both, carried them with him to university, on his marches, then across to Europe, perhaps even further – Japan, Australia, that tiny cove in South America they had always talked about.

His beloved had been a dreamer. Back then, everyone seemed to be passionate about something, but when he had seen those eyes, Hamish had known that this one was different. That he had found a person who not only aspired but achieved. An adventurer, an explorer, discovering the world and its truths. Just like the heroes of the books the fisherman had read to him. Just like Noa, in fact. Hamish still could not fathom what she thought of him, why she had decided to trust someone so quiet, so dull, who had spent his life trying to redeem his past by planning an impossible future. It was no lesson for a child to learn, especially not someone so admirable as his daughter.

With a fierce jolt, Hamish woke up for his nap, the empty mug escaping his fingers and rolling to the floor, the room now chilled and lifeless, no longer cocooning but claustrophobic. If the curlew's call and the dead bird outside the church had been omens, then the beluga whale had to have been a blessing. A kind of symbol, even a sacrifice, from whatever gods were out there in the oceans and the sky, showing the people of the land what to do, where to look. It had washed up on the beach below the cliffs, the cliffs where the cottage had been. That was where the story had started – now Hamish realised it must be where the story would end. The charms, the books, potentially even the man himself. This was it at long last. The final chapter.

Fuelled with adrenaline, Hamish scurried to the kitchen and searched in the cupboard under the sink, retrieving the little-used torch with its battery still working. He had not been up to the top of the cliff for many years, not since they had fenced off the land and declared the area highly hazardous, the fisherman's home included. It was only a matter of time until it slipped away into the water and vanished completely. He had to hurry.

Having changed into shoes and put on a coat, Hamish scrawled a brief note for his daughter, his mind too focused on what he might find to consider the potential consequence of his absence. He was running out of time. The town had already lost several houses due to erosion – it was possible that the cottage could be crumbling right now, right at that moment. The thought spurred him on as he hurriedly switched off the lights, left the flat and locked the door behind him, his entire body pulsing with energy, feeling like a scientist on the edge of a great discovery or an explorer at the mouth of an ancient crypt.

He marched through the narrow lanes without a

glance to the people or places he passed, along Church Street, then up the hundred and ninety-nine steps two at a time. As his heartrate quickened and his skin began to burn, Hamish found himself relishing the pain of his exertions, made all the more brutal by the increasing wind whipping across his face, blowing across from the expansive sea. He briefly took in the sight of the solemn church, striding past the familiar tombstone on his left, sensing its silent encouragement as he continued onwards and upwards, dedicated to his cause.

Past the abbey and across the clifftop, the path became replaced by dense clumps of dying grass and ambling weeds, their tendrils clinging to his feet and ankles as he tried to follow the barely visible track, stumbling over discarded polystyrene trays and drinks cans among lumps of mud and rock. He was close now, the closest he had come in years, the fear he had previously felt up there now replaced by determination. The cliff held so much history – not just his own memories but decades, centuries, millennia more, all conjured into reality by his imagination and studies during his younger years and as a journalist. The stories he held close to his heart were not his alone but part of a wider world, a place of myth and legend, of the land and sea, of the creatures that thrived and the vast skies that continued to turn from dawn to dusk as time ticked by.

Overcome with fatigue and feeling, Hamish paused to take in the view, his audible breathing lost to the boom of the ocean and the lash of the wind. The scene below reminded him of the wooden ark, quaint and colourful, a town painted in miniature. And there he was, reigning above it all. Yes, that was how it felt, back then as it did now. That day when they had sat side by side in the garden overlooking the rugged cliffs and the waves stretching out. Not another soul to disturb them. No sense of time nor routine. Just the endless hours to bask in the beauty of their surroundings, as if on their own island, their shared home. And now he would see it again, have the chance to remember, to find out more. To put the fisherman and his memory to rest.

Hamish walked on, the torch held firmly in one hand like a weapon. The wire fencing appeared, taller and more menacing than he had thought it would be. Could he climb it or perhaps tug it down? he pondered. He might need cutters or even to dig underneath. His footsteps hastened, his heartrate thudding in the rhythm of his tread, until there it was. The cottage.

He continued walking. Walking, walking, on and on, until his nose almost touched the fence. His chest heaved, his calves burned, his eyes moistened as he prised them open against the wind. The torch fell from his hand, his fingers moving to grip the mesh, shaking, urging, fighting against the desperate desire to scream. The cottage was there, but it was not as he had anticipated. Not at all.

While it was as deserted and derelict as he had expected, it no longer had windows or doors. There was no chimney on one side, no outbuilding pungent with the aroma of kippers. No herbs grew wild and no curtains lined the windows. No wooden hatch led the way to a hidden bunker. There were not even any walls. The fisherman's home had been reduced to rubble.

Nothing more than a pile of rocks. Hamish rested his head against the barrier, wishing he could wake up, chastising himself for ever going up there in the first place, for daring to imagine it might be worth his while.

The disappointment was soon replaced by anger. He stormed around the fence perimeter, eventually finding a weak spot, an opening large enough for him to crawl through. Marching over to the mound, he started searching through the debris, looking for any sign of familiarity – a flash of colour, the hint of a form, the weave of a fabric that he could remember from his time there. But he could see nothing of recognition, no furniture or fittings, no books or stones shaped like whales. Nothing to even suggest that someone had lived there, that he himself had once called the place home. It was all gone.

Hamish walked back to the fence, began pulling and pushing against the mesh, his fingers gripping tighter, the wires pressing into his skin. A low feral growl throbbed in his throat. He retrieved the torch from the ground then walked further round the periphery, banging the light against the bars so that they clanged and shook like a beast trying to escape its prison, the noise mirroring his own internal screaming. The wind cried around him, another witness to his grief.

Eventually, he came to a laminated notice headed with the council's insignia and an address he knew all too well. He had been in touch with them on a regular basis ever since the site had been deemed unsafe and cordoned off. He had known the day was imminent, that the cottage would need to be pulled down, but had not known when. He had thought there would be time, opportunity to build his courage until he felt confident enough to return to the cliffs, to walk back into his former lodgings, into his past life. But that day had not come. As his online research had grown, his contact with the council had become less and less frequent, until it had finally been forgotten; now, he had lost his chance. The house was a wreck, his hopes in ruin. Like the tombstone above the empty grave, the mound that had been a home now marked nothing more than a forgotten soul, another relic of history reduced to a lump on the landscape.

Hamish made his way back through the darkened streets, wondering if Noa would be back at the flat. On opening the door, he noticed her jacket on the banister, but he did not feel any comfort or relief from her return. There was the smell of tomato sauce and an unfamiliar perfume, hints of coconut and vanilla; the aroma of something changed, of someone else. Walking stealthily along the corridor, he heard faint rustles from behind her door but did not say hello or pause to knock, walking on in silence to his own room, where he hoped to fall asleep and forget the past few hours.

It was cool and dim in there, and the air felt thick with dust and decay in a way he had never noticed before. Stooping, he slowly slipped off his shoes, a few broken roots still clinging to the laces, before shrugging off his coat and letting it fall to the floor in a crumpled heap. He lay down on the bed without changing, careful not to disturb the aged springs beneath, then curled up, knees to chest, still clutching the torch he had not used.

He gripped it to his body like a child with a favourite toy waiting for a dream to begin. But for Hamish, he could think only of nightmares.

The following morning, he awoke early, surprised to find he had slept at all. Leaning against the kitchen counter, he tried to focus on his morning coffee, head pounding, hands shaking, but Fin's words pulled at his memory in an endless repetition. The pallid face and haunting voice of the boy at the door had echoed in his mind long into the night, resonating round and round like a circling predator. Hamish had truly thought the fisherman had been discovered – his father, his friend, the rescuer he had nearly given up hope of ever seeing again, had at long last been found. He had been so willing to believe, so eager to reach an end. Even now, the humiliation stung like a burn.

His usual coffee tasted bitter to his tongue, the kitchen light too bright, the cry of the gulls outside too brash. Hamish felt hungover without having had even a drop of alcohol. Maybe that should have been his plan, he thought; he could have joined the revellers, raising a toast to the poor creature on the beach. A more fitting finale compared to the evening he had endured.

Looking out of the window, the clouds outside seemed set on predicting a storm. He longed to go back to bed, to rewind time to yesterday morning, where he would ignore Fin's knocking and remain in the attic with his daughter, would never have to see nor hear of the beached whale, would not have taken a call from Rosa or have thought to go up to the cliffs. Instead, he would have disregarded the boxes of books and the envelope of photographs and have taken Noa to a café again, tea and lemon buns at Botham's, then a walk to the archway to have vegan ice-creams with raspberry sauce. They could have each shared more stories, enjoyed one another's company, just as they had on their first day. Have pretended that life was ordinary, that he was normal – just your average father doing his duty. He wished he could start again even further back than yesterday, to have done everything differently. To have focused on the living instead of trying to raise the dead.

The phone on the table buzzed, bringing Hamish back to the kitchen, back to the frustrating reality of his life. He threw the remaining half of his cold coffee into the sink and filled the mug with an inch of water, throwing two painkillers into his mouth before taking a sip. He retrieved the phone, reading through the first message from Adrian. They were going to remove the whale that morning and tidy up the area. He sent no reply. The second message was from the newspaper editor, thanking him for his work and assuring him that a local photographer would get some shots for an update, which Hamish would need to finish by nine. Again, he sent no response.

Flicking on the kettle, he slipped some fresh bread into the toaster and placed a selection of plates, cutlery and food on the table, including the raspberries he had forgotten about yesterday. Noa soon joined him, casually talking and smiling as she sat in her black pyjamas and fluffy slippers sipping a herbal tea, lulling Hamish into a state of ease as he munched on his toast.

He could not help noticing her face again, still taken aback by the likeness, and wondered if she knew, if she had ever seen photos of her maternal relatives in their younger years. It made him all the sorrier that he had so few images of his own to share.

Tucking into one of Fin's homemade scones, he listened as Noa told him all about her visit the previous day and what she had seen of Woody's collection, including the scrimshaw. There were many more examples of it in the museum, Hamish replied between mouthfuls. Maybe they could go together, he wanted to add, but Noa had already moved onto a different topic of conversation, brightly suggesting that her new friend could take her so that Hamish could work in the flat in peace. He nodded stiffly, wondering if his 'work' was a reference to the whale story or to his attic collection. She now seemed disinterested in both, and he could not blame her – it had not been the fresh start either of them had envisioned. Noa was right; she would have a much better time with Fin than with him.

Hamish quietly attended to the washing up, listening over his shoulder as Noa spoke to Fin on the phone. Her easy patter, her tinkling laughter. He kept his eyes fixed to the foaming water and the circular motion of his sponge, nearly missing the screech of the chair, the breezy thanks and the swift slapping of slippers as his daughter left the room. With a silenced sigh, he turned to the table to pick up the remaining dishes, noticing that Noa had stacked hers neatly with not a single crumb or spilled drop on the table. The raspberries had been left untouched.

Once Noa had left the flat, Hamish felt a strange sense of loss. He wondered if it was just the emotions of yesterday resurfacing, if perhaps writing about the demise of the whale for a second time was bringing too many old memories to mind. His daughter's travels and the framed illustration. The sighting on the boat and the day of the regatta. The drawings on the wall and his missing wooden toy. His life had been populated by whales for as long as he could remember. There was even the story he had read about of the souls of slain animals manifesting into human form. Maybe that was what the fisherman had thought when he had found a child outside his front door. That he, Hamish, was the spirit of a whale. The idea made him smile, brought a warmth to his fingers and a glow to his cheeks, the sorrow of the previous evening finally dispersing. He opened his laptop and began to type.

Hamish finished his story within the hour, phoned his editor and Adrian, and even sent a text to Rosa reassuring her that Noa was safe and happy. He could not be sure of the latter, but there had been no sign of tears or tension at breakfast. She had talked quietly but openly, seemingly unphased by her casual clothes or the tiny belch that had escaped her mouth after downing her drink. And he in turn had felt quite content too. As they had eaten and sipped, the pain in his head had eased, the shaking sensation disappearing. Despite the shock of the cottage and the knowledge that he might never find the missing fisherman, Hamish had realised that he was not sad. He did not feel the knot of fury and frustration as keenly as before, nor the usual desire to return to his research. It no longer seemed vital, not when he had something more important to concern himself with.

With a flask of tea in one hand and half the packet of ginger biscuits in the other, Hamish scaled the stairs to the attic, tiptoed around the rows of books still littering the floor and switched on his desk lamp. He set his provisions down then took one final look at the collection spread out on the wall before him. Everything seemed so familiar that he was sure most of the words and images were committed to memory. He bent down to look closer at the toy ark, lowering the little drawbridge so that he could reach the animals inside. He moved an elephant next to an antelope, a giraffe in between the two monkeys. The single whale he placed on the deck at the prow, as if staring out to sea, ready to shout 'land ahoy!' to his comrades. The simple act of rebellion pleased him immensely.

Then he stacked the books into three boxes – to keep, to take to charity and to pass on to Noa. He tried to resist sentimentality, knowing the important stories were already inside his head, engraved onto his bones like scrimshaw. He retrieved the envelope from the floor and placed it on the chair, undecided about its contents, drawn between Rosa's warning and his own sense of moral duty. Hamish realised he had been living his life as a lie – with the fisherman, with his former lover and now with his daughter – to the point where he had come to wonder about his soul. He had told himself time and again that he did not believe in God, but there was still something inside of him, some form of compass telling him the way. Now, despite being a middle-aged man with a career and a flat and a teenager under his roof, Hamish felt he needed such guidance more than ever; a way to know which path to take towards becoming a better father, to inspire the same sense of hope and pride in Noa that had once been instilled in him.

After pausing for refreshments, Hamish stood in front of the collection on the wall rereading its contents, but still, he could see no solution. With his hand lightly shaking, he leaned forward and gently peeled away the central page. The newspaper clipping came off easily, the photo of his six-year-old self and the fisherman curling and rolling, hiding the past from view. He had often imagined the pain the older man must have felt that day at the police station, seeing his young friend taken away by his mother, never to share stories or mealtimes or drawings with again. He sorely wished he had been able to say a proper goodbye.

Hamish unfurled the four corners and peered into the two faded faces. In all the times he had looked at the article, he had never been able to recall posing for the photograph, or where it had been taken, or even why they had decided to hold hands. The picture was proof of the event, but it was not a solid memory, not like the others from his time with the fisherman. Yet despite this, there had grown a sensation, a perception; the feeling of gentle warm fingers in his own. Whether real or imagined, he no longer knew nor cared. He had used the idea, that symbol of affection, to convince himself to carry on, to believe that hope, and perhaps love, could still be found.

In the top drawer of his desk, Hamish retrieved some plastic wallets and a thin roll of bin liners. He took one of the wallets and slipped the article inside, placing it carefully on the desk in the middle, as if inside a giant wooden frame. He looked down at the image for a moment longer, then turned to the unopened envelope on the chair. One he would keep for himself, tucked somewhere safe and out of sight, but always within reach. The other he would give to his daughter, placing his trust in her hands. As the ruined cottage had shown, Hamish could not control the future any more than he could erase the past. He had already done enough hiding to last a lifetime. It was time for Noa to learn the truth.

Retrieving the bin bags, Hamish tugged one free and shook it open. Piece by piece, he removed every single item from the wall.

Eighteen

Having returned to her room, Noa had settled under the duvet and fallen asleep within minutes. Her last view had taken in the framed drawing propped where she could see it from her bed, the stack of books from Woody nestled neatly by the wardrobe, and the tiny photo of her mother and great aunt placed against the shell-covered lampshade. Even though Hamish had not returned, the few trinkets had made Noa feel safe and calmed. She no longer saw his absence as another episode of abandonment; instead, it had given her some time alone in her new home, a chance to think through everything she had seen and heard and experienced in the past few hours. She had gone to bed with a feeling of gladness rather than regret.

The following morning, Noa felt just as buoyant, a spring in her step and a lightness to her thoughts that made the previous few days feel like months ago. As she was arranging her hair in the mirror, she heard her father in the kitchen and could smell the tempting aroma of toast. Not bothering to change out of her nightwear, she promptly joined him, basking in the normality of a shared breakfast. Hamish's mention of the museum had been a welcome one, especially when Fin confirmed on the phone that he had the day off work and would be glad to accompany her. Perhaps not everyone of her generation was obsessed with watching crazy cat videos or moseying around town centres, she thought with a smile. Spending a morning looking at old stuff in glass cases could be cool too.

Fin arrived at the flat an hour later wearing his usual ensemble of head-to-toe black with a few silver accessories. Noa invited him in to speak to Hamish and hear the latest on the whale, a topic Fin was already up to date with having been to the beach earlier that day to assist with the clean-up. After saying goodbye, the pair left the flat and headed towards the town, already locked deep in conversation as they discussed what they hoped to see. It was only as they walked past the station that Noa realised how far she had come. Her footsteps slowed as she thought back, picturing herself silhouetted against the building's exit, a tumult of feelings racing around her body, her feet momentarily glued to the ground as she considered her decision. It had been such a short journey, but that day when she had arrived in Whitby, she had never felt so many miles away from home.

Of course, the distance had been negligible compared to those she and her friends had traversed in Europe, their backpacks bobbing above their heads, walking boots growing ever more worn along the soles, cheeks permanently flushed with exertion and exhilaration. As they had stepped onto the train a little over two months ago, Noa had felt entirely capable and comfortable, able to handle whatever lay ahead. She had never been the top student or won any academic prizes, could not describe herself as witty or wise, sporty or creative, despite her desperate desire to succeed. But when she travelled and put her thoughts onto the page, Noa felt accomplished, as if she had found her reason for being. She tried to find that passion inside her once more as they walked past the station.

They reached Pannett Park just as the clock struck ten. Fin paused by the entrance of the gardens with Noa coming to an abrupt halt by his side, suddenly realising she had been talking the entire time during their walk. Having mentioned the train journey from Leeds, she had then rambled on about the summer and her great aunt, her ecological interests and her hopes of becoming a writer. Too much information, she thought, feeling her cheeks flushing. But Fin did not seem to mind – he had simply stopped to appreciate the view.

Taking in the scene around them, Noa felt as if they had left the coast and wandered onto a grand estate, the numerous neat green beds and borders each flawlessly manicured into smart shapes with blocks and bands of colourful foliage, a gravel path leading them round and up to the museum.

"You should maybe try writing poetry," Fin suggested as the museum façade came into view. "You just have this… skill with language."

Noa did not know how to reply. She was sure her tirade had been a revelation too far, but perhaps she had let her love of adjectives and allegory slip through in her words. It was strange; she was never usually so vocal with people she had just met. She was glad they had arrived so she could direct her attention elsewhere.

"So here we are, Whitby Museum," Fin announced, expanding his arms like a circus showman before the majestic structure in front.

A set of steps led the way to a red brick building with off-white pillars and a grey roof. A few benches were positioned looking out towards the park and a couple of hanging baskets in full bloom hung either side of the double wooden doors, one of which had been propped open for visitors. A guide dressed in a navy uniform had just amended the admissions sign and caught sight of the couple, grinning and giving a small wave in greeting. Noa smiled back as they began climbing the steps.

There was something about looking around a museum with a local history expert that made Noa enthused and fascinated by every display case they passed. Fin spoke in a low whisper, offering both noteworthy facts and random questions for them to muse over, sometimes in silence, sometimes with words. What was the woman like who owned that bone comb? How old was the little boy who played with the worn wooden abacus? Who made the bizarre and fascinating invention known as a leech barometer? And why on earth was there a withered hanged man's hand? There were stories everywhere, causing their imaginations to run riot. It was a rare freedom. Complete escapism.

Hours felt more like minutes, each room and gallery providing a cool cave of isolation and introspection with no other soul to disturb their thoughts other than the odd gallery attendant carefully pacing past. Sometimes Noa and Fin stood side by side, lost in their own ideas, each wondering what the other might be thinking, until they heard the distinct clang of a clock somewhere inside the building chiming twelve. They were both ready for an early lunch but reluctant to leave – there was one more exhibit they wanted to see.

In one of the furthest rooms, they found a single case set aside from the others with a banner that read 'Lost and Found'. A laminated page tacked to the wall explained that the cabinet contained items that had been recently discovered in the local area but with no known provenance. They had once belonged to someone somewhere but were now kept by the museum – small mementoes of people and places from a past that might otherwise be forgotten. Noa could not help thinking of Hamish and his collection, how much it meant to him yet would likely be worthless and meaningless to anyone else, perhaps also destined for a life behind glass.

As she neared the centre of the case, she stopped to peer at one particular piece. It was a rectangular tin with a lid, about the size of a bank card, rusted and dented but with remnants of colour across the surface. It was open to reveal what was inside – two small objects, one made from stone and the other carved from wood, their shapes so unique that Noa gasped aloud. Fin joined her side, giving a little laugh as he looked behind the glass.

"Whales," they said in unison.

But these were not just any whales, Noa knew. They had found the charms Hamish had described, his eyes having gone misty with the memory. First the books and now this – her father was going to be thrilled, she thought. Another part of the puzzle solved. Noa retrieved her phone and took a photo.

"Wonder where they found them?" Fin whispered over her shoulder.

"I think I can guess," Noa replied, picturing the cottage on the cliff.

As they walked back through the rooms, Noa began to tell Fin about the wall. She spoke slowly, choosing her phrasing with care – she had decided her father was justified in his investigations and hated to think that a neighbour, her new friend, might think of him badly or suspiciously. They had both seen the way Hamish had looked and spoken when they visited the beached whale. Even that morning, Noa had noticed the sadness in his eyes as he updated her on what would happen to the beluga, his plans for a follow-up article, his hopes that it might prompt people to take more responsibility for protecting the oceans. It was with the same emotion, the same sense of duty and concern, that he used when he talked of finding the fisherman. His quest, Noa now realised, was fuelled not only by grief but by a moral obligation. Over the past two days, Hamish's plight had become her own.

The friends left the museum and headed back through the park. As the gate leading to the pavement came into view, Fin slowed his steps and took a seat on one of the benches. Noa joined him, feeling wearied by their adventure, weighted down once more by the thoughts and feelings that continued to spin in her mind.

"I meant what I said earlier, about the poetry," Fin said, looking out across the greenery as a squirrel bounded from one tree to another.

"Well, that's what I'm here for. To write," Noa

replied, though she was conscious of an undercurrent of guilt to her words.

Could she write what she had experienced? Would she even want to try? Maybe she was not good enough, smart enough, strong enough. Look what a lifetime of research and writing had done to her father. What if she also fell to the same fate, ended up lost and lonely in an empty flat, driven only by a slim possibility and a fading hope. Would it be worth it? She slumped down a little further in her seat, feeling the collar of her coat slipping up against her neck, her gaze downcast.

"So write," Fin shrugged, as if it were the most simple thing in the world. "It doesn't have to be meaningful. It doesn't even have to be good. Just write what comes to your head. Write what you know. Write what you feel."

The reply caused Noa's eyes to sting, the hands in her lap go from cold and clammy to a brilliant warmth. Her shoulders eased a fraction, her brow loosening, her smile widening, but before she could respond, Fin began fumbling around in his coat pocket. Eventually he pulled out a paper bag, the kind Noa remembered getting from the local newsagents when she was younger, filled with as many cheap sweets as she could afford. Fin opened it up, holding it out towards her. She peered inside.

"No way! These are my favourites!" Noa exclaimed, reaching in to retrieve one of the familiar black shapes, tossing it into her mouth. The salty liquorice tang made her tastebuds tingle, her memory flooding with joyful images and echoed laughter.

"I think they're from Norway. Vegan, of course,"

Fin replied, slipping a couple of the sweets into his own mouth.

They chewed and rested, taking in the flora and fauna of the surrounding garden; the thick gnarled tree trunks and the dew-dappled branches, the rainbow-hued flowers and the clots of muddy soil. Blackbirds flitted up and down the lawns while endless gulls streamed back and forth above. Time stood still, the pair cocooned in their individual thoughts, until the sound of Fin's voice shook them both back to reality.

"Noa, you know about the fisherman's cottage, right?" he began, his tone low, his eyes avoiding hers as he fumbled for another sweet.

"What do you mean?" she replied, feeling the panic starting to bubble inside.

Fin did not want to be the one to tell her, but he knew it was the most likely explanation for the two talismans being in the museum and not in someone's home. He swallowed, moving his gaze across the sky to follow a passing crow.

"It's gone. They knocked it down a while ago." He could only just see Noa out of the corner of his eye, but he could tell she had grown still and stiff. "It's not safe up there. The land's falling away." There was an uncomfortable pause. Fin forced himself to continue. "Hamish probably knows about it…"

He turned to look at his silent companion. Noa kept her eyes facing forward, her expression blank, but Fin could sense her emotions, the effort it took to appear neutral when inside it felt like a volcano about to erupt. She had not known about the cottage, he realised. Either

Hamish had not told her, or he did not know either. The gap between them on the bench suddenly seemed wider, the air a little cooler. He heard her sigh, long and soft.

"At least the charms are safe," Noa replied, her mind elsewhere, her body suddenly yearning to head home, to check if Hamish was ok.

She had thought his sullenness at breakfast was on account of the stress from the previous day, writing his article and worrying about the whale, but maybe there had been more to it. Maybe he had found out about the cottage. Maybe it was something else entirely. She could never tell with him, could never understand what he was thinking or feeling. He would always be a closed book, but at least she was there. If he ever needed help, a confidant, a friend... she would be there.

"Come on," she said suddenly, rising to her feet with renewed determination. "Let's go back to mine and make something amazing for lunch."

Noa waited until Fin had joined her side to tuck her hand into the crook of his arm, just like the courting couple she had spotted in one of the museum's oil paintings. She could quite easily picture her friend with a top hat and cane, idling along beside the neatly mowed lawns, telling her stories as they admired the flowerbeds.

"Back to yours," Fin agreed, wondering whether Noa had realised her words.

They returned to find the flat empty, a note on the kitchen table reading 'Back Soon' in Hamish's hastily scrawled handwriting. Fin began unpacking the groceries they had picked up on the way while Noa busied herself with the cupboards and drawers, pulling out various pots, pans and utensils in dull shades of brown and beige plastic – relics from the Seventies or Eighties, she guessed, no doubt picked up from charity shops. She gave them a quick rinse before joining Fin at the hob, barely noticing her quiet contentment as she focused on the instructions for his 'top secret' recipe.

As the friends tucked into their first portion, they paused mid-bite on hearing the front door opening. Noa shouted a greeting, feeling something like excitement at the thought of her father joining them for lunch – a meal she had prepared herself, in his kitchen, for their mutual enjoyment. A muffled 'hello' followed from the hallway before the sound of fading footsteps headed away, headed upwards, telling Noa everything she needed to know. Her heart sank like a pebble tossed in the sea. She settled her fork on the plate, her appetite vanished, the flat returning to the cold and unwelcoming place she had always known.

Sensing the edge to Noa's silence, Fin filled her empty cup with more tea then placed his upturned palm on the table in the space between them. Noa traced her eyes around the inked compass, wondering where her own marker might point, wishing she had some way of knowing where to go and what to do. About her father, about her feelings, about her lack of direction in life. Fin curled his fingers into a fist and pointed at the half-finished meal. She managed a small smile then began eating again just as the sound of steady steps descended. Hamish appeared at the doorway of the kitchen looking dishevelled, his expression one of mild surprise.

"Are those pancakes?" he asked.

Noa nodded, rising to attend to the hob. She reheated the pan, melted a wedge of vegan butter and poured a ladleful of batter in as Hamish took a seat. As her father inquired about the museum, Noa focused on cooking, watching the little bubbles appearing across the pale wet surface of the mixture, the smell of cinnamon and sugar filling her head with thoughts of home, old and new, and her place within them both. No longer in between but now straddling two worlds, two places of belonging. She shuffled the pancakes onto a plate and set them down on the table.

"And there's homemade raspberry sauce," Fin noted, handing over a jug.

Hamish shuffled a little where he sat before bringing the small ceramic pot up to his nose, inhaling fruit that smelled as fresh as the day he had bought it, as if he had merely walked into a back garden and foraged for his own crimson gems. The image of spooning a dollop of jam onto a plump plum came to mind, the same joy of feasting accompanying every bite as he worked through four pancakes layered with Noa's sauce. Now as then, there was something in the simplicity of eating a homemade meal that made Hamish feel comforted and cared for. It was an act he had hoped to provide for his daughter, yet here she was, in his own kitchen, making him feel at home. An olive branch, a sign of forgiveness perhaps.

Sliding his knife and fork carefully onto the plate, Hamish took a final sip of tea and dabbed his mouth with a paper napkin, biding time as he thought carefully over his words. He rose steadily to his feet, fingertips pressed into the tabletop.

"Noa, there's something I'd like you to see." He realised only too late that his tone was unintentionally ominous, but perhaps the warning would be welcomed. He knew that what was about to come would be difficult for them both.

He led the way out of the kitchen, hoping Noa would follow. Recognising a family moment, Fin began collecting up the plates, busying himself at the sink with the washing up while Noa followed in her father's footsteps, out of the kitchen, along the corridor and up the stairs. She spotted his slippers – he was going into the attic.

As Noa neared the top, she could sense that something was different, that the atmosphere had somehow shifted. The stark lighting that had before given her a cool chill had been replaced by a softer and more subtle luminescence, growing steadily brighter as she climbed the steps. She could hear the seagulls outside, something she had not noticed before when she had been up there, but now their calls were sharp and certain, almost as if the house had been shifted closer to the sea or had become a ship sailing to a distant shore. It made her feel both peaceful and elated, her feet quickening as her curiosity grew.

She reached the room, pausing to turn in a slow circle as she took in the transformation. The sunlight was coming in, flooding in, as if a barrier had been broken, the skylight in the ceiling having been uncovered and opened to let in a silken breeze along with the sound of the seabirds. One wall had been painted a pale blue, the shade of a spring sky, with a long sandy-coloured rug positioned in front. In the right-hand corner stood a circular table painted deep turquoise, the wooden ark sat on top, as if afloat. The desk had been moved across to the left, unmistakable in its form but now topped with a thick piece of black felt and an assortment of accessories – a smart new lamp, a tiny cactus in a ceramic pot, a copper tin filled with stationery, and a silver laptop.

Noa touched each object in turn, stroking her fingertips back and forth over the base of the lamp, the length of the fabric, across the laptop's keyboard. Her mind felt feverish with thoughts, her mouth unable to form words. She made her way to where Hamish's papers and pictures had once been, but the mosaic of memories had gone. She peered closer to the wall in disbelief; not even a pinhole remained to prove its existence, though there was one new addition that hinted at its past.

In the very centre, positioned exactly where the image of boy-Hamish and the fisherman had been, was a drawing in a frame – the beluga sketch Noa had loved, the one her father had made. She leaned in, observing the fine lines and faint shading of its curved body, prominent head and dainty rosebud eye. And the smile, the same one she had seen on the beach, worn by the poor creature she still thought of with sadness and wonder. Noa took a few steps back, her eyes unable to leave the whale picture, her voice too lost to emotion to respond. She knew Hamish was hovering somewhere behind her, but she could not turn to look at him, not until she had worked out a way to say thank you, to express how it felt to see the collection not only removed but replaced, for her.

"I thought perhaps the laptop could be my belated birthday gift," she heard him say, his shuffling footsteps indicating movement towards the desk. "I realised that a book was maybe not quite enough for your eighteenth. And, of course, you need a place to write. A room of one's own, as they say."

Noa turned in time to see her father gesture to the space, a soft smile on his face. The attic was hers – a place in which she could work, to create her own stories, to put all her thoughts and experiences on the page. Somewhere she could belong. She could feel the gratitude swelling inside, but still, the words would not come – she could only hope her silence conveyed everything she wanted her father to know in that moment.

"And there's this," Hamish continued, holding out a familiar object.

It was an ordinary envelope, with no name or distinguishing markings, but Noa recognised it immediately. Her father turned it between his hands, his smile now fading, his brow becoming ever more furrowed. This was the real gift, the one he had been meaning to give his daughter for a decade, all those many years ago when they had first met under the whalebone archway.

Noa had already guessed what the packet contained – photographs. Her history. She took it with a trembling hand and made her way to the desk, her father walking past, towards the staircase, his back turned and his voice quaking slightly as he spoke.

"I think you should know the truth."

Nineteen

After leaving the police station, Emil drove back to his cottage, barely taking in the people and the traffic, the buildings and the daily bustle all around. He felt as though he were sleepwalking, that soon he would wake up from a dream. From a nightmare. Parking unevenly beside the outbuilding, he walked up to and entered a dwelling that did not feel like his own. There was a strangeness, a sense of displacement, as if he had wandered into someone else's home, as if something was missing. Or someone. He closed the curtains, made up the fire, then prepared tea and a slice of toast. But the sparse meal did not interest him. The armchair did not seem as comfortable as before, the warmth of the flames stifling rather than soothing. The fisherman sat there in silence, his eyes unfocused, staring ahead into nothingness.

Earlier that morning, before they had left, Emil had folded and stacked the blankets and towels on the arm of the sofa, the drawings neatly arranged on the edge of the table, the thick black pen resting on top. He could not help but look across at them now, willing his mind not to reimagine the scene as it had been before, only a day earlier, his home filled with joy and laughter, company and hope. He would put the blankets and the papers away soon, store them in a cupboard to be forgotten. Out of sight, out of mind.

Emil then thought of his boat, of heading out onto the water, inviting the sea and the air to restore his sombre soul, to remind him of why he was there. But he could not move, every bone in his body begging him to remain. The fire crackled, the wind lightly rapped against the windows, the gulls screeched, over and over, but all the fisherman could hear was the sound of a boy shouting across a busy street, along with the echo of the words he wished he had replied.

First his parents, then his beloved, and now a child he had found outside his home. He had forsaken them all, every person he had ever loved – mother and father, future wife and child, and the surrogate son he had named Noah. He had never even been able to say goodbye. Emil opened his mouth to whisper into the frigid air, to let his lungs pour forth the agonies of his mind, to alleviate the tension, ease the pain, but he could muster no sound. Not even a gasp. He sat there, less a man and more a prisoner than ever before. Up there on the cliffs, in the isolation of his cottage, he was completely alone.

Emil awoke late morning on the following day, stiff and sore from sleeping in the armchair. The fireplace was black and empty, the tea and toast untouched. The curtains were already open, day having become night having become day once more, though the light seemed muted. He could not feel the cold nor the hunger, no longer sensed the passing of time or the call of his vocation. Just the bitter sting of solitude he had thought long subdued, one of the many ghosts that would only reveal itself in the bleakest of moments. Now, they were all around him. The cottage had become his tomb, a final resting place among the past departed; he could no longer find peace within its walls, only a suffocating, endless terror. It was as if he had stumbled into the bunker once more, the steps reduced to a wall of mud, the hatch door above locked from the outside by some unknown force, providing no escape.

With the difficulty of a man three times his age, Emil managed to rise from his makeshift bed and shuffle forlornly across to the kitchen. The fish in the fridge was still fresh; he ate it raw with his fingers, stooped over the counter, his stomach aching with release. It bulged out after his meal, yet inside he still felt empty. Carrying a mug of cold water, he walked through to the bedroom at the back and peered out of the window to the harbour where his boat had been moored for days, waiting patiently for his return. But he could not bring himself to go to her. It was as if he feared accusation – he could feel her shame, her disappointment. The windfall of herring had seemed miraculous, but he should have known. Fairy tales did not have happy endings, and this story would be no different.

With his income and food source secure for the coming months, there was now no purpose to the fisherman's days, no motivation to succeed. He did not have to fish nor even to sail. He could remain concealed in his cottage without seeing a single person all autumn and winter, perhaps even into spring. Financially, he had been saved from ruin, but on seeing his lonely vessel, Emil realised the true cost of his good fortune. Something inside had faded. A part of his soul had been erased. He had lost all sense of self-worth.

He walked back through, closed the curtains and returned to the armchair. The stacks of blankets and papers were still waiting to be cleared, but his mind and body felt too weary to move them, his memory too hesitant to take away the last traces of the child. In the darkened room, the shadows turned into spooks, his imagination adding detail to their forms – the tuft of sandy hair, the chubby fists by his sides, the treacle-coloured eyes staring out from the blackness. The fisherman could remember his voice, the little lisps and strange sounds all his own, the rhythm of his laughter and the bouncing creases of his brow. There was still something here, Emil realised, becoming more settled in the gloom. The boy had gone from his world, but the dream remained – it had been real. They were recollections that could not be taken, that he did not have to forget.

As the fisherman rested, he began to think of the stories he had shared with Noah, the fictions and facts he had intertwined for their mutual enjoyment, each narrative becoming vivid once more in his mind. With a sudden impulse, he rose and went to the bookcase, pulling out the volumes they had read, opening each and squinting his eyes across the text and illustrations, drinking them up. Succour for his spirit. To his surprise, Emil found that he could now repeat many of their lines and phrases in perfect English. 'A man can be destroyed but not defeated,' he said to himself, mulling over its meaning. The words came alive once more, refreshing the stale air around him. Suddenly, he found he could breathe again, almost as if he had been reunited with the spirit of his companion.

Within one of the books, he found the story he himself had written, the tale he had hoped never to remember again. Yet now, as he looked down at the lines, he was filled not with sadness but with acceptance, a gentle easing of his grief. He said a final goodbye under his breath and slipped the pages back inside, replacing the book on the shelf. He looked up to the row above and noticed the tin, realising it was in the wrong place. Then he recalled what had happened to his talisman; he had given it to Noah to join the wooden whale the child had brought. Emil looked across to the coffee table, along the sofa, around the surrounding floor. He could not see the charms anywhere. Perhaps the boy had taken them home, he thought with gladness. Two small tokens of the time they had spent together. Emil no longer had any need to keep his own, not now so much had changed.

Feeling wearied once more, he settled back in his chair and allowed his eyelids to lower, shapes and shadows dancing across his thoughts, enticing him into sleep. The visions came steadily, seeping one by one into his consciousness, growing brighter and bolder as his imagination embellished the details. From that first sighting of the boy's tiny form on the land to the scurrying sound of the pen as he drew, the mumbles and hums as he tried to learn the names of the birds through to the waving motion of a single hand as he said goodbye. If this were to be his dreamworld for ever more, then Emil would be happy never to awaken.

Just as he was recalling the time they had spent in the garden, a noise caused him to shift in his seat. The bang had been singular but loud and strange enough to have startled him into full consciousness. The fisherman looked around in the darkness, trying to make out any other movement or further sounds. He knew he was not dreaming by the rapid beating of his heart and the rush of pulsating blood pounding in his ears. Not daring to move, he peered around the bleak room, but did not notice anything out of the ordinary. Cold, dark and empty – just as it had always been. Though the banging had been real.

Easing himself to standing, his ears and eyes alert, Emil lumbered towards the nearest window, pulling back the drapes to stare across at the scene. The sky was already fading into darkness, a heavy wind whipping its way across the land, disturbing the grass and foliage while the sea remained eerily calm. Everything looked as normal, yet he was filled with foreboding, as if a storm was approaching once more. He moved across to the kitchen, tugged on his boots and coat, then went to unlock the door. Just as he reached for the handle, he stopped, eyes on the floor. On the worn wooden boards was a white square.

Emil stooped to pick up the small sheet of folded paper and looked across to the door. The metal letter box. He was usually out on the boat whenever something was delivered; he could barely recall the noise of it, the squeal and crash as it opened and closed, but now he remembered. He peeled open the paper – delivered by hand, with no envelope or address – and slowly read the message inside. Five words in English, written in thick capital letters in black ink. Emil felt his throat tightening, his palms growing moist. Logic told him to screw up the paper and go back to his private musings, but instead, he read the note again, slowly this time, so that there could be no misunderstanding. Despite his language skills, he knew that he had understood each word perfectly. A practical joke or a childish game, the voice of reason told him. But inside, he knew otherwise. It was a feeling he knew too well to ignore. Emil was afraid.

The fisherman reached out a faintly shaking hand and tested the handle. Locked. He sighed with relief, then crept across to the kitchen back to the window. Night had fallen rapidly, a bright full moon now gracing the sky, glazing the surroundings with a pearlescent sheen, including the solitary body mere inches from his front door. He could tell that it was a woman, standing perfectly still and staring straight at his home, at the window. Glaring at the man inside. In the moonlight he could see a mane of light hair surrounding her head like a halo, the ends spreading out over the collar of a fur coat. In one hand dangled a black bag, in the other a single speck of orange light; a flame with a whisp of smoke slowly curling upwards.

Two moments of Emil's life suddenly merged into one, their meanings revealed with the flourish of a conjurer's trick. Poison Ivy. Noah's mother. They were one and the same.

The fisherman swiftly stepped back from the window, the note in his hand as he hastened towards the armchair. He sat down silently, keeping his body as still as possible as he listened, for footsteps or shouting, for glass smashing or fists pounding. Violence and anger, destruction and retribution. But all was quiet. Staring into the blackened embers of the fireplace, Emil strained his ears, noticing a faint whine down the chimney and a droning beyond the walls, setting his teeth on edge, his pulse racing, his underarms pooling with sweat. He sat rigid, not daring to move, not wanting to know what might happen next.

An hour passed. Emil heard nothing more. Cautiously he returned to the window, looking out into the gloom. He exhaled, feeling his body finally easing, though his heart still beat fiercely. He was sure the woman had gone. The message, he realised, was all she had come for. It was still there, crumpled and damp in his hand. He peeled it open again, taking in each word. He understood the warning but did not know where to begin with his reply.

Walking over to the fire, he hurriedly scraped out the charred remains and replaced them with new coal and fresh tinder, lighting and blowing on the tiny sparks as quickly as he could. As soon as the flames had sprung, he flung the paper onto them, watching the heat and light devour the note. Though it burned almost instantly, he did not feel at ease. He could still sense its presence between his fingers, could still clearly picture its text – just five little words, as if they had been scorched into his flesh. The fisherman moved onto the sofa, pulling the blanket from the top of the pile over his shivering legs. His mind was still piecing together the scattered facts, aligning them into a new formation, an explanation he could never have imagined yet knew to be true.

When the child had first woken and looked into his rescuer's eyes, Emil had known. They had stared, locked onto one another's gaze, seeing not a stranger but a likeness, as if they had been viewing a magic mirror; one reflection showing the past, the other the future. Older, younger. Father, son. Made from the same cut, woven with the same thread. As he closed his eyes and prayed for sleep to take him, all the fisherman could think of was the child's face, those small wide eyes watching him intently, two drops of nectar identical to his own.

Despite the conflict of his thoughts and the aching of his body, Emil fell into a deep sleep. In his dream, he saw that the home he had known for ten years had been changed, stripped bare, the furniture and fittings removed, ripped away by some invisible brutality he could sense rather than see. He looked above to find that the roof of his cottage had also disappeared, so that the stone walls stood lurching upwards into the sky. He could see the sun and the clouds, feel the faintest specks of rain amid the harsh breath of the wind. Squinting into the light, Emil rose a hand to shield his eyes, eventually picking out what else had begun to amass above him.

Seabirds. Hundreds of them. Moving, shifting; closer they came. He had never seen creatures as big as these, like an albatross mixed with a type of eagle or hawk. They swooped and circled, then hung in the air as if immune to the forces of nature. Indeed, there was something unnatural to them as they observed their prey, great wings stretched wide, eyes bulbous and glinting. Like a startled rabbit, Emil could not move, his heart beating in his mouth, legs longing to collapse beneath him. He could feel the blood rushing from his cheeks, pulse pounding in his neck, one hand still quaking against his forehead as he continued to stare upward, while the fingers of the other – fully formed, somehow, as if they had been that way all along – clenched against his thigh in fear.

Soaring in endless figures of eight, more birds flocked from higher and wider, the sky suddenly heaving with them like a swarm of insects, vibrating with their combined presence and force, their determination and malevolence, pressing further and further down on the terrified fisherman. Their voracious calls and frenzied shrieks became synchronised, swelling into a deafening chant, causing Emil to cover his ears and cower in fright. But even then, he could still hear them – shouting, screaming, not sounds now but words, talking to him in the new language he had learned, repeating the phrase he had thrown into the fire. The letter, her threat; they were wailing with its warning, ensuring he would never forget.

As the last sunlight vanished from the sky, Emil fell to his knees in terror, mouthing the words from the note in time to the rhythm of the gulls' cries: *Dead men tell no tales*.

Twenty-One

The photographs sat side by side in the middle of the desk. Noa knew each of the three faces, could easily recognise parts of herself within them all. Her distinctive nose and the width of his jaw. Her thick dark hair and his sullen stare. The arch of their eyebrows and the curve of their smile, for she could identify similar features in the third person too. Her mother and her father, and the man who had brought them together. A beloved brother and an adored lover; pictured alongside her parents in every photograph was Uncle Jonah.

In each of the images, the trio stood closely huddled together, almost cheek to cheek, their arms entwined, seemingly the best of friends, but their forced smiles and overly wide eyes hinted at the truth. It had taken Noa around twenty minutes to piece the parts together, to understand why her father had been so reluctant to show her the photographs, why her mother had never said more than two words about their relationship. Rosa and Hamish had been in love, but not with each other. It had been Jonah who they had both worshipped, Jonah who had been the light of their lives, Jonah who they had lost when they were all so young. Two people brought together in the most painful of circumstances, with the most unexpected of outcomes. A child.

That child now counted on her fingers – eighteen

years since her birth and nineteen years since Uncle Jonah's death. Aunt Isobel had mentioned the date of his funeral years ago when Noa had been delicately probing her for family stories, but she had not realised the significance until now, the revelation seeming to scream at her – the total of nine months exactly between his demise and the day she came into the world. It seemed so obvious, but with the combined silence of her mother, father and great aunt, it had been a well-kept family secret – until now.

As Noa surveyed the photographs over and over, a great surge of emotion welled up inside, all she had ever felt and more. Clenching her eyes shut and open again, she tried to drive away the hurt, the helplessness and hopelessness that seemed to creep back every time she attempted to move forward in her life. Wiping angrily at her eyes, she attempted to think of a practical plan. She could leave the attic, go downstairs and demand that Hamish tell her the truth, call Rosa and berate her until she confessed everything, or find Fin and walk with him as far as the coastline could carry them. None of her options seemed appealing.

As she leaned forward to stare into the three faces, she could more clearly imagine her mother as a young woman, imbued with the same yearning for life that she had inherited and that had once made Rosa so cheerful and confident. How devastating it must have been, Noa thought, to have heard the news. A bright and sunny day in June, when everything and anything seemed possible to the twenty-something siblings, living separate lives but always connected. Had her mother been at the hospital when it had happened? Or at the other end of a phone? Maybe with friends, or even Aunt Isobel – a boyfriend, perhaps? However she had heard, it had detonated her world, broken her in two, with only one other person who might understand that loss – the one she called 'Rebel Man'.

The former partner, the person her brother had tried to keep secret, but he had been too elated with his newfound love to be able to lie, to hide from his twin. From that very first encounter at City Hall, Rosa had known. Jonah's face had told her everything, his heart as familiar as her own. She had watched him day after day, month after month, seeing all the tell-tale signs from a discrete distance, the love almost glowing from his smile and his eyes, glazing his voice, changing his words. And the sadness he had felt when the relationship had ended. Her heart had bled just the same. Rosa had not kept in touch with the man her brother had brought for lunch on a few occasions, but she knew he had returned to the coast to become a writer. She even had his new address, kept in an old diary in the bottom drawer of her dresser. It had not taken her long to find it again after her brother's death.

Though not exactly happy, Hamish had found comfort in returning to his hometown, the place he knew so well yet where few seemed to know his name or remember his story. He grew content with his small-time job and his unassuming flat, spending his spare time alone fixating on an old forgotten mystery in the attic to fill his spare time, to mask the aching loss within, all those harrowing thoughts of what might have been.

Then she had appeared – the sister, the twin, a woman he had met only a handful of times and always with him – now in Whitby and at his front door, crying, weeping. She had not known what else to do, where else to turn. Hamish had managed to find the words to invite her in, made them both a cup of sugary tea. He had sat, unable to feel the mug as it scolded his fingers, while she talked and he listened. The illness, the medication, the hospital and the final fight.

Through tears, Rosa told the near stranger that the doctors had done all they could. That her brother had not passed in pain. Sitting rigidly upright with his drink growing cold, Hamish could barely comprehend her explanation, was unable to offer any reply of consolation or care. He thought he had already lost everything and everyone he cared about, but he had been wrong. The wound ached afresh.

How easy it must have been for them to fall into one another's arms, Noa thought. The grief, the hurt, the relief of having finally found a supportive embrace, a shoulder to cry on, someone who understood. Though she had yet to discover the cruelty of losing a loved one, Noa could imagine their agony. It was pain, not love, that had driven Rosa and Hamish together, and she could not blame them. Yet there was still a discomfort inside her, a sense of something amiss. Despite feeling able to forgive, Noa was still aware of being the outsider, the other, the unexpected arrival in her parents' past. No doubt they had thought their tryst a mistake, an impulse fuelled and excused by their loss – but then there was her, their child. Rosa and Hamish had chosen to lie not for her benefit but to protect themselves. Were they embarrassed by their decision, their blunder? Did that mean they regretted her too? Did they look at her face, their combined features, and wish their union had never happened? If Uncle Jonah had lived, Noa realised, she might not even exist.

Just as the heavy swell of tears began forming again, she heard footsteps coming up the stairs of the attic. Quickly, she fumbled to replace the photographs in their envelope, though she did not know why – Hamish clearly knew what they were, and she had no plans to hide her feelings from him. But the voice rising from below was not that of her father's. Noa watched as a head appeared in the floor, a pair of jauntily angled goggles followed by a flame of dark hair. Kind eyes and a skewed grin. A calming voice saying her name. She gave a weak smile as Fin stepped into the room, her fear and frustrations soon replaced by relief and gratitude. She watched him take in the space, though he would have no knowledge of how it had looked before.

Fin walked across to join her at the desk, peering down into the three faces. Speaking quietly and with care, Noa began to explain her version of the history she believed the images proved. Her friend listened intently and without comment, waiting patiently as she wiped away the evidence of her emotions once more, moving across to the skylight to open it further, letting in great wafts of cool air to calm her thoughts. It was only when she finally collapsed back into the desk chair that Fin ventured to share his perspective.

"That's a pretty amazing story," he said, looking

down at the middle image, almost as if he were speaking to the people from the past. He was surprised at how different Hamish looked and by the uncanny resemblance between Rosa, Jonah and Noa. They were not a conventional family perhaps, but Fin knew from his own experience that there was no such thing, and that Noa, like himself, would be all the better for it.

"I mean, they must have been devastated about your uncle," he continued, his voice low and thoughtful. "Completely destroyed. But they came together and had you. And you're... well, a brilliant person. And they love you. That's a beautiful thing."

Noa returned to the desk. "But they lied," she thought aloud, her eyes tracing the happy images. Fin may have been right, but she could not dismiss the fierce anger within, the unceasing sting of hurt. "Why couldn't they have told me?"

Fin shrugged then began to roam round the room, realising that it had recently been redecorated, the smell of paint and polish still sharp in the air. Perhaps Hamish had created it for Noa, he realised, though it seemed a grand gesture from someone who lived his life in such isolation. Almost as if he wanted her to stay.

"Sure, maybe they weren't honest," he finally replied, turning to face his friend, "But they wanted to protect you. They've tried. They're still trying."

Noa considered his words. Two parents who loved her, who were both too ashamed and maybe too saddened by their past to share every detail of their former lives with their daughter. Rosa had been trying to live through Noa by encouraging her independence and ambition, while Hamish had been trying to find his former father figure by sharing his love of stories through his gifts of books. Both had suffered, but they had tried, just as Fin had said, perhaps hoping to navigate their way through lives they had never expected to lead. But did that mean that Noa was wanted?

"You're the best thing they have," Fin added, as if hearing her concerns. He was now standing in front of the beluga sketch, eyeing it intently. "You're their lucky talisman."

At those final words, Noa gave a small startled cry and launched to her feet, sweeping the images back into their envelope before swiftly making her way to the staircase, shouting an apology to her friend as she went. She had almost forgotten about the photograph on her phone, the one she had taken in the museum earlier that day. The two miniature whales that had once meant so much to Hamish and which had now come to mean so much to her. After everything, all she had seen and discovered, remembered and understood during the past few days, she knew her father was a good man. An honest man. A man who wanted to be there for his daughter, despite – or perhaps because of – having no one else he could love.

Noa found him at the kitchen table, the dishes put away, the surfaces wiped, the man silent and morose as he stared down into an empty mug. Hamish looked up as she entered the room, his face gaunt with worry, his lips already moving, mouthing his confession. Could words ever be enough? he wondered.

"It's fine, I know what happened," Noa began, taking

a seat and placing the pictures one by one on the table. She was concerned her father would be upset, but she needed to know the truth. She looked across to him, the smile on his face indescribable.

"You loved him. Mum's brother. My uncle," Noa said, holding back more tears.

Hamish exhaled before replying. "Very much."

Noa felt something like relief washing over her, calming her, bringing a clarity to her mind and body, as if nothing else mattered. Hamish had loved him, and she knew that Uncle Jonah had felt the same. Then the memory of the man from the protest appeared in her mind.

"You know Mum calls you 'Rebel Man'?" she grinned. Her father's sudden laugh, natural and almost musical, was something she had never expected to hear.

"We were very political," he replied, smiling despite the pain of his memories. "We used to go to rallies and meetings, make banners and write letters. Always with Jonah leading. He was like that – a beacon. A light that would never go out."

Noa glanced down at one of the images. Her uncle was wearing what looked like a homemade t-shirt with 'Rainbow Warrior' written across the chest. She decided she did not need to know anything else; she would not make Hamish reveal what had happened word for word. Hearing every detail would not change anything, could never heal old wounds, nor take away what they had already shared as father and daughter. What mattered now was how she could help him to move on, to find value in his life away from the wall and its secrets. She pulled out her phone and brought up the picture from the museum.

Pulling his gaze from the table, Hamish peered into the screen and let out a low moan. He leaned closer, as if unable to trust his own eyes, looking up at his daughter with a puzzled expression. She smiled and nodded until his face softened with understanding. The two talismans had been found, and they both knew what this meant – that the recollections of Hamish's six-year-old self were real. The fisherman was not a figment of his imagination, nor a kidnapper or criminal. The man and the boy had met after the storm, shared their stories and their thoughts, finding a peace with one another they had barely experienced before or since, their whale-shaped tokens having remained together even when they were apart.

Noa was talking but Hamish could not hear a word. His mind and hands were too busy working over the imagined objects, one cooler than the other, one natural and the other manmade, unique versus commonplace, given and stolen, but their importance had been the same. It was as if he could feel them both again, their curves and textures, their weights and temperatures, so familiar to his fingertips despite their age spots and wrinkles. Now he knew that the charms were safe, he suddenly felt settled. One piece of the puzzle complete.

The moment was interrupted by the creak of the door, Fin's cheerful face appearing from behind. Hamish and Noa both reached for the photographs, feeling strangely protective of their past. Fin pretended not to notice as he took a seat.

"Great job on the writing room, Hamish," he said, absentmindedly running his left forefinger in circles across his right palm.

"Thank you," came the bashful reply as Hamish rose to fill the kettle. "Just a few bits to add. A blind for the window, a couple of shelves next to the desk. For all your gifts and future publications." He turned to smile at his daughter.

"And the books Woody found for you," Fin added.

Noa gave a gasp as Hamish looked between the two youths, perplexed. She slid off the chair, racing to her bedroom where the books still sat in a pile on the floor. Scooping them into her arms, she headed back to the kitchen and set them on the table, remembering the many more that had once almost entirely covered the floor of the attic, a time that now seemed a distant memory.

The kettle had boiled but the three mugs Hamish had set out remained empty. He moved to Noa's side, hovering the fingers of one hand over the covers displayed before him, titles and images he had tried so hard for so long to recall with accuracy and which had now reappeared with complete clarity, as if he had been looking at them only a few evenings ago. They were his books. His and the fisherman's. The exact ones they had shared, treated with silent reverence as they slowly turned the pages, anticipating the next part of each story. He could remember it all so clearly.

Hamish could barely hear Noa's excitable explanation or notice Fin's actions as he completed the trio of teas. He was at a loss for words and understanding, having searched for these very objects for so long, each failed attempt draining his belief, obscuring what he could recall of those few days from his childhood. But now they were here – physical, touchable, and all his own. He picked up the largest, the book of photographs, turning to find the shot that featured the forest and the water, with the little cabin nestled in the landscape. The one that had sparked the first tale from Emil Kleve's history and homeland.

Meanwhile, Noa retrieved the novel she had hoped to begin reading soon, the one that promised a saga of daring adventure, of one man against the wild seas and the creatures of the deep. It fascinated her to become immersed in such fictions, to question her own responses, to wonder how it might have been written from another perspective, that of the victim and not the victor. Perhaps she could write a book review, feature it as the first entry of the new blog she planned to start, adding her own experiences to begin a conversation with her readers.

As the thoughts flourished, Noa's fingers worked through the pages, picking up odd words and phrases as she went, the spine gradually easing open to the centre to reveal what had been concealed inside for nearly fifty years. She muttered a thank you as Fin set her cup down on the table, her eyes transfixed on a folded piece of paper in the book. She picked it out carefully, as if handling a precious relic, and opened it up. The writing was small and cursive with a few spelling mistakes in each line and what seemed to be some words in another language, which Noa recognised as Norwegian. It was a story, though whether fictitious or factual, she could not be sure. The beginning had the feel of a fairy tale, but as she continued, the narrative grew darker and more ominous, before becoming poignant and upsetting. She had to read the last few lines several times to make sure she had understood.

Pressing a hand to cool her flushed cheek, Noa felt suddenly anxious once more. A touch against her elbow caused her to flinch and look up at the two concerned faces opposite, bringing her back to reality, to the enormity of what she had found. She quickly nodded – yes, she was fine – then handed the paper to Hamish. She pretended to drink from her mug as she watched him read, wondering what his reaction would be. It was undoubtedly the hand of the fisherman, his sorry tale in his own words, maybe even written when her father had been there at the cottage. It had been hidden in a book for all these years, and Noa knew why.

The narrative of a young man in love with a woman called Marna, a woman he had planned to spend the rest of his days with – a marriage, a home, a little boy they would both adore. Perhaps she had been too young, too scared, pressured by expectation and responsibility. She had taken her life and the fisherman had blamed himself. It was painfully sad, the writer's words swollen with grief and regret, giving Noa the unmistakable feeling that the note was something more than just a story. It felt like a final goodbye.

In his isolated cottage with no one else to tell, Emil Kleve had written down his memories so that there was something he could leave behind, something that would remain when everything else had gone. The fisherman had known his days were numbered, Noa realised; his disappearance had not been an accident. She glanced across at her father, waiting for his response. Hamish set the paper carefully back on the table, raising a hand to slowly stroke the base of his chin. Noa could not bear to meet his eyes now that they both knew the truth – that the fisherman had planned his vanishing act, that he had ended his own life.

The tea proved a welcome distraction, all three of them poised with their mugs against the mouths, making sharp sipping sounds to cut through the silence, until Hamish gave a long sigh that seemed to lift the veil of unease. He set his cup back on the table and began making an odd sound that eventually revealed itself to be laughter. Noa frowned at him, bewildered. He had read the note from the fisherman yet somehow seemed pleased, or else the story had been the final straw and he had gone mad. She still could not look at him, nor find the words to question his sudden and unwarranted glee.

"Well, that's the end of it," he finally said, slapping the table jovially before releasing another steady exhalation. "Now we finally know."

His daughter remained incredulous. Had they read the same piece of paper? Had Hamish mistaken the words and their meaning? Or perhaps he was just so grateful to finally have an answer that he could not help but feel glad of it. He slid the note over to Fin while Noa busied herself with taking their mugs to the sink.

"I knew there had to be a reason," Hamish continued, steepling his fingers like a detective having solved a challenging crime. "There must be hundreds of Kleves in Norway, no wonder I couldn't find him."

A teaspoon clattered across the draining board and fell into the suds in the bowl. Noa did not retrieve it, her attention distracted by her father's words. They had both read the tale but had come to two opposing conclusions: death and life. Yes, it was possible, she thought. Maybe meeting her father had made the man long for home, for Norway, for the land of his family and community. It was a far kinder way to think of the fisherman's grief than the other option. Maybe the truth did not really matter anyway, not now Hamish had an answer. He had the collection of books and knew where the talismans were. He would have notes and records on his computer, along with memories that were now more vivid and precious than ever. Believing that Emil Kleve had returned to his native country seemed a tidy end to what had been a complicated and exhausting mystery.

Noa picked up the story again, a piece of evidence that neither she nor her father could ever have imagined finding. A real life fairy tale written in Emil Kleve's own hand; a memento Hamish could keep and remember him by forever. Noa did not know if it was the happy ending her father had expected, but from the way he now acted, striding and humming around the kitchen cupboards as he planned what to cook for dinner, she knew it was the long awaited close of a difficult chapter of his life. It was time to begin anew.

Twenty-Two

The note had been right. Emil Kleve had always been a dead man walking. Even as a child, he had known that he was different, a stranger to an otherwise typical family – what some might have called a 'changeling'. An interloper. A parasite. He was not the son they had wanted. He had looked and seemed like any other little boy at birth, the same as his brothers had been, until the doctor had taken him away to study his hand, or what was left of it. And though his mother had loved him, and Marna after that, and the boy he had called Noah had not even flinched at the sight, still, the fisherman felt marked, a being more befitting the myths and legends of his grandfather than the biography of a valuable soul.

Unworthy. That was what the note had made him feel. Though the fire had long since crumbled it to ashes, the scorched remains of the paper still seemed etched into the dust, their words hissing in the air like a wheezing bellow, in and out, timed to the fisherman's own heavy breaths. This was an altogether different form of haunting, a darkness more absorbing than anything he had experienced before. The loneliness had become all-consuming to the point where no thought or daydream, no action or utterance, could shake him from his spiralling descent.

In the time between leaving the police station and

receiving the message, there had been the faintest feeling, deep inside his chest, which had been keeping Emil alive, urging him to continue breathing and to stay within the cottage. He had forgone his fishing trips and resisted returning to town; he had not even ventured to the outbuilding or paced around his newly weeded garden. He had kept to the house for one reason only – to wait for his son.

There was a flame, as tiny and as fragile as a struck match in a storm, burning in his chest in the place where a heart should have been. Despite all he had suffered, all he had felt and come to understand, Emil wanted to keep that delicate light alive. The belief, faint but tangible, that Noah would return. That he would open his eyes, walk to the door and find the boy stood outside, awaiting rescue once more. An adventure story. A perfect fairy tale. The fisherman still hoped for a happy ending. But in the cold light of a new morn, things were different. Like the note and the fire, the spark inside him had been extinguished.

Only hours had passed since he had returned the child to his mother, the moment they had been forced to say farewell, but already, Emil felt aged as if years had gone by. He could feel a weariness to his bones and within his blood, as if his whole body were in the process of decay, fading with great speed while his mind and heart had relinquished their hope. Emil now knew there would be no second coming, no second chance. His options were few. The fisherman could either give up and return to his homeland in the hope of forgiveness, or he could stay in Whitby and live a life of solitude, patiently awaiting his fate.

After three days alone in his cottage, Emil woke to find that the heaviness had finally eased. His soul seemed to have quietened, even brightened, lifted ever so lightly by the plans he had slowly contemplated during the long drawn-out hours of the passing time. He yawned, rising sluggishly from his armchair to slope across to the window, a pleasant autumn morning greeting him from beyond. After a much needed wash, shave and a change of clothes, Emil felt ready to accept his destiny. He replaced his coat, gave his boots a quick polish, then paced across the room to unlock the front door and step outside.

Squinting into the misty light, he took in deep breaths of the salted air, peering around as if in an unfamiliar place. The atmosphere had changed once more. He could sense it in his skin, in the unnerving shiver across his entire body, in the altered beat of his heart. A warning. The landscape seemed old and new at once, both friend and foe. The sky weighed heavily on the horizon, bleeding into the sea like a stain. All around, scraps of vegetation were being whipped up by the intermittent wind, grazing his cheeks, settling into his hair, adhering to his lips. Just like when the storm had come.

He raced as swiftly as his stiffened legs would carry him to the back of the house. Still his ever loyal companion, the little boat with the emerald green hull remained secure in the harbour. He watched her rhythmical rocking side to side, impatient, wishing to be released. He had betrayed her, hoping and dreaming of a different life, forsaking the only future that mattered. He had forgotten his place.

Then it came – the sound. Low and dull, yet mighty in its power. The cry of a beast, the language of another time and place. The light wavered as dense clouds obscured a pale sun, the air growing ever more feverish. His gaze followed the bend of the path from his cottage to the bay below, where he peered, trying to focus on the landscape. The branches were forced into a flutter then slapped into a stiff stoop, the towering reeds shaking as if in fright, every element becoming steadily silhouetted as the light lessened. It was happening again, Emil realised. Retribution.

He had thought his noble deed would be enough – caring for the little boy, becoming his saviour, his provider, then returning him to his rightful place. Had that not been plenty to show the goodness of his heart, the purity of his spirit? *Selfish*. The word erupted in his mind, a fierce accusation spoken in the language of his forebears, using the distinct drone of his father's voice. He had kept a child locked away for days, had denied him his freedom, had resisted trying to find out his true family and caused a mother anguish. He had failed once more: now his punishment approached. But this time, Emil decided, he would not hide away in his bunker like a coward. This time, he would weather the storm.

The fisherman turned from the harbour and concentrated on the horizon, making his way across the land before heading steadily down the cliff path towards the sea. The way became thick with matted yellow grass, then chunks of mud and stone growing finer and denser as he continued down, down, down into the small secret cove, a way to reach the water from his clifftop home without risking injury or needing to head into the town. His own private nook, a place where he could be alone with his mistress.

Underneath his feet, the clatter of rock finally gave way to the crunch of grit as he reached the beach. Emil slipped off his coat and sat on a flat boulder. He pulled off his boots and tucked his socks inside before easing his toes into the sand, wondering when he had last felt such cool softness against his soles. Slowly walking forward, he allowed himself to notice and enjoy the shifting sensation below each step until his toes curled sharply on meeting the icy foam. He took a few more paces forward into the mouth, into the icy water that began fervently sucking and nipping at his skin, the current surging around his ankles, happy with their new companion, pleading him to move closer, to go deeper.

Steadily edging further, Emil secured himself against the punch and smack of the waves into his shins, the breeze now laced with brine. He could just make out the shadow of a single trawler ahead, swaying softly in a lulling motion. Behind it, the sky formed a thick bruise across the horizon, the ocean a slick of oil beneath, the two blurring into one as the light continued to fade. Then in the distance, he saw it – the steel-coloured flesh shimmering with moisture above the waterline, disturbing the perfect symmetry for a few rare seconds before receding again, dissolving into the swell, vanishing as quickly as it had appeared. The fisherman stared after its presence, at first with doubt then with a burning desire, his gilded eyes straining for another sighting, for further proof.

"Hush, *mitt barn*," he said to the waves. He was no longer alone.

Emil could remember each of their faces with the accuracy of an artist. Their eyes, their hair, the shape of their noses and the colours of their skin. Mother, lover, and his two sons, now side by side. Against the roar of the elements and the surge of both the sea and his own blood, he could hear their voices once more, calling him, pleading with him to listen. *Listen*. He knew these phantoms were not like the others, those taunting ghosts trapped within his home. There, the cries had kept him awake at night, their screams filled with anger and aching, lamenting the loss of his love, the many lives he had ruined. But now among the waves, the words were warm and welcoming, full of forgiveness and frivolity. It was almost as if they had been reborn, were now living figures before him, urging him to join them, so that he found himself walking further into the water.

A sudden wave of freezing cold soaked the fisherman up to his neck, its swift force and bitter sting bringing clarity to his wandering mind, the voices suddenly gone, the vision having disappeared. Closing his eyes, Emil waded on with greater resolve, determined to find them, to be reunited with the long-gone souls whom he had never forgotten, would never cease to love. He moved forward, the water at his waist, then his chest, the growing waves hitting him like boulders, bruising his flesh, pounding his bones. On he went, digging his toes into the sand to force himself further, the surge splashing his face, rising higher, higher.

Another step, another inch – he was almost there. The gulls above him circled and cried as he strode on, focused on the point where the sea met the sky, so close he could almost taste it. The more he moved, the calmer he felt, his body comforted by the strident tug and push of the tide, his spirit eased by the sound of the wind. Then there, straight ahead, Emil could see them as clear as day, their heads and shoulders bobbing above the surface, each wearing a docile smile of familiarity. Silently, they beckoned.

He struggled on, his legs slow and cumbersome against the powerful force of the water, stepping then swimming before finally he was floating. He was so close he could almost hear their breaths, four trailing whispers on the wind, the faint shadows of their bodies faintly visible below the waterline. The four people he had loved and lost – two drowned, two disappeared – yet now they had returned. He had been forgiven. And among their calls, their echoes of his name, Emil could also hear the cry of the beast, the mysterious creature that had haunted him for so long.

Another wave enveloped him, leaving him gasping but elated, his eyes and ears trained on the phantoms he longed to follow. As the sea wrapped itself tighter around his body, the fisherman could feel himself sinking, his limbs lightening, all his anxieties finally ebbing away. Lost in a heady state of euphoria, he did not sense the figure on the beach behind, nor hear the muffled footsteps as they strode slowly but purposefully

across the sands, a cigarette in one hand, a kitchen knife in the other.

Twenty-Three

Noa closed her laptop with a contented sigh, slipping it inside its case before placing it in the top drawer of the desk. The article was finally finished, the images had been uploaded and the emails at long last replied to. She checked her phone: ten minutes to go. Her father would be back on the hour, ready to take her out for the rest of the day before her final farewell. The six months had passed as effortlessly as a cloud drifting across the sky, with Noa barely noticing the time ticking away. Weeks had become months, autumn turning to winter, before all too quickly March had arrived.

Each night, Noa had taken the time to find and observe the subtly changing moon as it grew and shrunk, morphing from great spheres of light into the faintest slip of a curve. She had watched the transition first from her favoured spot beside the bridge and then from underneath the skylight using her new telescope. In the day, the weather had helped her to find a sense of balance and calm. There had been rainstorms and dense snow, gloriously clear skies and scatterings of cloud, all captured on her phone and shared across social media and blog posts, the days once so distinct yet now blurred into a single hazy recollection of her time in Whitby.

Looking back, Noa realised she had viewed that long stretch ahead as a process, a pathway, leading from her old self to the new. She had come to learn how to write – it was what she had told others and herself about her planned six months in Whitby – but soon after her arrival, she had discovered that both the ideas and the ability were already inside her, making the journey not one of learning but of self-discovery. Hamish had only needed to offer a little light encouragement to coax out her natural flair, until Noa finally recognised her own talent and began to feel comfortable enough working in her own way.

It had been after reading her father's published reports on the beached beluga whale that Noa felt compelled to write. Ever since visiting the museum with Fin, her mind had felt swollen with stories, each itching to make their way into words. She had noticed how Hamish had managed to turn a trying encounter into a delicately detailed account, balancing fact with emotion, honesty with hope, a complex issue becoming an engaging conversation. Noa had written her own version for her blog, nervously sharing the link with family and friends – her first tentative step towards becoming both a writer and an activist. Her work and her ideas had not stopped since.

While her online posts had been a productive way to practice, Noa had sought other opportunities to not only write but to help her new community. She had penned articles on conservation for the local newspaper and had helped to promote an anti-littering campaign. She had spent a week volunteering at the museum during the February school holidays, then had worked with a local librarian to help digitalise some rare documents.

She had interviewed fishermen on sustainable produce and had even helped with the advertising campaign for the town's prestigious regatta, which she planned to attend in the summer. As well as building an admirable portfolio of work, Noa had also made lifelong connections and friends.

With so much activity, the refurbished attic became not only a writing room but a sanctuary. Helped by Hamish, Noa had added a few more practical and decorative additions to the space; a standing lamp and a star chart, new shelves and a small armchair, plus some more framed pictures, including two of her own drawings made during another visit up to the abbey ruins. Noa's bed and belongings had soon been moved up so that she could wake early to write, making the most of the soft dawn glow that filtered through the skylight. And, of course, Emil's collection of books took pride of place behind her desk.

Though Noa had tried to keep her writing area tidy, the number of trinkets had soon grown – another potted plant, a fossil paperweight gifted by Fin for Christmas, and a small framed photograph perched in her eyeline, the three familiar faces providing a constant source of support as she worked. After she had learned more from Hamish about his past and the time he had spent with her uncle and mother, Noa had shown the images to Rosa on a video call, hoping it would break down the invisible barrier she had built between her own history and her daughter's future. Over several emotional catch-up calls, Rosa had finally revealed the truth, carefully recalling her fragile memories, both happy and sad, and sharing with Noa some of the mementoes from her younger years – CDs and clothes, a fabric protest banner Jonah and Hamish had stitched, along with a sketch Rosa had made of her daughter as a new-born. Noa had not even known her mother could draw.

Following her move to the attic, Noa's former bedroom had been fitted out with a sofa bed, a bookcase in place of the wardrobe and a second-hand easel. Without his research to occupy him, Hamish took to spending his spare time sat alone on Tate Hill beach, looking out across the sea like a forlorn old man. Noa had found him there one afternoon and had taken him over to Woody's house for some company, watching across a cup of ginger tea as her father had become engrossed with the collection, particularly a newly acquired series of landscape watercolours. Hamish had been so inspired that he had signed himself up for art classes at the local community centre and was soon using his evenings and weekends to capture the natural beauty and wildlife of the area on canvas. He had even sold a few at a seasonal artists exhibition, gifting his favourite picture – a freshly caught red lobster – to Noa for Christmas. She had wrapped it up that morning ready to take back home to Leeds.

Home. A word that had once filled her with so much conflict but now made her feel both relieved and grateful. As she had reflected on the word, Noa had come to realise that she had not one but many places she belonged – with Rosa and Aunt Isobel, with her father and her new friend Fin, and with old friends too – Rowan and Al had both sent invitations for her to stay with them over Easter and she regularly wrote letters to Mo and Hem. And there would always be Whitby, a place Noa now felt a part of. A home she was proud of. From the daughter of a single parent, she had formed ties with people and places across the world and from different walks of life, each making her feel all the more complete, somehow more like herself.

She would never forget Fin's parting words the day before he had left for his travels: 'The past is history, tomorrow's a mystery, the present is a gift.' It had made them both laugh, but the sentiment had been clear. The mantra had been scribbled into Noa's notebooks and across pages of her diary so many times that it almost felt etched into her very skin, like her own tattoo. Her own magical talisman.

For Hamish, the six months he had spent with his daughter had been a time of revelation, reflection and transformation. After the discovery of Emil Kleve's story in the pages of a book, he had settled on the conclusion that the fisherman had returned to Norway, as Noa had once suggested. He liked to imagine him forging a new and successful life there, perhaps reunited with his brothers or even parents. Maybe he had fallen in love and got married, he often wondered. He could even have had a son.

The child that had once been called Noah now felt at peace with his past. The recovery of the hidden papers had triggered a lifetime of grief and guilt to slowly disperse, leaving Hamish feeling both lighter and stronger, mentally and physically. He had become a new man with changed priorities, able to do as he pleased, to choose how to spend his days without the wall absorbing his attention. Untethered from history, he had been released into possibility. It was only on very rare occasions when he would retrieve the file and allow himself a brief glance at the newspaper clipping or the letter, their power having evaporated. Nothing more than distant memories now.

As well as his newfound interest in painting, Hamish had also had his kitchen and bathroom updated, turned vegetarian, and had begun spending more time with a local conservation group. He would join them for nature walks and wildlife counts, or for afternoon lectures and debating nights. He had even been down to the pub for a pint or two, enjoying the company of others for the first time since university. In addition to his new friends, he had also tried to mend some of the broken threads of attachment from his younger days, making regular visits to Mr Marshall at the newsagents, emailing a journalist called Tom he had once worked with, and speaking to Rosa over the phone. The latter had been the hardest reconnection of all, but over stilted conversations and awkward silences, the pair had set their differences aside and moved forward, for the memory of Jonah as well as for their daughter.

Hamish looked at his watch, the time seeming to tick by even more quickly now that Noa was about to head home. Back to her mother, back to her former life, the one he had known so little about but now felt closer to, even a part of. He could feel the familiar hollowing of his chest, the impending sense of loss, along with the steady waves of panic as he wondered what he would do without his daughter. At least this time he would not be left completely alone. And unlike those moments under the whalebone archway – when he would watch the young girl look left then right then left again before crossing the road, back to the hotel – he now knew that Noa would soon return.

As the day of her leaving had crept ever closer, Hamish had tried to put into words how he felt. The pride, not only of his daughter's writing and sketches, but of who she was as a person, the passion and motivation she brought to every aspect of her life, all carefully contained behind her cool and calm façade. Walking down the street on their way to the beach or the café, the shops or the arcades, it would always be Noa that the locals would greet first. She had formed a connection with seemingly everyone in the town, as any local journalist might do, with a skill for communication and compassion that Hamish, in all his years of work, had still never mastered. He would not be the only one to miss Noa's presence, to feel the absence of her light.

Though he was never one for spontaneity, Hamish thought he had finally come up with a way of making his daughter's final afternoon in Whitby one to remember. He had departed the flat early, leaving his usual curtly factual note of apology in the kitchen. They had already agreed to have lunch and a long walk together, but he hoped Noa would not mind the change in plans – if he could make them a reality, of course. At just after twelve, he bundled through the front door and shouted a 'hello' up to the attic, idling by the staircase as he listened for the now familiar thudding of descending footsteps.

On hearing the front door opening, Noa kissed the tips of her fingers and rested them against the glass, leaving a set of three smudges against the faces in the photograph. Having already put her shoes, coat and scarf on, she hooped her satchel over her head, slipped her phone inside and made her way down to meet Hamish. There was a bounce in each step but also a feeling of apprehension, an awareness of the emotional weight of what was to come – this, their last afternoon together before she would take the train home. To the big city, the old life, a world that had so suddenly felt a thousand miles away and which now seemed to be claiming her back. It was inevitable, she knew, but there was still a reluctance, a tether tugging her in both directions between one home and the other.

Noa hid her thoughts behind her usual bright smile, following Hamish out of the door and turning left in the expectation that they would be heading to The Crow Nest. A sharp whistle caught her attention and she turned to see her father, fingers hovering in front of his lips, still waiting outside the flat. She retraced her steps, noticing now that he held a small canvas bag in one hand, clutched tight in a fist. She watched it start to swing as Hamish walked the opposite way, towards the bridge. A frisson of excitement swept through her body as she followed, curious and keen.

She wanted to burst out with questions, like a child being led on an adventure, but Noa knew her father well enough by now – he was a man of few words and a master of secrecy. She would just have to hope that this time it would be a welcome surprise rather than one of worry. They turned left again and continued walking along the road beside the bowl of water where the boats were moored, a crisp chill to the air but with enough sunlight to feel as if spring were about to blossom at any moment. Noa wished she could see the town when it did, having already had a taste of autumn and winter. Maybe she would ask Hamish to paint her a picture of the newly emerged season, giving her another excuse to make a return visit in a few months' time. She was already beginning to miss the place before she had even left.

A little further ahead, Noa noticed a handsome vessel tethered to the dock, its distinctive glistening red hull nodding happily in the wide pool of water, which today looked more like mercury, molten and vivid. A young man stood on its deck wearing a thick sweater, heavy-duty cargo trousers and sturdy black boots that seemed to anchor him against the rocking motion. As she and Hamish walked closer, the man followed their path with his eyes, until finally they were close enough to hear him.

Hamish responded, raising a hand in greeting before stepping across and down into the boat, as effortlessly as if he were a seasoned sailor. For a moment, Noa wondered if this might actually be *his* boat – the fact that her father was doing something seemingly sporadic had ruffled her senses. Flushed with exhilaration, she made her way across the deck, already eager for the journey to begin. The man on board, Matthew, shook her hand with a surprising lightness before motioning for his guests to take their seats. With an unpretentious ease, he then carefully coerced the vessel away from the mooring and out towards the open water.

Taking a trip to sea was something Hamish and Noa had repeatedly talked about but had somehow never found the right moment to do, particularly with the severe weather that had darkened their November through to February. But now that the skies had cleared and their last day loomed, Hamish could think of no better way to treat his daughter, a trip that he thought would symbolise everything they had experienced and achieved over the six months together. He had made use of his contacts as a journalist to arrange the boat ride, but there would be one or two more surprises in store, including inside his canvas bag.

Placing the weight down on the bench between them, Hamish removed a flask, two old-fashioned enamel mugs and a lunch box, which he opened to reveal two generously sized scones sliced and layered with homemade jam and vegan clotted cream. He had used Fin's now famous recipe, adding his own touch with a few dried raspberries. Without a word, Matthew slowed the boat and let it bob softly on a serene stretch of water, the town and the cliffs on one side and nothing but endless ocean on the other.

Once the motion had settled, Hamish carefully poured out two mugs of peppermint tea and wrapped one of the scones in a paper napkin for himself, then handed the box containing the second to Noa. Though the surrounding expanse seemed calm, the deck occasionally swayed and jolted, sending crumbs and splashes into the air and across the bench. A rogue kittiwake swooped down in pursuit, managing to amass its winnings before any other birds could take advantage, leaving father and daughter to finish their lunch in peace with idyllic views in every direction.

As Matthew set them back on course, Noa realised why her father had arranged the excursion. *The whales.* Amid all her animation, it had only just occurred to her why Hamish might go to so much effort, especially when none of the other tourist tours had started running again. She had hoped to return in late summer when there would be a better chance of seeing one, but she also knew that no amount of planning or preparation could predict the motions of wild animals. That had always been part of the allure for her – the dual sense of consistency and unpredictability, the natural world's enduring ability to surprise, startle and delight. While her mind told her there was little possibility, her heart remained filled with hope.

They were now the only ship within sight, the harbour becoming ever fainter with only the green and grey cliffs and the two white curves of the piers defining their view – two white curves, just like the whalebone archway. The place where it had all begun. Noa's first experience of Whitby, her first understanding of whaling history and the first time she had ever met her father. Now here they were, potentially about to see the very creature that had come to mean so much to their reunions, past and present. She could feel her heart pounding, her eyes searching.

Whale watching had been Hamish's intention on

booking the trip, though he knew a spotting would be rare at this time of the year. Yet there was something about Noa leaving, a feeling of urgency tinged with regret, that had convinced him to take a chance. To put a little faith in the impossible. After all, surely it was the same optimism that had led him to pursue the missing fisherman for so many years. He could feel it now as he gazed across the expanse – the anticipation, the yearning for discovery. Perhaps Emil had felt it too, during the endless hours spent on his boat or observing the view from his cottage high up on the clifftops. There was a certain joy in simply watching, passing the time in the company of nature. Whether they saw a whale or any other creature, it did not really matter. The boat trip meant much more than that. Their mutual love of wildlife and conservation had brought Hamish and his daughter closer, as well as helping him to forge an even deeper connection with the town he had grown up in. He could allow himself a certain pride in that. Perhaps he had become a decent father after all.

They both suddenly lurched to one side as the vessel began to turn, racing against the tide as Matthew steered them back towards the land. Hamish watched his daughter adjust her position, wind whistling through her now shoulder-length hair, a broad beam stretching almost from ear to ear, as if she would not want to be anywhere else, with anyone else. Happiness. It was something Hamish had long thought unattainable, something he had found and left behind long ago. But here it was again, and all because of her.

As the journey neared its end, Hamish reached

into his pocket, drawing out a small black box. Noa looked between the object and her father's face, unable to read anything from either, but coming to her own understanding that this was a gift – and not a paperback book, this time. She took it, her fingers faintly shaking, her mouth suddenly dry, and opened the lid with a gentle pop. Inside was an antique pendant made from Whitby jet with a silver clasp and chain, cushioned beneath by black velvet. She knew the shape immediately, instinctively, as if she were looking into a mirror. Her father had bought her a whale's tail. A talisman of her own.

The cry of surprise faded into the wind, but Hamish could tell he had made the right choice. He watched as Noa removed the necklace from the box and attached it around her neck, her hands still quaking, smile wavering, eyes growing wider and filmed with moisture as her wordless mouth opened and closed. No, he would never understand much about women, but he had known that the whales meant as much to her as they did to him.

For luck, Noa thought, running the smooth shape through her fingers, oblivious to the bay that now surrounded them once more. She wanted to say so much, to express everything that hurried through her mind, not only this minute but in all the moments she had spent with Hamish. The hurt and the confusion, the comfort and the contentment, every emotion possible during those first few days alone, before she had settled, before he had accepted her. The calm after the storm.

And there would always be Emil Kleve, the fisherman

she never should have known about but whose mystery had changed the path of her life in remarkable and unexpected ways. Now she was on her way towards a new adventure, with her new lucky charm – not the pendant itself, but the person it represented. Her father.

When Hamish had purchased the necklace from the jewellery shop, he had wondered if it might be seen as an emblem of good fortune, a protective trinket, but he did not believe in fairy stories anymore. In the past six months, he had learned of something far more powerful than the knowledge or conviction he had clung to for so long. He now knew of a different kind of magic, one he had seen and experienced with his own eyes, with his own heart, ever since Noa had entered his life. It was not a symbol of luck, he wanted to tell her. It was a sign of his love.

But, as always, Hamish kept his thoughts to himself as they alighted onto the quayside, the salted breeze whistling, the drifting seagulls cawing, the life of the town all around, vibrant and celebratory. As they reached the path, father and daughter both turned to take one last look out across the water, to form one last memory before they had to say goodbye. And as they gazed, both bodies paused, their eyes caught on what they had silently been hoping to see all along.

An arch, a curve, slicing through the sparkling ripples, up and over, before vanishing. A thing unseen, like a wisp of silver smoke, but it had been there, they both knew, out where the sea touched the sky. A fleeting glimpse, a sign from beyond – a being waving one final goodbye.

Author's Note

While this novel is a work of fiction, its themes have been informed by a variety of historic and contemporary sources. Having decided to write about a Norwegian fisherman in Whitby, I was lucky enough to read a dissertation on the bond between humans and whales, which proved hugely inspiring and informative – thank you, Elodie. I consulted several books about whaling practices, most notable of which were *Fathoms* by Rebecca Giggs, *Memories of the Yorkshire Fishing Industry* by Ron Freethy, *Spying on Whales* by Nick Pyenson and *A Life on Our Planet* by David Attenborough. Literary quotes and references within the novel include *The Old Man and the Sea* by Ernest Hemingway, *The Salt Path* by Raynor Winn, *Dracula* by Bram Stoker and the poems 'The Rime of the Ancient Mariner' by Samuel Taylor Coleridge and 'The Seafarer' translated by Ezra Pound. Also included are references to stories from Whitby, Norway and Sami traditions.

Ingram Content Group UK Ltd.
Milton Keynes UK
UKHW040007070723
424696UK00004B/155

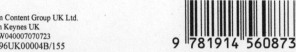

9 781914 560873